# TOUCHING INFINITY

## MARK O'BANNON

Published by MEOw Publishing.

Visit our website at: www.MEOwPublishing.com

First published in 2024



ISBN 978-1-933888-35-4

Printed in the United States of America

This book is dedicated to my friends,

Sarah Crowne and Ira Drower

**Books by Mark O'Bannon**

**IMPERIUM PREQUEL SERIES**
*(May be read in any order)*
Pirates of the Imperium
High Salvage
Touching Infinity


**IMPERIUM SERIES**
Imperium – Return of the Archons (Coming in 2025)


**SHADOWS & DREAMS SERIES**
The Dream Crystal
The Dark Mirrors of Heaven (Coming in 2025)


**AIA THE BARBARIAN SERIES**
Aia the Barbarian – The Fallen God


**WHISKERS**
Whiskers (Coming in 2025)

# CONTENTS

Go To:
www.MEOwPublishing.com
to see a high quality map of the Imperium

# PROLOGUE

## Pleione

**3220 A.D. — YEAR OF THE METAL RAT**

**VERMILION BIRD OF THE SOUTH**

**HD 69830 / PLEIONE**

The couple trudged through the snow towards an ancient city of stone. A woman, carrying a sleeping child in her arms, dropped down into the snow, exhausted. The man took the child into his arms and helped the woman to her feet. Anger flashed in his eyes as he looked skyward. The night was illuminated by a bright band of zodiacal light which crossed over the River of Heaven. He took a deep breath and let his fury drift away into the icy wind.

He returned his gaze to the frozen highlands up ahead and they marched forward.

Howling winds brought death to an icy wasteland. Dead trees stood rooted to the ground where they had relinquished their lives. Icebound animal carcasses lay just under a white blanket. The imperial colony was already covered in ice. Beyond the dead city, a massive crater stretched across the horizon. The snow that came down after the comet's impact would never melt.

The couple trudged purposefully towards the stone terraces set into the side of a hill where hundreds of prehistoric buildings lay in ruins. At the top of a long flight of stairs carved out of the rock there was an ancient circular building, still intact. They climbed the stairs and approached the primeval structure. The walls were made from stones of different sizes, fit together without a crack or seam. It was as if they had been molded into place. Light came from inside one of the stone archways.

The scent of ash from the recent firestorms was still heavy inside. He led his wife and brought the sleeping child down a long hallway and paused at the entrance to a huge chamber at the heart of the structure. Silver light fell into the chamber through high skylights. Prehistoric inscriptions covered the walls.

"Wait," the woman warned. "Are you sure this is the only way, Mauritius?"

The man looked down at the sleeping blonde girl in his arms.

"The High Augur was clear, Lucienne. One day, the ancients born in the darkness will rise out of the abyss to devour everything. This is the only way she will survive the day of their coming."

"The High Augur is dead now," said Lucienne, "along with everyone else."

"The Sibylline Oracle said the Augur's prophecy is connected to this prehistoric temple. Sibyl Helene can operate the ancient machines," he said. "We should have done this long ago, before the asteroid shifted the planet's orbit."

Lucuenne looked pensively into the chamber.

His voice was gentle, but firm. "It's the only way."

"Give her to me." Lucienne took the girl into her arms and hugged her close. "How can you trust an android?"

Mauritius rubbed his chin, breathing out a cold vapor into the chill air. "She's more than a simple android. Sibyl Helene is connected to the greatest computer on Pleione. Like all the other Sibylline Oracles in the Imperium, her calculations are never wrong. She predicted the comet's impact, didn't she?"

Lucienne held the girl tightly in her arms. "Not in time to get help. The Imperium won't know about this disaster for at least another two weeks."

The colonists of Pleione had sent a drone to the Ming Sha colony. L744-10 was the closest star with an imperial colony. At ten and a half light years distance, it was only four days away. But it was impossible to help three hundred million people. Ming Sha didn't have the resources.

"Did you send the courier drone to your brother on Scylanthia?"

He nodded.

But he knew it would take at lease twenty days for his brother to get here with help. He glanced out at the frozen wasteland through one of the windows along the far side of the chamber. By that time, everything would be under a hundred meters of snow.

Their world was dying.

Lucienne glanced around. "This equipment is very old."

"It will work," said Mauritius.

"I won't let her go," said Lucienne.

"Then she will die here with us."

Tears fell from Lucienne's cheeks. "Can't we go with her?"

"There's only enough power left for one."

"She will be all alone."

"There are others there," he said.

"How many have gone before her?"

"Over a hundred thousand," said Mauritius. "The others will help her after she passes through the gateway."

He listened to the howling windstorm outside. It was so intense that it could be heard here, in the heart of the ancient structure. Their world of green hills and beautiful valleys was covered in a massive sheet of ice now. Like a skeletal hand of death, he could feel the cold reaching out, promising eternal sleep.

Lucienne leaned against the wall as drowsiness threatened to overcome her.

Mauritius shook her. "Wake up, Lucienne. It's just a little further."

Lucienne nodded.

Mauritius led them into what the Sibylline Oracle had called, the 'Transference Chamber.' It was a huge room devoid of contents, except for a circular dais in the center of the room, and an energy projection device in the ceiling. Embedded in the roof was a large crystal, five meters high. It was similar to the large sunstone crystals which were used to power starships. The light inside the crystal was very dim.

Sibyl Helene, having the appearance of a normal young woman, stood in the chamber, unaffected by the cold. She smiled as they came in. "Welcome to the Transference Chamber. I'm so sorry, though. There is not enough power to transfer all of you."

Mauritius shook his head. "No, not us. Just the girl."

Sibyl Helene tilted her head slightly, considering. "Yes, there is just enough power remaining for the child."

Lucienne glared at the android. "How do you know that this device won't simply disintegrate her?"

"This technology was designed to open a gateway to another place," said the android. "The ancients called it the 'Requiem.' Those undergoing transference are prepared for existence in the Requiem. Their souls are—"

"Stop," said Lucienne. "I've heard enough."

Lucenne turned away towards the frozen hallway. She took a few steps and stopped in her tracks, defeated. Ice had formed on the walls. The howling wind whistled through the night. There was nothing out there. Nowhere to go. She closed her eyes and held her face against the girl in her arms.

Mauritius stepped up behind Lucienne and brushed a strand of blonde hair out of her eyes.

Lucienne stopped crying. Her face filled with anguish and resolve. She walked back into the room, past the android and over to the dais. She hugged the girl tight, one last time.

The little girl woke up. "Mommy, I'm cold."

Lucienne knelt down, her voice trembling yet soothing. "Sweetheart, we're sending you away, to a place of safety."

"No, I want to stay here with you."

Mauritius came over and picked up the little girl to give her one last hug. He put her down. "Alastriona, you need to be brave now.

I need you to go over to that platform. Can you do that for me?"

The little girl nodded, looked over at the android standing next to the platform and ran back to her mother. "No. I don't want to go."

Lucienne hugged her tight, tears streaming down her cheeks.

Mauritius put his hand on her shoulder and Lucienne let go of the little girl. "Alastriona, sweetheart, we love you so much." She kissed the little girl's cheek, holding back sobs. She picked up the little girl's doll and handed it to her. "Keep Nanette safe for me, will you?"

The little girl nodded.

"Be brave, darling. We'll find you soon."

The little girl walked over to the platform and sat down, cradling the doll in her arms.

Mauritius nodded towards Sibyl Helene.

The android activated the ancient machine. There was a hum, and the girl vanished in a blue-white flash of light. The radiant glow inside the crystal powering the machine went out.

Sibyl Helene's voice was lighthearted. "All done."

Mauritius glared at the android. "You don't have to be happy about it."

"I'm sorry," said the android, still using a cheerful tone. "May I assist you?"

Lucienne and Mauritius sat down onto the icy floor and hugged each other.

The android repeated her question, "May I assist you?"

They sat there, listening to the howling storm outside.

The end would come soon.

* * *

# TEN
## Fantôm de Lumière

**3230 A.D. — YEAR OF THE METAL DOG**

**VERMILION BIRD OF THE SOUTH**

**HD 84117 / SCYLANTHIA**

The cathedral was bathed in heavenly silence. A breath of tranquility swept down the nave past white marble pillars and reached up to the sexpartite vaulted ceiling. Quiet shadows lay in the aisles and covered a dozen bays full of votive candles. Rose windows of stained glass at the four ends of the cathedral let in a rainbow of light that banished the darkness. Silence was a balm that promised rest to the weary.

The tall doors opened, revealing a storm from a noisy city just outside. Alastriona DeTroyes entered the cathedral and marched down the nave towards the altar, fracturing the silence inside. Alastriona had an ethereal kind of beauty, as if she had descended out of heaven. Tall and thin, she had the look of a fashion model. Long blonde hair fell in a wild entanglement over her shoulders. Her face was as delicate as a porcelain statue. But her face was frozen into a stony expression, to hold back a wave of discouragement.

Alastriona had blue, intelligent eyes with a gleam of superiority. It was not a judgemental or an arrogant kind of look, but rather a certainty that she was above mere mortals who spent their days pursuing meaningless trivialities. *Cute sheep,* she thought. She didn't criticize them for it, though. She was simply above them all.

Alastriona wore an anti-gravity belt over a white peasant blouse and leggings. Her tall white boots thundered out a storm of rhythmic footsteps that echoed inside the cathedral. The whole outfit was topped off with a short white jacket.

Closing her eyes for a moment, Alastriona inhaled the sweet aromas of frankincense and myrrh as she strode down the nave. Before she reached the transept, which formed a cross inside the cathedral, she entered a pew, went over to the aisle at the side, and then turned into one of the bays. She dropped a coin into the collection box, picked up a beeswax candle, placed it on the stand and lit it. "As I light this candle, I wish to stand in your presence to be consumed in the light and warmth of your love."

Alastriona knelt down, put her hands together and closed her eyes. A heaviness came over her. She wanted to be alone, but for some reason, solitude was more frightening than simple disappointment. Opening her eyes, she prayed in a soft voice, "God, please help my stupid sister, Julie, who has completely lost her way."

She closed her eyes and remained there for a time, wishing the news wasn't true. Her sister had a boyfriend. *How can she be so foolish?* She took a deep breath and opened her eyes again. She crossed herself and said, "In the name of the Father, and of the Son and of the Holy Spirit. Amen."

Alastriona stood up and marched back down the aisle and out the doors of the cathedral.

The city hovered above the world on a massive antigravity platform. White puffy clouds drifted through the city, like little whiffs of fog. The city had dozens of tiers, up, up, up to a central tower at the top. The sky was full of the balloon-like natives of the planet, who drifted all over the skies. Alastriona emerged from the white marble Gothic cathedral in the center of a plaza. She inhaled the clean sweet air which one gets after a rainstorm and marched away from the cathedral.

While she was strutting down the street at a quick pace, a man approached with one hand behind his back. She tried walking past him, but he had the audacity to speak to her. "Can I ask you a question?"

Alastriona stopped in her tracks and took a longer look at her accoster. He was taller than she was, and had the look of an athlete. His blue eyes radiated intensity, honesty and strength. One could get lost in those eyes. He wore a dark suit and a black newsboy cap. True, he was quite attractive, but that didn't matter at all. "Yes?"

He took out a bouquet of flowers from behind his back, smiled, and handed them to her.

Stunned by the kind gesture, she took the flowers into one hand. A trace of a smile touched her lips. She resisted an urge to smell their aroma, though. Instead, she looked up into his beautiful eyes just as he asked another question.

"What's your name?"

"Alastriona," she replied.

"I saw you walk into the cathedral," he said. "So I wanted to meet you."

She gave him another shadow of a smile. "Well, now you have."

"Would you like to have coffee, sometime?"

*Is this what happened to my sister?*

"Thank you, no," she said. *Better to let him down fast.* "I don't wish to be unkind, but I do have an appointment." She gave him another quick smile to soften the blow. "Thank you for the flowers."

Before he could respond, she walked away. Whether he was shocked by her abruptness or for some other reason, he didn't try to follow her. Alastriona went over to the edge of the city and peered down through the clouds at the ground two thousand meters below. She dropped the bouquet over the edge. The flowers were caught in a draft and the pretty arrangement disintegrated as it went down. With a sigh of disillusionment, she muttered, "Yet another man who's not good enough."

Following the flowers, Alastriona stepped off the edge and plunged down hundreds of meters. After passing through a few clouds, she activated her antigravity belt and came to hover just a few meters over another road on a lower terrace of the city. She adjusted the controls and lowered herself softly down onto the street.

She went over to the wall at the edge of the tier she was on. With the grace of an acrobat, she jumped over the impediment and down onto the roof of a building on yet another lower level of the city. She walked across the roof and when she came to the end, she slid down to the lower edge. She jumped off the roof onto a balcony and dropped down onto another wall further down.

Cat-like, she walked over the top of the wall until she came to a rope attached to another terrace. She walked across the rope and stepped onto the platform which overlooked the ground a thousand meters below.

Alastriona raised her eyes to the skies, which were filled with thousands of the huge, balloon-like Scylanthians, peaceful beings that spent their time drifting over the planet. They came in every color of the rainbow.

Noticing one going in her direction, Alastriona raised her hand. A turquoise and white Scylanthian came down to the platform. She could feel the hot breath of the Scylanthian against her face as it blew her hair into a tangled mess. The Scylanthian let out it's long tail which curled up into a convenient perch. She jumped onto the end of the tail and held the rope-like appendage for stability. She pointed in the direction of another floating city and the Scylanthian drifted away towards it.

* * *

The Scylanthian set her down onto a high platform of Lisieux, a floating city that hovered over a major river down on the surface of the planet. Shaking her head, Alastriona walked over to a waiting hovercar where her sister Julie stood by a quiet man. Julie couldn't contain her excitement and jumped up and down slightly.

Withholding a grin, Alastriona hugged her sister and whispered, "Salut toi."

"Salut," said Julie.

Alastriona released her sister and stepped back a pace. Nervousness mingled with excitement in Julie's eyes. Her sister turned to the man, who had a wild, flamboyant look in his eyes. He wore a white stetson hat and had a suit to match it.

Julie introduced him, "Alastriona, this is my fiancé, Healer Decimus Salvius Mirium."

Alastriona was too stunned to respond. *Fiancé? It's even worse than I thought.*

With a smile, Decimus took off his hat, swept his hand down in a dramatic arc, bowed deeply and then placed the hat back onto his head again. He greeted Alastriona in French, her native language. "Bonsoir, enchanté."

Alastriona's soft voice reflected the reticence in meeting her sister's boyfriend, but she offered her hand nonetheless. "Bonsoir."

Decimus took her hand into his and kissed it. Before letting go, he examined a silver ring on her forefinger. He switched to English. "Quite an unusual ring," he said. "Where did you come by it?"

Alastriona glanced down at her ring. A delicate tracery of writing in some unknown language was engraved upon it's silvery surface. She remembered suffering from horrible nightmares as a child, but after she had received the ring, they had all gone away. Alastriona had the habit of gazing at the ring whenever she was nervous. It always seemed to calm her down.

Alastriona said, "My aunt gave it to me when I was a child."

"We're not really sisters," said Julie. "We're cousins. After

Alastriona's parents died in the disaster on Pleione, my parents took her in."

"My condolences," he said.

"I barely remember my real parents," said Alastriona. "But I call Julie my sister and her parents are my mom and dad now."

"Your ring is exquisite," he said. "It's very old. It may even be an artifact of the ancients."

The ancients were powerful god-like beings that ruled the galaxy millennia ago. Their prehistoric cities and pyramids were found all over the galaxy. Surprised, Alastriona looked down at her ring. "Really?"

"Yes," said Decimus. "I'd love to show it to Captain Black."

"Who?"

Julie couldn't keep the excitement out of her voice. "Decimus works for a famous treasure hunter, Captain Black. He's an expert on the Archons and all the other ancient races."

"Oh."

A mischevious smile lit up her sister's face. She withdrew a little box from her purse and handed it to Alastriona. The present was wrapped in silver tissue and it had a gold ribbon curled into a bow on top.

"What's this?"

"A present, silly," said Julie. She lowered her voice down to a conspiratorial whisper, "Don't open it until your birthday."

Alastriona raised her eyebrows, wondering which birthday her sister was talking about. Pleione, Scylanthia and Earth all had different calendars. The math was simple enough, though. Scylanthia, which went around the white star HD 84117 once every 550 Solar Days, had 18 hour days. Her birthday was in 19 Scylanthian days, or 342 hours. Earth had 24 hours in a day, so her birthday was two weeks from now by Sol's calendar.

Her sister giggled, "I can see you thinking," she said. "Your 18th Earth birthday of March the twelfth, of course."

Alastriona raised her eyebrows. "On Scylanthia, I'm still just 12." She looked at her sister and broke into a smile. "You shouldn't have."

"Yes, I should."

As Alastriona put the small box into her purse, she noticed Decimus staring at her. The odd expression of his was disquieting. As a healer, he was also a trained scientist. This scientist was studying an experiment, an amoeba.

His words interrupted her thoughts. "I wonder if I could get a sample of your brain tissue?"

Alastriona wasn't sure if she heard him clearly. "Quoi?"

Julie laughed. "He's only kidding."

"No, I'm not."

Julie glared at her fiancé. "Decimus does genetic research, like me."

"I've heard that you have a very high IQ," he explained. "I'd love to measure the neuronal and glial cell densities in your cerebral cortex. Super soldiers and others would benefit greatly from an analysis of your DNA. I'm studying human-machine interface technology, and I'm developing ways to help Enhanced Humans, in my spare time."

"He doesn't have any spare time," said Julie. "Not if I can help it."

Because of their cybernetic augmentation, Enhanced Humans had extremely short life spans. Age regression technology didn't work on them. No Enhanced Human lived longer than a century. Most were in the military and lived glorious days of success and power before they died. *That's what the Imperium needs, more deranged lunatics in the military with longer lifespans.*

Alastriona bit her lip. *Our parents are going to love Decimus.*

"Come on," said Julie. "Decimus is giving us a lift."

Alastriona was both relieved and surprised. "You're not coming to dinner?"

"No," he said. "I have business in the city. I'll drop you off."

Decimus opened the doors of the hovercar. They all got in and he drove the vehicle through the streets of the cloud city. Julie sat in the front seat by her boyfriend, holding his hand.

Alastriona closed her eyes. *They're both crazy.*

* * *

The house occupied the upper class neighborhood of Lisieux. Windows encircled the round dining room at the top of her parent's house. Outside, Scylanthians drifted through gray storm clouds.

Alastriona sat at the dinner table with her parents, along with her sister, Julie. Alastriona crossed her arms and looked over at her sister, who remained silent. *How can she be so senseless?*

Their mother, Chantel DeTroyes smiled at Alastriona, who was fresh out of the military science academy. "It's good to see you."

A trio of shiny chrome robot slaves entered with silver trays to serve dinner. Alastriona glanced up at one of the female slaves, who was no more than a smooth metallic body with a humanoid face peeking out of a chrome helmet. The slaves brought Boeuf Bourguignon stew made with red wine, pearl onions, mushrooms and bacon.

After their father, Théophile DeTroyes said grace, they all started eating. Julie and Alastriona exchanged clandestine looks. *Is she going to tell them about her boyfriend?*

Julie sat there, eating silently.

Determination mingled with disappointment. *If she won't do it, I will.* Alastriona spoke up. "So Julie, tell me more about Decimus."

Julie gave Alastriona a dirty look.

"Who's Decimus?" asked Chantel.

Between bites of stew, Alastriona said in a matter-of-fact tone, "Julie's boyfriend."

"Alastriona!" shouted Julie. She glanced left and right at her parents and went silent.

Their parents were speechless for a moment as they took in the news.

Finally, Chantel grinned. "Don't be silly, Alastriona. Julie is far too young to have a boyfriend. We haven't even started searching for her husband yet."

"It's true," said Alastriona.

Chantel pretended not to be angry. She stiffened slightly and turned her nose up just a little bit. "You shouldn't engage in inappropriate behavior like this, Julie."

"I don't see a problem with it," said Théophile, "as long as it's not serious. But you should be careful not to indulge too long in these childish games, Julie."

"It's not childish at all," said Julie. "I love Decimus and he loves me."

Chantel, Théophile, and Alastriona all broke out in laughter.

Taking pity on her moronic sister, Alastriona hoped she would pay attention. "Everybody that's anybody gets an arranged marriage,

Julie."

"That's right. We'll decide what's best for you," Théophile said. "The Chinese call these types of marriages, 'máng hūn.'"

"Yeah, that translates as, 'blind marriage,'" said Julie. "Not for me, thanks."

Their mother shook her head in exasperation. "No one wants their children making rash decisions to marry someone because of passion or lust. In an arranged marriage, you will stay together forever."

"What about love?" asked Julie.

"Don't be naive, Julie. There's no such thing as true love," said Théophile. "That's just a silly romantic fantasy."

Julie stopped arguing and devoted her attention to her food.

Alastriona tried to get her sister to understand. "There are two kinds of love: The first kind is frivolous, romantic love. That kind of love leads to madness and suffering. The second kind is the stable form of love that is the result of careful planning."

Julie found her voice. "But love isn't supposed to make sense. If you start a fire, you can't control where it goes. You should follow your passions, sis. Don't you want to fall wildly in love with someone?"

Alastriona shook her head. "Of course not. I have no patience for crazy love. It's pointless and irresponsible."

Chantel, chimed in. "Husbands and wives fall in love with each other after the wedding takes place in order to sustain their marriage. You know the divorce rates for provincials are over fifty percent. Arranged marriages rarely result in a divorce. You know the statistics as well as anyone, Julie."

"That reminds me," said Théophile. "I have an announcement to make."

Théophile waved over a slave. The robot came over with a bottle of wine, which he displayed with a slight bow. Théophile nodded. The slave opened the bottle and poured him a sample. Théophile breathed in it's aroma, tasted it, and smiled. He motioned for the slave to fill everyone's glass. "Since this is a special occasion, I have brought out a bottle of Burgundian Pinot Noir all the way from Earth."

The slave went around pouring. Alastriona watched the robot fill her glass. She picked it up and inhaled the aroma, which reminded her of cherries and strawberries. She took a sip and closed her eyes, tasting mushrooms, pine, and just a hint of anise. It tasted like sunlight shining down on a grove of cherry trees.

"What's the occasion?" asked Julie.

"Alastriona is getting married," said Théophile.

Alastriona nearly choked on the wine. She set the glass down and coughed. "Désolé."

Feeling as if she had just been shoved off a high platform without an antigravity belt, Alastriona took a moment to regain her composure.

Chantel asked, "Aren't you excited, Alastriona?"

"Of course," she said. "It's just a surprise, that's all."

"We've spent months searching for just the right man," said Chantel. "We found one. He's a Pure Strain Human from Earth."

Théophile huffed. "You're being redundant, Chantel."

Pure Strain Humans where those who were born on Earth. They enjoyed more benefits than the provincial citizens who were born on colony worlds. Pure Strain Humans were the highest class of elites in the Imperium.

Picking up her glass of wine, Alastriona leaned back in her chair. She looked outside at the storm raining down on the Scylanthians. The star HD 84117 was going down and the horizon was full of colors. Light glittered off wet bodies of the balloon-like people. The French colony world Scylanthia was warmed by a white F8V main sequence star in the constellation of Hydra. At 6,100 degrees Kelvin, it burned hotter and brighter than Sol, the homeworld of humanity. A world that she could never go to because she wasn't a Pure Strain Human.

Théophile reached out and took Chantel's hand into his. "That means your children will be allowed to visit the Forbidden Palace.

Earth."

Chantel smiled warmly at her husband. "Your father and I met in Paris for the first time after our parents arranged for us to be together. I wish you could see it. It's such a beautiful city."

Théophile squeezed her hand. "Our family will finally be secure once again."

Alastriona nodded. Colonies were well protected by the Imperial legions, but they were far from impregnable. All of the frontiers were on fire with the wars of expansion. Occasionally, a colony would be decimated. The safest place for humans was the Earth itself. Since Julie and Alastriona were not born there, it was essential that they marry Pure Strains, so that their descendants would have the greatest chance of survival.

Théophile gave Alastriona a sober look. "Until Julie comes of age, the fate of the future of our entire family rests with one person. You."

Alastriona took a deep breath. She knew how important it was. She would do the right thing for their family. She smiled. "What's his name?"

Her father smiled. "Maximo."

Alastriona took another sip of wine and tasted the name. *Maximo.* She wasn't sure if she liked it. The name meant, "The greatest." *He's probably full of himself.*

"Your compatibility profiles match perfectly," said Chantel. "He's ideal for you."

Alastriona raised her eyebrows and tilted her head slightly. "May I see the algorithm you used to calculate the biographical correlates?"

"Certainly," said Théophile. "Here are the formula specifications. My grandfather developed them out of the compatibility matrices used on Old Earth." He waved a hand and the data was transferred onto her device. "I have also included a Cost Benefit Analysis report."

"Thank you."

Alastriona spent a few minutes reading the reports. Core values, communication styles, personality types, interests, hobbies, music, conflict resolution styles, family backgrounds, financial goals, future plans, physical traits, astrological synastry. His Chinese astrology sign was metal rooster. She was a water dragon. A perfect match. "Very nice," she said. "How did you find someone with an overall 93% compatibility match?"

Théophile stopped eating and picked up his glass of wine to take a sip. "I assure you, it took some time. There were three other high probability correlates, but none of them had as high a rating as this one."

With a cheery, "Hmm," Alastriona put her hand computer

down, satisfied.

"Soulless, computer generated love," muttered Julie. "How romantic."

"It's not supposed to be romantic," explained Alastriona. "It's supposed to be practical."

Julie turned to their father, "Will she get to meet this man, before she marries him?"

"Don't be ridiculous," said Chantel. "Of course she will."

Théophile couldn't keep the excitement out of his voice. "You're an astute girl, Alastriona. You have one of the highest IQ's the Imperium has seen in the past hundred years and you weren't even the result of genetic modification."

Alastriona interrupted by teasing her sister. "Julie modified my DNA, didn't you sis?"

Her sister was one of the top genetic engineers on Scylanthia. Julie giggled. "Yes, I modify everybody's DNA these days. Decimus—"

Julie stopped talking after she mistakenly mentioned her boyfriend's name. Alastriona motioned for one of the slaves to refill her wine glass and a robot came over to pour. Alastriona gave her foolish sister a sharp look of discouragement.

Their father didn't notice the exchange. "The point, Alastriona, is that you're a natural genius. This man is the smartest detective in the entire Imperium. He's almost as intelligent as you are. You'll get along just fine."

"He's a police officer?"

"Not just that, he's a specialist," said Chantel. "Maximo is a Chief Inspector. He tracks down the most notorious criminals in the Imperium. He's famous."

"I've never heard of him," grumbled Julie between bites of stew.

"Julie, love matches out of passion rarely work," said Chantel. "Arranged marriages create the only kind of love that will lead to happiness."

Alastriona nodded in agreement, but despite her outward appearances, she suddenly became aware of the emptiness in her heart. She was reluctant to get married. She looked at her parents, who sat there, smiling. Were they truly happy together? They had always gotten along fine, but there had always been a clinical feeling between them. *That's because we're a family of scientists.* No, the statistics never lied. She looked into her mother's eyes, not sure if she believed her own words. "That makes sense, of course. You're right."

"I know you're feeling a little worried, Alastriona," said Chantel. "That's all right. I felt the same way when I first met Théophile."

Alastriona didn't want to think about marriage now. "I don't know if this is the best time," she said. "I have my career. I've made an important discovery."

"You just received your military commission," said Théophile. "It's the perfect time."

*Maybe they're right,* she thought. *I should let them plan out my life for me. It's the smartest thing to do.* Alastriona let out a loud sigh. "All right. If you think he's good enough for me, fine, I guess."

Julie added a comment, "But if she doesn't like him, she has the right to say no."

"Of course she does," said her mother. "But we know she won't."

Alastriona brushed a strand of hair out of her face, overcome with a sinking feeling. She wondered if she was doomed to spend the rest of her life feeling alone, even when she was with someone. *Will it be a loveless marriage?*

A slave entered with an envelope on a silver tray. He walked over and presented it to Alastriona. She picked it up, opened it and read. It was a report from the supercomputer on Scylanthia, which had finished analyzing data from a long range probe she had sent out a year ago. A rush of exhilaration swept through her body like an electric shock. In a soft voice, she whispered, "Confirmation, at last."

"What is it?" asked Theophile.

"It's a data report from a long-range science probe. It's also an invitation from the Imperial Science Institute," she said. "They've asked me to speak at a conference on Galileo."

"Isn't that a chandelier city hanging down into a gas giant?" asked Julie.

"No, Galileo is the name of the second planet around the star Copernicus," said Alastriona.

"Copernicus," muttered Julie. "I don't know it."

Putting the letter down, Alastriona shook her head in exasperation. "It's the provincial capital, stupid. Don't you know the planet, Maria Celeste?"

"Of course I know about Maria Celeste," moaned Julie. "You said Copernicus."

"A thousand years ago, the star was called, '55 Cancri.'"

"Oh, that helps," said Julie. "What they called stars a thousand years ago is so informative. Copernicus is a better name, though."

"Stop arguing, you two," said Chantel.

Alastriona stopped eating and regarded her sister. *Will she run away with Decimus?* She looked away, outside where Scylanthians drifted through the clouds. The storm had passed away but the sunshine was fading. A forbidden thought touched her mind. *I would love to run away with someone.*

Théophile asked, "What's the conference about?"

"Hmm? Oh, I've found an anomaly with the progenitor of a supernova."

They were all silent, obviously wondering what she was talking about. Alastriona returned to her diner, refusing to worry anymore about her future, or her sister's, no matter how idiotic she was behaving. Finally, Julie asked the question on all of their minds. "What's a progenitor?"

"It's a star that's approaching the end of it's life. This one is going to explode into a supernova soon."

"Soon?" said Théophile. "How soon?"

Alastriona shrugged. "It could happen tomorrow."

Silence filled the dining room as they all took it in.

Their mother broke the silence first. "Tomorrow? Is that normal? Do stars explode all the time?"

Alastriona shook her head. "No, it's quite rare in a single galaxy. We only have one or two supernovas every century."

"So what's the big deal?" asked Julie.

"It could endanger some of our new colonies at the edge of the Imperium," said Alastriona, "and it's happening a billion years before it's supposed to."

*Just like my upcoming marriage*, she thought.

"Oh," said Julie.

Her sister never mentioned her plans to get married. The idea of a wild, romantic tryst was absurd, but there was something appealing about it, too. It was like breathing in the clean air of a primordial planet. But would it be a paradise world or a nightmare?

Alastriona realized that she didn't want to get married. Not yet. She had an impulse to run away from here as far away as she could.

"When is the conference?" asked Théophile.

The Copernicus star system was 40.9 light years from Scylanthia. Alastriona calculated the travel time in her head. "In about two weeks. I'd better leave for Copernicus tomorrow."

*    *    *

After dinner, Alastriona went outside alone to watch the sunset. The skies were full of a brilliant array of Scylanthians drifting among the clouds. The pink horizon was turning into twilight. The star HD 84117 which warmed Scylanthia came out from behind a cloud, throwing bright light into her face. She squinted, wondering if she would ever find love.

A ball of light appeared on the horizon, seeming to emerge out of the star. It rapidly approached, swerving back and forth a little, like a drifting firefly caught in the wind. As it advanced towards her, Alastriona realized that it was a tiny ball of fire. It approached like a playful puppy, moving quickly, pausing and then coming closer.

As it came up to her, Alastriona caught her breath and took a step back. No larger than an marble, the little ball of fire halted just in front of her face. For some reason, it reminded her of the star IK Pegasi, the one she'd been studying. Blazing with a blue-white flame, she could feel the heat of it on her face. Another kind of warmth came from it, too: Love. Alastriona felt her heart racing. She smiled. "Hello."

The little ball of fire exploded into a bright burst of light.

Instinctively, Alastriona brought her hands up in front of her face and shut her eyes. When she opened her eyes again, the little ball of light was gone. After a moment of darkness, her scientific curiosity came back. *What was that?* After it had vanished, a powerful impression lingered: Desire. Alastriona wished that it would come back.

The star HD 84117 over Scylanthia went down. Shadows turned into night. The empty darkness brought loneliness. As night came, she saw the first stars come out. Although it wasn't visible from Scylanthia, IK Pegasi could be seen on Earth as a tiny light in the constellation of Pegasus. Soon, it would explode into a supernova.

A billion years before it's time.

Why?

*   *   *

# NINE
## Progenitor

**VERMILION BIRD OF THE SOUTH**

**COPERNICUS / GALILEO**

The armored launch emerged from the starship *Klein Frisia* and dropped down into the bluish-purple atmosphere of the enormous gas giant planet, which was named Galileo. The launch combined the functions of a shuttle and a submarine. It was designed to fly into space and also to submerge down into the thick, high pressure atmosphere of a gas giant. The launch approached an orbital ring, which looked like the blade of a chainsaw from a distance.

Suspended from the ring was Spiralis, a beautiful city that hung down like a chandelier, sparkling in the darkness. The towers of the city were arranged in two descending spirals, made to imitate DNA strands. In the center of the city was a massive dome made out of diamonds. Underneath the dome, several towers descended from it like icicles. It looked like someone had taken a snow globe of a city and had turned it upside down. Many other chandelier cities stretched out over the horizon, suspended from the orbital ring like icicles along the edge of a roof. The star Copernicus emerged over the horizon.  It's light turned Spiralis into a glittering jewel.

After a leisurely two weeks spent inside a hyperspace wormhole on a starship, Alastriona sat calmly in her seat on the launch with a book on her lap: *Bioluminescence and Chemiluminescence—Atmospheric Ghost Lights Explained.*

Stretching, she raised her arms up over her head and yawned. She put a hand into the pocket of her jacket and touched something. Curious, she withdrew it and found her sister's present. A little smile lit up her face. It was her birthday today.

Unwrapping the box, she opened it. Resting upon black velvet was a golden bracelet with an infinity symbol studded with diamonds. She took it out and fastened it around her left wrist. Holding it up to the overhead light above her seat, she smiled. She was about to close the box when she noticed that there was a note inside.

*Happy Birthday, Alastriona!*

*This infinity love bracelet was part of a treasure hoard from the San Augustin, a shipwrecked starship that had been trapped inside the atmosphere of a gas giant. They used a Deep Space Recovery Vehicle with a solid diamond hull to access the galleon. Decimus thinks this bracelet may even have come from the ancient race of the Archons! I hope you like it. What better way is there to symbolize everlasting devotion?*

*Love,*

*Julie*


Alastriona shook her head. *My sister is as witless as she is naive. Romantic love indeed.*

A pleasant tone sounded in the cabin, indicating that they had arrived in Spiralis. As the other passengers got up, she checked her phone, waiting. With an impatient sigh, she stood up, and retrieved her travel bag from the overhead rack. After disengaging the safeties, she activated her hyperspatial pouch and deposited her travel bag inside. Just as she was closing the hyperspatial pouch and folding it up into a little piece of cloth, her phone finally dinged, indicating that it had just connected with the local planetary node. She put the pouch inside her pocket and checked her phone. A message appeared from Dr. Binu Pillai: *Hello, Dr. DeTroyes. Are you coming to the conference? People are here, waiting to see you.*

Alastriona rolled her eyes, wondering how such an empty-headed man could become the director of the Imperial Science Institute on Galileo. The Klein Frisia had first stopped at Maria Celeste, the main provincial colony world in the star system before making it's way to the gas giant Galileo, which orbited closer to the star. With a sigh, she typed out a reply. *My transport was delayed. I'm on my way and will arrive presently.*

This morning, knowing that she was late for the conference, she had dressed in riding gear. Wearing black leather pants, boots, a white peasant blouse, a black leather jacket and gloves, she strode towards the exit of the Sky Palace. The gravity on her homeworld Scylanthia was .8G's, or twenty percent lighter than on Earth. So she always wore a contra-gravity belt to compensate for gravity that was heavier than she was used to.

Alastriona exited the Sky Palace and went outside, into the upside-down city surrounded by an energy dome. Disoriented, she paused to get used to the vertigo sensations. She closed her eyes, waiting for the dizziness to subside. A moment later, she reopened them.

Withdrawing her phone, she quickly located a rental agency and made her way over to a counter where a robot customer service representative waited. The robot's gold chrome body gleamed in the light of the sunshine coming in through the outer dome. "May

I help you?"

"I'd like to rent a hoverbike."

The robot waved his metallic arm and a hologram of the latest model appeared. It was a sleek and agile machine designed for swift travel through the city. It's matte-black exterior was adorned with subtle blue accents. The soft azure glow from the contra-gravity generators kept it suspended a few feet above the ground. "The I-13 Skyrider uses a powerful anti-gravity propulsion system, with twin repulsorlift generators."

Unwilling to listen to the entire sales pitch, she interrupted the robot. "Fine. I'll take it."

A few minutes later, Alastriona zoomed through the chandelier city on the I-13 Skyrider. The directions to the Imperial Science Institute were displayed on the inside of her helmet's Heads-Up-Display. With a deft tilt and a burst of acceleration, the skyrider executed hairpin turns and sharp maneuvers, weaving through the hovercar traffic effortlessly. She located the immense circular tower and drove into the parking lot at the top of the structure.

Alastriona pressed a button on her collar and the helmet withdrew into a pocket dimension. With a toss of her head to free up her hair, she got off the hoverbike and went inside the lobby. She took off her gloves, put them inside her jacket pocket and ran a hand through her hair, hoping it wasn't too messy from the ride on the hoverbike. She surveyed the lobby and noticed an Asian woman wearing a blue jacket over a white blouse and blue skirt standing at a desk.

As she approached the counter, the woman behind the desk put on a happy expression. "May I help you?"

Noticing that she was a cleverly disguised android, Alastriona smiled back. "Could you tell me where the science conference is being held?"

"The Imperial Science Instutute's conference is in the lecture hall on level 80."

"Thank you." Alastriona idly wondered why she was being polite to an android. Most people would not recognize the woman as a machine, of course, but she could tell.

Resisting an urge to rush, she walked swiftly over to the elevator and got in. A moment of disorientation returned. She was on the top floor, which was labeled, "1." All of the numbers got higher the further down they went. She pressed the "80" button at the bottom and the elevator descended. As it went down, she sang a pleasant melody to herself.

Through the transparent glass walls of the elevator, she looked at the immense purple-blue gas giant far below the city. Swirls of methane, ammonia and sulfuric acid were visible through the dim, dusky light. The old helium-3 refineries along the orbital ring still operated. Giant mining vessels, attached to the orbital ring's transport system swept down into the lower atmosphere and dipped into massive clouds of volatiles, such as nitrogen, carbon dioxide, ammonia and methane. The transport system brought the mining vessels back up, and the gasses were refined along the way.

As the elevator descended, she continued to sing to herself while looking outside.

Helium-3, the preferred fuel for aneutronic fusion was still in great demand in the provincial colonies. A single tanker could deliver enough helium-3 to power a colony for centuries. Despite the newer technologies of light sensitive crystals used to line solar sails, which were used to get to light speed quickly, the older aneutronic fusion economy transports were still used.

Giant mirrors operated as pushing stations for the old laser superhighways. Immense transport vessels full of refined helium-3 and deuterium slowly traveled along these highways which led beyond the astrosphere. Once the transports had gone through the terminal shock wave, the transports were picked up by starships and taken to their destinations through hyperspace wormholes.

She stopped singing and thought, *Galileo is such a pretty planet.*

Exiting the elevator which led onto the floor at the bottom of the tower, Alastriona strode towards a set of wide doors that led into the circular lecture hall of the Center for Astrophysics Research. The spacious room was already full of people. More than five hundred scientists and military officers were present. She strutted over to a seat next to the circular platform, sat down and crossed her legs.

With a look of relief, the Director of Astrophysics Research, Dr. Binu Pillai, nodded to  her and stepped onto the circular dais. The crowd quieted down. He spoke for a few minutes about her career. He talked about her high IQ, how she had earned her doctorate in astrophysics at such a young age, and her entry into the Imperial Star Force.

Alastriona sat there, checking the notes on her hand computer, not really listening to his introduction. The list of her scientific accomplishments had already become too long for brevity. *I guess that's what happens when you're smarter than everybody else.* Strangely, she had always been comfortable speaking in front of an audience and wasn't nervous. *They rarely understand me anyway.* Her sister had once said that she was fearless in front of crowds.

Unless the science didn't hold up.

*Am I a piece of meat being thrown into a river full of ravenous piranha?*

A slight frown touched her face. Such a strange thing, doubt. Still, she decided to recheck the data one last time, just to be safe.

Yes, it was all correct.

With a sigh of satisfaction, she closed the hand computer

and glanced around the vast lecture hall, wondering what kinds of people were here. *Brainless fools with little minds full of small ideas, probably.* A smirk slipped into her face just as Dr. Pillai called out her name, "Dr. Alastriona DeTroyes."

Standing up, she stepped onto the platform and inserted her mini-computer into a slot of the holographic projector. A green light indicated that it was connected properly. A friendly applause greeted her and she said the things you're supposed to when you take the stage. "Hello, everyone. Thank you for the kind introduction, Dr. Pillai."

With a wave of her hand, a giant hologram appeared in the center of the circular area. Although most of the audience sat in a semi-circle, there were some people behind as well. So she deliberately walked around the circular platform, pacing back and forth with purpose.

A hologram of stars appeared over the stage. The stars rotated around until the Pegasus Constellation was centered in the view. The viewpoint of the hologram rapidly zoomed into the constellation until one star was centered in the display. It slowly grew larger and larger until it filled the space above the platform. It swelled up into a huge red star.

In a soft-spoken voice, Alastriona began, "I'd like to introduce you to the scene of the greatest crime in the galaxy. This is

IK Pegasi A, a red giant star 184.02 light years from Copernicus. It's 154.2 light years from the Forbidden Planet, Sol. Just two thousand years ago, an examination of the spectrographic features of this star showed that this was a hot, type A8 star in a binary system with a white dwarf."

The hologram of the massive red giant star floated in the room. "As you can see, it's no longer a hot blue star. It has quickly evolved into a red giant, hundreds of millions of years ahead of it's time."

Murmurs swept through the audience.

Alastriona's gaze swept over the crowd. Her eyes touched a man there and her heart skipped a beat. He looked back at her and she felt an electric shock. There was an air of mystery about him. His chiseled jawline and sharp cheekbones were accentuated by the flickering glow of the hologram which cast a shadow across his rugged features. Under a pair of round glasses, his eyes held a hint of mischief, as if he knew something that nobody else did. There was an intense focus in his gaze that sent shivers down her spine.

The hologram shifted to display a small white star inside the outer envelope of the red giant. The white star was surrounded by a disk of hydrogen and helium which was being pulled onto it's surface from the red giant.

Alastriona forced herself to look away from the man and continued, "The star's companion, IK Pegasi B, a dense white dwarf, is surrounded by a gaseous accretion disk. I thought it might have become a cataclysmic variable but the current data does not support this."

Curiosity drew her gaze back to the man and when their eyes met again, her heart raced. She became keenly aware of her pulse, her breath and her every movement. It was as if his presence had ignited a fire within.

Trying not to lose track of what she was talking about, she glanced up at the hologram and with a wave of her hand, the view shifted. The image of the white dwarf grew larger and larger. "Over the past thousand years or so, the white dwarf has been steadily accumulating mass without erupting as a nova. In fact, it has nearly reached the Chandrasekhar limit."

There was an audible collective gasp of surprise from the audience. This meant that the star would soon explode. One man raised a hand, prompting her to pause. She tried to keep the irritation out of her voice and raised her eyebrows. "Yes?"

"That isn't possible. This white dwarf isn't likely to detonate into a supernova for another two billion years."

Alastriona took advantage of the pause to regain her composure. "That's what everyone thought," she said. *These simpletons call themselves scientists?*

With a wave of her hand, the hologram shifted again, focusing on the center of the white dwarf, whose core flashed and burned brightly. "A robot probe has just returned from the region. The data shows that the core of the white dwarf is not made up of magnesium, neon and oxygen. Instead, it has a carbon-oxygen core. Therefore, the pressure and temperature will soon reach the ignition temperature for carbon fusion in the core. It should be sufficient to unbind the star."

A burst of whispers swept through the room as the implications of this were keenly felt. The white dwarf would become a supernova. If the star had evolved as it should have, the binary system would have moved hundreds of light years away before the white dwarf exploded. This would be close, too close, to the Imperium.

Alastriona's cheeks flushed and her heart raced. She closed her eyes for a moment and took a deep breath, wondering who the man was. *He's probably not even a Pure Strain. He's not good enough.* She opened her eyes. *Impossible.* In that moment, she desperately hoped that she would see him again.

Collecting her scattered thoughts together, she waved a hand and the hologram vanished. "The question is, why? Something killed this star. Was it deliberate? This region of the galaxy was where the ancients fought massive battles. Has an ancient piece of technology been discovered? We need to find out who or what killed this star because there is no natural explanation for why this happened so quickly."

Silence filled the room. Normally, she would have expected a nice round of applause at the end of one of her presentations. She glanced around the room, self-consciously wondering how to end her speech. She found something to say. "I have written a paper on this with all of the relevant details. Feel free to examine the data. That's all I have for now. Thank you."

Dr. Pillai got up and clapped, which was followed by an uncomfortable applause from the rest of the room. Most of those present were used to scientific discussions on stellar evolution or other subjects, but this talk unsettled everyone because a supernova could threaten the Imperium.

Flustered, Alastriona looked back to where the man had been sitting, but he was no longer there. She took a deep breath, both disappointed and relieved. She was here to realize her destiny, not to get involved with a mystery man. But she closed her eyes again, just for a moment, to bathe in the remembrance of the radiance of the encounter again.

* * *

The warm glow of candlelight cast long shadows across the hotel lounge where a woman sat, playing a Spanish guitar. The delicate notes filled the air with an ethereal beauty. With her eyes closed, the musician was lost in the music. Small groups of people

45

sat on couches or stood, enraptured.

Just outside the lounge, Alastriona was standing near a group of scientists, not really listening to their discussion, while she looked up and down the hallways, inquisitive. The mystery man was nowhere in sight. She lowered her eyes, disappointed. Then she noticed that someone was walking up to her.

A high ranking officer approached. Tall and broad-shouldered, he exuded an aura of strength and leadership. His dark skin was the color of rich mahogany and his voice was deep and resonant. He wore the white uniform of the Imperial Star Force and held the rank of Legatus Legionis. He halted in front of her. "Lieutenant DeTroyes, I presume."

Alastriona smiled. "Yes, sir."

"You're out of uniform."

"Oh?" His remark caught her off guard. "But this is a science symposium."

"You are a second lieutenant in the Imperial Star Force," he said. "That's what your dossier says. In the future, I expect you to wear your uniform during these events."

"To a science lecture, sir?"

His sigh was audible and indicated his annoyance. In a corrective tone, he said, "Tell me, Lieutenant, what is the Imperial Star Force?"

A memorized reply came to mind. "It's a uniformed scientific and military organization."

"What is it's primary mandate?"

"Exploration, research, diplomacy and peacekeeping, sir."

"That's right," he said. "Scientists conducting research here are under the command of the military and don't you forget it. Report to my office tomorrow morning at zero six hundred."

"Yes, sir."

The man walked away, leaving her shaken. *Oh, God, please save me from these rigid military minds.* Too often, during her military career, she had encountered imbeciles who enjoyed using their power to demean the ones that threatened them. She shook her head and muttered, "Arrogance and stupidity, what a nice combination."

Dr. Binu Pillai approached her with two glasses of champagne. He held one out.

She took it with a smile. "Merci, Dr. Pillai."

"Thank you for such an enlightening discussion, Dr. DeTroyes," he said. "Do you really think the star IK Pegasus A will explode into a supernova during our lifetimes?"

An irritated frown touched her face. "IK Pegasus B, the white dwarf." She sighed in exasperation. "It may already have happened."

"Oh, I never thought –" he paused to collect his thoughts. "That's right. It's a hundred and eighty light years away, isn't it?"

She nodded. "A hundred and eighty-four point zero two light years."

"Then we won't know anything for a long time," he said. "The Imperium is safe."

She shrugged. "For now, yes."

Dr. Pillai chuckled. "I do love your sense of drama, Dr. DeTroyes. I thought we were all in trouble. Once again, I must congratulate you on your presentation. These events are usually quite dull."

Suddenly, she realized that she had no idea who that officer was or where she was supposed to report to in the morning. "Dr. Pillai, could you tell me the name of that man I was just talking to?"

Dr. Pillai grinned. "That was Legatus Legionis Itoro Oliha," he said. "He's the commanding officer of the Imperial Star Force on Galileo. He's the highest ranking officer on this planet."

"Oh."

Alastriona drank down the glass of champagne, wishing it was something stronger.

Dr. Pillai laughed.

Feeling self-conscious again, she asked, "How long is a day on this planet?"

He waved at a passing slave who was carrying a tray of glasses filled with more champagne. The robot walked over and bowed slightly. Dr. Pillai took Alastriona's empty glass out of her hand and placed it on the tray. "Twelve hours."

He drained his own drink and put it on the tray as well. He picked up another pair of glasses and gave her one. "Don't worry, Lieutenant. I think he likes you."

*  *  *

Under a thick diamond dome that covered the city Spiralis, dozens of buildings occupied an immense circular plaza. Beyond the dome, immense clouds of blue and purple swirled over the planet Galileo. The star Copernicus lit up the dome, which sparkled in the daylight. One of the larger buildings, the Principia, was the planetary headquarters for the 14th Legion, which was stationed in this star system. It had the look of an ancient roman temple with immense white pillars and statues outside. Next to a formal garden, poplar trees lined the road leading up to the building, as if they were soldiers standing at attention.

Alastriona arrived in a hovercar, which dropped her off at the entrance. She wore a high-collared white military coat, trimmed in gold, over a white blouse, pants and boots. The jacket held the rank insignia of a Second Lieutenant, along with the gold emblem of a science officer of the Imperium.

A gust of wind caught her long blonde hair and blew it into her face just as she entered the building through the Porta Caeli, the Gate of Heaven. Brushing her hair out of her face, she walked with a brisk, confident stride across the polished marble floor of a courtyard lined with marble pillars.

Finally, she came to a door, wondering if the commanding officer was as senseless as the director of the Imperial Science Institute. She took a deep breath, straightened her hair, smoothed out her uniform and knocked.

The door opened and a gleaming silver robot came out, carrying a hyperspatial briefcase. As it walked by without making a comment, she glanced after it. It went down the hallway and out of the building.

She heard a man speak from inside the office. "I don't know about this, sir. We've never gone out this far."

Another voice, which she recognized as belonging to their commanding officer responded in an impassioned tone, "Come on, Karl. After what happened, I think you need something like this."

Alastriona remained still, wondering what to do. Oliha called out to her, "Come in, Lieutenant."

The white circular office was surrounded by glass windows interspersed with marble pillars. Several potted plants gave the room some color. Outside, one could see an immaculate garden full of flowers. The room was dominated by a white desk on top of a circular platform that had a turquoise light under the single step.

Legatus Legionis Itoro Oliha sat behind his desk, where a

hologram of IK Pegasi was suspended above it.

Sitting on her side of the desk was another man. He appeared to be middle aged and had a sturdy physique that bore evidence of countless days under the starry heavens. He black hair had a distinguished touch of silver at the temples. He had piercing blue eyes that held an unwavering focus, as if he was charting the course of a vessel. A small, well-kempt beard gave him the air of an aristocrat. He wore the uniform of a captain and emanated an aura of command and quiet resolve. But there was a trace of pain in his eyes, which only made him appear more mysterious.

Exuding a sense of calmness and control, she came to attention and saluted. In a confident voice, she said, "Second Lieutenant Alastriona DeTroyes, reporting as ordered, sir."

Oliha saluted back and repeated her name, "Alastriona DeTroyes. Thank you for joining us. At least you're on time, I'll give you that."

He deliberately mispronounced her first name, "Alas-tree-ONA," instead of saying it correctly, which sounded like, "Alas-TREENA." Officers sometimes did this to annoy their subordinates and to assert their dominance. He was baiting her. She resisted an urge to smirk at him, knowing he would want to play the power games that all military commanders enjoyed. *I shall endure his petty discipline and then we'll see how bright he really is.*

He sized her up and down. "Where is your thunderbolt, Lieutenant?"

Vajra Thunderbolts were small batons that held spiritual powers, if you could figure out how to unlock them. They were symbols of imperial authority given to commissioned officers.

"I thought Vajras were purely ceremonial, sir."

"They are not," said Oliha. "When you're in uniform, I expect you to be wearing it."

"Yes, sir."

"When I first heard your theory about an impending supernova, I thought it was a joke. But for some reason, Dr. Pillai says that your research on IK Pegasi is sound," he said. "However, I'm not so sure you're the best candidate to study this."

Alastriona lost her composure and relaxed her gaze. "I don't understand, sir."

Oliha jumped down her throat. "You're at attention, Lieutenant," he said. "Did I give you permission to speak?"

"No sir.

"Scientists!" he complained. He stood up, turned his back on her and went over to the window, muttering to himself. "No discipline at all. Every one of them has an attitude as big as this planet. If only they spent more time doing real science instead of admiring themselves, maybe we would have more progress in the Imperium."

He stood there, silently gazing into the carefully manicured garden inside an artificial dome over the chandelier city above a gas giant. The familiar surroundings were a lie. Beyond the artificial dwellings, the universe was full of cold darkness. They were surrounded by death. After a time he seemed to come to a conclusion and turned around. "At ease."

Alastriona adopted a parade-rest posture. She avoided making eye contact with him, not really interested in his military opinions.

"You're only a provincial citizen, is that right?"

"Yes, sir. But I'm from a Pure Strain family."

"Pure Strain Humans understand what it really means to be part of the well-honed machine of the Imperium," he said. "In my experience, provincials are undisciplined, reckless adventurers. They get us into more trouble out on the frontiers than even our inferior subjects do."

"Inferior" was the name given to all of the conquered alien races. Mostly it was correct. Inferiors were rarely as intelligent as their human subjugators. Aliens were full of problems. They actually warred against each other. Many of their worlds were full of famine, disease, poverty and suffering. The Imperium, once they had conquered an inferior world, became their guardians and protectors, guiding them into a better future.

He asked, "What makes you think you're the one that should

be conducting an investigation into this star system?”

“Permission to speak freely, sir?”

“Granted.”

In a dismissive tone, she spoke with cold honesty. “Respectfully, sir, you’re not a scientist. You’re a bureaucrat. You’re no more than a menial cog in a huge galactic wheel. I’m smarter than you are. Those with slower minds need to give smarter people everything they want. No one should ever disagree with them. When you understand that, it will make things much simpler. The truth is, you need me. The Imperium needs me.”

To his credit, he silently took it all in.

She pushed harder, looking into his eyes. “Don’t you agree, sir?”

He nodded. “Perhaps, I do,” he said. “But understand this: I expect all officers serving in the Imperial Star Force to conduct themselves with discipline and self-control at all times, both in their personal conduct and in their adherence to military regulations and standards. One of the most important of these standards is respect for your superiors. Is that understood?”

*Another insecure officer, obviously.* She raised her eyebrows. “Yes, sir.”

Oliha nodded and turned to the other man. “This is Captain Karl Winters, the best explorer in the Imperium. He’s your new commanding officer. I’m assigning you to his starship, the Tycho

Brahe. It's one of the fastest science vessels we have."

Captain Winters stood and offered his hand. She took it. As they touched, she noticed that his hands were icy cold. He said in a chilly voice, "Lieutenant."

Oliha sat down, all business now. "Your orders are to go to IK Pegasi to discover what is happening to the stars there, whether it may pose a danger to the Imperium and how much time we will have to prepare, if indeed, the star turns into a supernova. Dismissed."

*   *   *

Imperial Courier Drone: 3A7B9F42

Origin: Copernicus / Maria Celeste — Galileo

Destination: Copernicus / Maria Celeste — HD 84117 / Scylanthia

March 15, 3235

*Dear Julie,*

*Ever since I set sail on the Tycho Brahe, I have been disappointed. I have no one near me who has a cultivated and intelligent mind. One whose tastes are like my own. Someone who can hold an intelligent conversation is, sadly, an unattainable goal on this starship. I am surrounded by educated fools who call themselves scientists. Their incompetence is only exceeded by the military geniuses I am forced to work with. However, my predicament was to be expected. I find myself concerned about you, though. I suppose you have the right to ruin your life with your silly ideas about love, but I wish you would see reason. Romance just isn't real. I will write again soon, but it will be some time before my letters can get there. Don't do anything crazy.*

*Love,*

*Alastriona*

Secure Data Transmission Encrypted

Imperial Regulations Compliant

*   *   *

Dozens of armored launches and smaller pinnace shuttles rested upon the platforms of the Sky Palace over the orbital ring. Starships rarely descended to the ring because of the heavy atmosphere of the gas giant. The launches served to bring people down to the ring, or brought them up to the starships anchored in a higher orbit.

Wearing her uniform, including the Vajra Thunderbolt baton which now hung from her belt, Alastriona sat in a monorail, looking out the window. A massive anticyclonic storm, twice the size of her homeworld Scylanthia, swirled a slow dance across the planet. *It looks like a blueberry smoothie.* She smiled at the comparison just as the monorail came to a rest at the sky palace. She exited the monorail, went inside and looked at the flight board. She took the moving walkway to gate 16 and boarded a pinnace shuttle that would take her up to the *Tycho Brahe.*

Though the pinnace did not have windows, a hologram displayed their approach to the starship. Like most vessels, the *Tycho Brahe* looked like an ancient sailing ship, except for three sets of three masts that were equally spaced in lines around the cylindrical hull. When the solar sails were hoisted upon the nine masts and unfurled, the starship would look like a flower in bloom. As an exploration vessel, it was heavily armed with a hundred and four guns. The pinnace approached and docked.

Stepping through the airlock at the ship's main entry port, Alastriona was greeted by three officers, one woman and two men. She came to attention and saluted. "Permission to come aboard, sir."

The senior officer present was a centurion. He was a ruggedly handsome man of African heritage, with a towering stature. He was obviously a man of strong discipline and unyielding loyalty to the Imperium. His uniform was well-tailored and meticulously maintained, all the way down to his highly polished boots. He had a finely etched scar along the side of his face, which gave him a forbidding appearance. "Granted," he said. "I am First Officer Salisu Tinibu."

He turned slightly and pointed at one of to the other two officers present. "This is our Chief Science Officer and your immediate superior, Lieutenant Nils Ostergaard. He will give you your assignments. Now, I have things to do."

Abruptly, Tinibu turned and walked away. He went up a staircase to the upper deck. Remaining at attention, Alastriona listened to his receding boots.

Lieutenant Ostergaard was a lean blonde man with a serene demeanor. When he smiled, his slate gray eyes warmed a touch. "At ease, Lieutenant."

Alastriona relaxed somewhat and looked around. Twenty-eight blaster cannons sat in two rows of fourteen cannons on either side of the middle gun deck. Shot garlands with projectiles – spheres of energized atomic particles referred to as, "round shot" – lined the grating and stairways at the center.

"It's good to finally get a top astrophysicist on the crew," he said. "You're on the larboard watch. Report to duty at the middle watch."

Alastriona nodded. That meant midnight to four in the morning, by Earth's calendar, which was used throughout the Imperium, even though every planet had different lengths for a day. She sometimes wondered why provincials weren't allowed to use their own day cycles. They all had to use Earth's, which no one had ever visited, unless they were a Pure Strain.

Surprised that she was being treated like a new recruit, Alastriona frowned. "I am to stand watch, sir?"

"Yes," he said. "The captain wants everyone to be familiar with all aspects of sailing a starship. Don't worry, Lieutenant. You will get plenty of time for scientific research once we're closer to our destination."

Ostergaard turned to a tall, thin blonde woman at his side. She had a stern disposition and bore a cool, distant look. "This is Second Lieutenant Saila Heikkinen," he said. "She's our contact scientist. Welcome aboard."

He offered his hand.

Alastriona shook it and glanced at Lieutenant Heikkinen. *What a perfect attitude for an Imperial diplomat.*

Ostergaard said, "Saila, why don't you lead DeTroyes to her cabin?"

"Yes, sir." She pointed to the left where a structure surrounded what looked like a meal preparation area. "That's the main galley for the crew. Beyond those doors at the fore is medical. Come with me please."

Saila led Alastriona down the corridor to the right, to the aft of the starship. They entered an area that looked like a common room. Eight doors lined either side. "This is the wardroom. Home for all of the junior officers."

Noticing an unfamiliar accent when Saila spoke, Alastriona asked, "Where are you from, if you don't mind my asking?"

"I'm from the city Oulu in Finland."

*Finland. I don't know that planet.* Alastriona bit her lip, not wanting to show her ignorance.

Saila walked up to the door on the port side, furthest aft of all the others. "This is you. You're already authorized."

"Thank you."

"Not at all." A mischievous grin slipped into Saila's expression, shattering her standoffish attitude. As if she was sharing a secret, she whispered, "I heard you came blazing into the conference on a hoverbike."

"Yes, my transport arrived late and I barely made it there on time."

"I bet that was fun," she said.

"Hardly. I hate being late."

"Oh," said Saila. "Make sure that your hyperspatial containers are all deactivated and stowed away before we enter hyperspace."

The special containers used extra-dimensional technology. You could fit an entire cargo hold full of goods inside of one. But a hyperspatial container would rip a starship in half if it was active while entering a wormhole. They were made with special safeties that automatically deactivated the devices when near a hyperspace vortex, which sent their contents into oblivion. Most starship captains required everyone to manually turn them off anyway.

Alastriona was irritated that anyone would remind her of something everyone knew about. *These military people are as dumb as rocks. I am not a child.* "Yes, of course."

Saila said, "When you're ready, I'll give you a tour of the rest of the Tycho Brahe. I'm free all afternoon."

"Very well. Just give me a few minutes to unpack."

Saila sat down in a chair by the table in the wardroom. "I'll wait."

Alastriona placed a hand on the lock and the door opened. She went inside and looked around the small cabin. A blaster cannon, turned to the side to make room, rested against the hull. She withdrew her hyperspatial pouch, opened it, placed it on the bed, reached inside and withdrew her uniforms, one at a time. She hung them all up in the closet.

As she turned around, the little ball of fire which she had encountered on Scylanthia was there, hovering in midair. Alastriona caught her breath.

The ball of fire radiated its warm light and she felt it on her face.

A great happiness came upon her at the sight of the little light. *So, you are a life-form after all. Fascinating. A being of pure energy.* She smiled. "Hello."

*   *   *

# EIGHT

## The Nameless Ones

**VERMILION BIRD OF THE SOUTH**

**COPERNICUS / ASTROSPHERE**

The little ball of light winked out.

Alastriona wondered if she had imagined it.

Saila called through the open doorway, "What did you say?"

Stepping outside, Alastriona closed the door behind her. "Nothing."

As the starship got underway, Lieutenant Heikkinen gave Alastriona a tour. The *Tycho Brahe* had eight decks. The hold at the bottom contained all of their supplies. The orlop deck above the hold had cabins for midshipmen recruits, the steward, purser, and the healer. Next to a medical dispensary, the captain and first officer had private storage rooms with encrypted locks. The orlop deck was lined with warbots standing in power bays. At the stem was robot maintenance, engineering and the power center, which held the 5 meter tall sunstone crystal that powered the starship. To the aft was the hangar bay, containing longboats and a pair of fighters.

The lower, middle and upper gun decks had crew quarters, along with the starship's main armament. For sublight duels, fifty-eight blaster cannons rested upon the lower two decks.

Thirty-two laser cannons for computerized light speed combat were on the upper gun deck and on the quarterdeck. There were two crew lounges on the upper gun deck, one for officers at the fore and a larger one at the aft for the rest of the crew.

Above the three gun decks was the science deck. This contained the stellar observatory, stellar cartography, a gymnasium, a garden, and hydroponics. Saila paused outside a hallway leading aft where a pair of Marines stood guard. "This area is occupied by the leader of this expedition, Legatus Kevin Von Meyer, along with his Executive Assistant, Elfriede Tischler. Von Meyer is the CEO of World Builders in the Pegasus Province."

"I thought Captain Winters was in command of this excursion."

Saila shook her head. "Your scientific paper on IK Pegasus

got everyone's attention. Von Meyer wants to know if it's safe to establish colonies in Pegasus, so he's accompanying us. Captain Winters has a cabin aft of the quarterdeck above us."

*   *   *

Stars glittered overhead. They had stepped out onto the quarterdeck, which was covered by a forcefield that held off the vacuum of space. They had sailed away from Galileo towards the edge of the star system, which was called the Termination Shock. The star Copernicus had already shrunk down to the size of what Sol would have looked like from Earth. Alastriona knew they wouldn't stop at Maria Celeste, the main colony world in this star system, but would head out beyond the astrosphere so they could enter a hyperspace wormhole which would take them to their destination on the other side of the Imperium.

Three of the starship's nine masts rose up from the quarterdeck and extended beyond the forcefield into space. The other six masts extended out from the lower hull and protruded "down" at 120-degree angles to either side of the centerline of the starship, in two sets of three masts. Tubes inside the masts allowed the crew to climb into the rigging where they could work on the solar sails. Alastriona noticed that they were currently sailing under topsails alone. She glanced at the orange star Copernicus and wondered if the  stellar winds were strong today. *Perhaps it's because Galileo is so close to the star to begin with, where the astrosphere is strongest.*

Saila pointed towards the front of the starship. "The cathedral is inside the fo'c'sle."

"I can see that."

For some reason, Alastriona had always hated the crimson gloom inside starship cathedrals. At the same time, she felt more protected in pitch darkness than anywhere else. It was like snuggling up inside a warm blanket. This was why she had joined the Imperial Star Force. Her dream had always been to immerse herself in an eternal night, sprinkled with stars. She leaned against a railing next to a sailor who was sitting on the deck, dozing. Even though she wasn't on watch, she chose not to disturb him.

Saila looked down at him and smiled.

Alastriona whispered, "Why did you join the Imperial Star Force?"

Saila looked outside the energy dome into the darkness. "My family was in Helsinki during the Hymenopteran War of Extinction," she said. "After the bugs nuked the city, I was all alone in the countryside. So I chose to become a contact scientist. I want to help us avoid unnecessary wars with aliens."

"Oh, I'm so sorry." Alastriona brushed a strand of hair out of her eyes. "I wasn't even born yet. My parents escaped the war by settling on the colony world, Pleione."

"Really? The captain is from Pleione."

Alastriona turned her attention to the aft of the quarterdeck where the captain's cabin was. All she remembered from Pleione was a terrible cold that froze you all the way down to the bones, and her mother's endless sobbing. The memory of it made her shiver.

Saila continued, "I just went through my first age regression treatment. I'm one hundred and eleven years old. Eleventy-one."

Alastriona suppressed an embarrassed smile. "I'm just twelve, by Scylanthia's calendar."

"How old is that on Earth?"

"Eighteen."

"How did you graduate so soon?"

They were interrupted by the ship's bell, which rang eight times, sounded in sets of two. Eight bells. It was time to change the watch. Crewmen came out onto the deck and climbed into the rigging while those above came down. The sleeping sailor didn't wake up.

A dark-skinned man with a wiry muscular build indicative of a life spent on starships came down the ladder from the poop deck. He roamed out onto the quarterdeck, giving out orders. He looked at the sleeping man and exclaimed, "Jonesy, bestir yourself."

The man woke up and jumped to his feet. "Sorry, sir."

"Aloft now."

The sailor ran over to the tube leading up the main mast,

stepped inside and went up. The dark-skinned man watched him climb. Even though he was using the intercom, he shouted to the crew, "All hands, make sail. Clap on sail, lads, and look sharp about it."

He put his hands on his hips and glared up into the main mast. "You there! I might with justice hang you from the yard-arm if you don't reeve off a new tackle. Quickly now."

His gaze dropped down to Alastriona and Saila. "Good afternoon, ladies."

"Good afternoon," said Saila.

The man looked at them with stern eyes. "It was kind of you to refrain from putting that man on report for sleeping on the quarterdeck, though I should think the captain would prefer we stick to stricter discipline."

Although he outranked them both, neither Alastriona nor Saila chose to explain themselves. Saila said, "Lieutenant De Troyes, this gentleman is our Sailing Master, Jabulani Dlamini."

Jabulani looked her over. "You the new officer everyone is complaining about?"

Alastriona raised her eyebrows. "Perhaps, yes."

"Good." He grinned. "What I hate more than anything else is complacency in our command structure."

Holding back an amused smile, she asked, "Sir, why don't we

use the automatic controls for the solar sails?"

"I want experienced sailors aloft, not push-button imbeciles," he said. "We'll be using the solar sails for another thirty hours before we hit the Termination Shock. Then it's a hyperspace wormhole for 20 solar days to 51 Pegasi. Once we get there, we haven't even begun our excursion into deep space yet. We're on a real odyssey this time. Good day."

* * *

**HYPERSPACE**

Over the time they spent in the hyperspace vortex, Alastriona did what was required by her commanding officers. She executed the orders from her superiors and stood watch, taking command on deck. While in a star system, the watch officer was responsible for ensuring they maintained their correct course and bearing, but in hyperspace this wasn't necessary. Standing watch in a wormhole was to remain in perpetual darkness. All you needed to do was keep alert for damage to the hypersails.

The majority of her free time was spent in the science labs, studying the data reports from IK Pegasi. The entity which she had encountered did not reappear, much to her dismay. She began to think she had imagined it's appearance altogether. She didn't encounter Captain Winters or Legatus Von Meyer at all, which was fine with her, since she had little patience for dullards in the military. *Best not to play in their silly power games.* A few days before they were to arrive at their destination, a star system at the edge of the Imperium known as 51 Pegasi, she went into the officer's lounge at the aft of the upper gun deck.

A woman played Bach melodies on an Italian lute, filling the lounge with pleasant music. Lieutenant Nils Ostergaard was sitting at a table next to a panoramic window looking out into space, or in this case, the hyperspace wormhole. No light came from outside, except for a dim red glow left over from the Big Bang at the birth of the universe.  Flickering candles cast a warm glow over the lounge. Amidst the gentle hum of conversation between a dozen officers there, a sense of tranquility pervaded.

Saila Heikkinen was seated next to Nils, holding a steaming cup of something warm. A partially sliced loaf of bread sat on a cutting board next to some cheese. Nils took a bite just as Alastriona approached and sat down. He said, "I thought I was a recluse. Do you ever stop working?"

Before she could respond, a robot slave sauntered over and said in a tinny voice, "May I help you?"

Alastriona looked at the gleaming silver machine. No attempt had been made to humanize it. Most places she'd been to employed human looking androids. Flustered, she stumbled out a reply. "I, um, yes please. What wines do you have?"

The slave waved a hand and a holographic list appeared with the available wines. The slave pointed at one. "I recommend the Imperial Reserve. Crafted from select grapes harvested under the radiant glow of Gliese 282's triple suns, this Cabernet Sauvignon exudes opulence and sophistication. It's bold flavors of ripe black-berries, cassis, and dark chocolate are underscored by nuances of espresso and toasted oak. A full-bodied palate, framed by supple tannins and vibrant acidity, leads to an enduring finish of black pepper and clove."

"Yes, please. I'll take a glass."

The slave went over to the bar, retrieved the bottle, opened it and began slowly decanting the wine into a glass vessel. Alastriona turned to look at Nils. "I'm sorry, what did you say?"

"Not very friendly," said Nils, crossing his arms. "That's what the crew says about you."

"Oh." She wasn't listening. With her mind elsewhere, she muttered, "Using the mass and chemical composition of IK Pegasi AB, I've constructed new mathematical models to compute what should be their proper evolutionary phases, but I've never seen such accelerated transformations in a star before. It's all happening, quick as a wink."

Saila and Nils exchanged concerned glances.

Alastriona leaned onto her elbows and put her hands on her

forehead, pushing fingers into her hair. "I've run extensive calcu-lations to determine the changing state of both of these stars over time, but the data just doesn't add up at all. It isn't natural. An external force is definitely involved."

Nils snapped his fingers three times in front of her face. "Wake up, DeTroyes."

Leaning back, Alastriona dropped her hands down and glanced around the bar. "Sorry. Just thinking out loud. I have a lot on my mind."

Saila asked, "Is this the first time you've come here?"

"Oui."

"We've been in space for nearly three weeks," said Saila.

The robot slave returned with the wine and placed a glass on the table. Alastriona picked it up. The slave poured. She inhaled the aroma and took a sip. Nodding, she held out the glass and the slave filled it. She glanced up at the machine. "Merci."

"Isn't that why we're going there?" asked Saila. "To figure out what's happening with the stars of IK Pegasi?"

"Of course," said Alastriona. "But there is a ton of preparation work to do before we get there. I'm excited to discover if the flare from runaway fusion of a supernova transforms into a supersonic detonation from subsonic deflagration or not. It's been an unan-swered question for thousands of years."

"This is an order, Lieutenant," said Nils. "Stop working so hard. You're to relax as least an hour every day. You don't have to justify your presence here."

"Don't I?"

"Not at all."

With a sigh, she muttered, "Very well, sir."

"After all," said Nils, "we're going to have to pass through an extensive expanse of Ash Worlds in order to get there. Though we probably won't stop at one of the burned out planets, I want everyone ready for whatever we may encounter there. This is the farthest any exploration vessel has gone out before."

"Ash Worlds?" asked Saila. "What are those?"

"In the days of the ancient races of the galaxy, there was a massive war fought in this region of the galaxy between the Archons and their most powerful adversaries, the Nameless Ones. The Archons destroyed them by burning down all of their planets. Today, nothing will grow on an Ash World. The planets are completely lifeless rocks now, tens of thousands of years after they were reduced to gray powder. They say the Nameless Ones nearly defeated the Archons, who had to take drastic measures to win."

"What happened to them, the Nameless Ones?" asked Saila.

"No one knows," he said. "Most believe they're all extinct, but I wouldn't bet on it. You'd have to be sharp-witted geniuses to outwit the Archons. There must be some of them still, lurking among the stars."

They sat there for a moment, trying to envision prehistoric clashes in the celestial realms and a galaxy ruled by the ancients. The Archons became the almighty rulers of the River of Heaven after their wars of conquest. They commanded fantastic technologies one could only dream of. After they had conquered the galaxy, they gave it all up and ascended into heaven, or so the legends said.

As she was daydreaming about divine beings, the doors opened and the attractive man she had seen during her lecture walked into the officer's lounge. Her heart skipped a beat. He looked at their table, smiled, walked over,  and sat down next to Saila.

"Hello Saila, Nils."

"Hi," said Saila.

Alastriona was too stunned to speak.

Nils introduced him. "Alastriona, this is Francois Chevalier. He's one of the Starsingers of the Tycho Brahe. Francois, this is Alastriona DeTroyes."

Starsingers were a kind of techno-mystic who tuned the solar sails of a starship by using extra-sensory perception to focus on the spirit inhabiting a star. They sang a melody which matched the precise frequency of a star at that moment in time. Special crystals lining the solar sails would vibrate to the harmonic frequencies from the music. This would tune the solar sails to match the light frequency of a star and it would vastly increase the speed of the starship.

Francois cut a piece of cheese and placed it onto a slice of bread. "I'm really just a painter and a photographer, but they liked my voice at the academy. So now I spend my time here, singing in the dark."

Alastriona glanced down at her glass of wine. "Oh?"

"I saw your lecture," he said, between bites, "at the Imperial Science Academy. Quite illuminating."

Alastriona felt her cheeks flushing. "Yes?"

Francois waved over a slave. The chrome robot came over. "How may I help you, sir?"

"Bring me whatever this woman is drinking."

The server went over to the bar.

Francois leaned back in his chair. "It's nice to be on a mission that doesn't involve the pacification of an alien planet."

Alastriona raised her eyebrows. "You don't agree with the Imperium's policy of expansion?"

He shook his head. "Warfare is a manifestation of all of our darkest impulses. We need to stop fighting aliens. I have always been against our wars of conquest."

Alastriona frowned. "The Imperium offers friendship, first."

She picked up her glass of wine but didn't take a sip. "It's sad that so many of them choose to fight. "

Nils nodded. "Alien inferiors usually can't appreciate our help until after they've been subdued."

The server returned with his glass of wine. Francois shook his head. "Is it better to be feared or loved? You can't have both."

Captain Winters entered the lounge. He paused in the entryway and looked around. Spotting the four of them sitting by the window, he made his way over to their table. He brought a chill in his wake.

Nils spoke first, "Good evening, captain."

Winters withdrew a pocket watch and glanced at it before speaking. "Lieutenant Ostergaard, I want you to prepare a courier drone for launch after we exit hyperspace."

"Very good, sir."

Alastriona raised her eyebrows. "A courier drone, sir?"

"Lieutenant DeTroyes," he said in an irritated tone, "I think you should know that I did not want you on this expedition. The Imperial Star Force is perfectly qualified to deal with this. Lieutenant Ostergaard and the rest of the officers know how things work on a military vessel and rarely get out of line. I only took you on because I was given an order by Legatus Legionis Oliho. A free-thinking scientist full of new ideas is a random element which could jeopardize our mission."

"I'm as military as you are, sir."

Winters let out a loud sigh. "New officers fresh out of the academy lack the experience which I require from those serving under my command on these long exploration voyages."

Alastriona objected, "With respect, sir, this task requires my expertise and insight. My involvement is essential to this mission."

Winters raised a hand before she could say more. He softened his tone. "Keep your peace, Lieutenant," he said. "As long as you stick to the trusted science and obey orders, I won't have a problem with you, even though you don't need to be here at all."

"Yes, sir."

Winters obviously didn't care what she thought. He addressed Nils. "We're due to exit the wormhole in a few minutes. We'll be switching from hypersails to solar sails soon."

"I shall inform Sailing Master Dlamini, sir."

The captain walked out.

For a moment, Alastriona felt like one of the Nameless Ones who fought against he Archons. She swallowed a gulp of wine, hoping to take the sting of his words away. She closed her eyes, feeling worthless and embarrassed in front of the handsome starsinger. *Do I really belong here?*

Francois got up and drained his glass of wine. "I'd better get back to the solar sails," he said. "Nice meeting you Lieutenant. You should come up to the cathedral sometime. I'll sing you a song."

As he went out, she heard him mutter, "Officers."

Alastriona looked after him.

Saila crossed her arms. "We're officers, too."

"Sometimes, I wonder how scientists ever survive in the military," said Nils.

Alastriona put her glass down and stood up. "Their lack of understanding only highlights their inferiority. I think I'll get back to the stellar observatory. I'll need to study the neutrino oscillations from the Pegasus Constellation before we proceed any further."

*   *   *

The hallway of the upper gun deck was lined with doors that led to the crew quarters,  communal rooms full of bunks. Laser cannons rested on the side of the hall closest to the outer hull. Her boots echoed as she strode through the upper gun deck. She reached a ladder, went up  to the science deck and went forward to the stellar observatory. While she was approaching the door, she sensed someone's presence behind her. She halted and turned around.

No one was there.

There was only the wind from the ventilators blowing through the hallway.

She heard the unmistakable sound of a hushed sigh. It was like a soft breeze, whispering something, but it was too quiet to make out any words. As the murmur of soft voices crept closer, her spine tingled.

Then it was gone.

Feeling suddenly dizzy, she leaned against the wall, shivering. The hallway was chilly, frigid even. The ring on her right forefinger became so cold that it sent icy tremors up her arm. She shook her arm like one does when it falls asleep and stared at her hand. It was shaking.

Rapid footsteps approached. It was Saila. "Alastriona, are you okay?"

"Yes," she said, dropping her hand down and standing up straight again. "I'm fine."

"The captain was a bit rough on you."

She turned to walk into the observatory. "That's his military prerogative, isn't it?"

Saila followed her inside. She put a hand on Alastriona's arm. "No, you don't understand," said Saila. "I think you remind him of his wife."

"So, the captain hates his wife?"

"No. She's dead."

The shock made Alastriona pause to consider. With a shrug and a shake of the head, she went over to the holographic controls and began entering data into the computer. "That doesn't give him the right to treat me the way he does."

Saila sat down at a workstation. "I know that. I just wanted you to know there's a reason he does what he does. He loved her more than anything."

Théophile's words came to mind: *True love is a silly romantic fantasy.*

Alastriona activated a hologram of the region of space in the Pegasus Constellation. Little colored lights floated in the air. "I'd like to do some work now. Thank you for telling me, Saila."

Standing up, Saila bit her lip and shook her head. "Very well. I'll see you later."

As soon as Saila went out, Alastriona sat down. A frigid heaviness weighed down her heart. A creeping tide of despair washed in from out of the depths of her soul, threatening to pull her away into oblivion. She took a deep breath and let it out again. *The captain's attitude is irrelevant.*

*   *   *

**BLACK TORTOISE OF THE NORTH**
**HELVETIOS / PEGASUS**

Alastriona sat at her desk in the observatory, reading. But she had trouble concentrating because she was annoyed by the attitude of the captain. In many ways, he was just like everyone else in the military. She closed the document she was trying to study. *Their lack of appreciation for my work is a testament to their narrow-mindedness.*

As if they had been listening to her thoughts, she was interrupted by the military. Over the intercom, First Officer Tinibu made an announcement. "Now hear this. Now hear this. We are exiting hyperspace."

There was a slight movement felt in the floor as the artificial gravity adjusted to the change when the *Tycho Brahe* passed out of the wormhole and into normal space. Alastriona waved a hand to activate the local sensors and a small hologram appeared. Because of the long distance traveled from Copernicus, 79.95 light years, all the way across the Imperium, they had arrived far away from the yellow star, 51 Pegasi. Sixteen planets encircled the star. Their destination, the Pegasus colony, was the sixth planet. With a wave of her hand, she sent their location data up to the command deck.

A bright light appeared and blinded her for a moment. Warmth spread from her face to her heart and the heaviness evaporated like snow melting in the sunshine. Alastriona smiled. Her little friend, the tiny ball of fire had reappeared. "Hello again."

Opening a compartment next to her workstation, Alastriona withdrew a hand scanner and took some readings. "So, you're a life form after all."

The door to the observatory opened and Nils walked in, accompanied by Saila. They both stopped in their tracks when they saw the little ball of fire. "What's this?" he asked.

Alastriona shrugged. "I first encountered it on my homeworld, Scylanthia. It seemed to have come out of our star. It hovered before me and then vanished. It appeared again on Galileo, just after I had come aboard. It vanished as quickly as it had appeared, so I thought it was just my imagination."

"I guess it wasn't," muttered Saila.

"No," said Alastriona. "I think it's a life form."

"How can it be a life form?" asked Nils.

Alastriona thought for a moment before answering. "Well, it can't be life that runs off biochemistry or chemistry. All of those kinds of substances have melting points lower than the temperature of a star. My scanner indicates that this is a form of energized plasma. I think it's intelligent, too."

"That's not possible," muttered Saila.

Nils glanced at Lieutenant Heikkinen. "You're the contact scientist," he said. "Do some contacting."

"Let's see," said Saila. She turned to the little ball and said, "Why have you followed Alastriona here from Scylanthia?"

The marble sized ball of blue fire moved over to the hologram of the star map. It went directly to their current location, 51 Pegasi and flashed once. Then it moved over to their destination, IK Pegasi.

As soon as it touched the light in the hologram corresponding to the star, the little ball of fire changed color from blue to red and expanded in size. Then it shifted down to a tiny white ball, next to IK Pegasi, mimicking the white dwarf. A steady stream of matter transferred from the large red star to the white dwarf. A moment later, it flashed so brightly that they all had to close their eyes.

When Alastriona opened her eyes again, the little ball of fire was gone.

They all stood there, at a loss for words.

*　　*　　*

Alastriona stood watch on the quarterdeck while the *Tycho Brahe* sailed towards the star, 51 Pegasi, which was also called Helvetios. She thought it odd, that they did not sail directly towards the colony world. Instead, the captain had ordered a leisurely approach, which would take them around the ninth planet first.

The captain came out of his cabin carrying an electronic spyglass. His magnetic presence drew her in like a moth to the flame. He climbed up to the poop deck, extended the spyglass and scanned the darkness.

A sense of longing which she couldn't quite understand stirred within her. Although she knew he loathed her presence on his starship, she wanted to see more of him. She walked up to the higher deck and glanced into the darkness. She could see from the starboard railing that the ninth planet, a greenish, ringed ice giant similar to Uranus, was growing larger as they approached. The captain stood on the opposite side, scanning space. She walked over to him and asked, "May I help you with anything, captain?"

"I'll thank you to mind your own business, Miss DeTroyes."

"Yes, sir."

Still, she lingered there, looking out into the darkness. The captain lowered his spyglass, shut it with a snap, looked up and called out to the lookout, on the intercom, "Look sharp. Do you see it?"

Over the intercom, she heard the lookout's reply, "Low contact, two points abaft the port beam."

"Well and good." A look of relief spread over the captain's face. He finally seemed to notice her standing there. He smiled, and she realized it was the first time he had given her anything resembling a friendly expression. He held out the spyglass. "Be so good as to take this down to my day cabin. Your watch is over now."

Alastriona returned his smile. "Thank you sir."

She took the spyglass, went down the ladder from the poop deck to the quarterdeck and went into his day cabin. It was the first time she'd been there. A sturdy wooden desk with a large, ornate chair offered a commanding view. A large wood table surrounded by four chairs was in the center of the room. Star charts covered the table. A leather couch occupied one wall and the other walls were lined with bookshelves that contained relics from the past. The desk had a computer resting upon it. Holographic projectors, now shut off, hung from the ceiling.

Upon the desk sat a woman's photograph inside a silver frame. Next to the photograph, a small sphere sat in a holder. It looked like a quartz crystal, but she had never seen anything like it before. A sigh, like a tiny breeze, emanated from the sphere. A chill surrounded it, as if it were made of ice.

Alastriona put down the spyglass and looked at the photograph of, presumably, the captain's wife. She was a pretty young woman of about twenty-five, though, with age regression treatments, one could never know how old someone was these days. Alastriona turned her attention to the crystal sphere. She brushed a strand of hair out of her eyes, wondering what it was.

Footsteps approached and she heard the helmsman greet another crewman just outside the door. Fearing the captain's displeasure, Alastriona exited the cabin.

*   *   *

The *Tycho Brahe* sailed towards the sixth planet, Pegasus, descended into the blue atmosphere, sailed over high mountains, lakes and forests and landed at the Sky Palace in the imperial capital city, Hua Zhi Cheng. They were here to resupply and prepare for the long voyage  into deep space.

The world was covered in lush forests, jungles and rivers. Along with two hundred million human provincial colonists, a billion native inhabitants lived there, spread out over hundreds of cities that blended into the natural surroundings.

They called themselves the "Anthousai" and were known to love flowers of all kinds. When the Imperium sent "Watchers" to scout out the planet with the aim of determining the world's viability as a colony, they were welcomed with open arms by the locals.

Off duty, Alastriona had an urge to free herself from the confines of the starship and so she went out into the city. Shying away from wearing a uniform, she wore a loose peasant blouse, a long gypsy skirt and a pair of sandals. Unable to resist shopping on a new colony world, she went to the beautiful outdoor mall, which was full of trees and flowers. All of the architecture on the planet blended harmoniously into the natural surroundings. Even the colonial buildings were full of greenery.

As she entered the shopping mall, she was enveloped in a serene atmosphere reminiscent of a lush garden full of towering trees. Cascading waterfalls and pretty gardens were everywhere.  One wall shimmered with holographic displays showcasing the latest in interstellar fashion, high-tech gadgets and the latest AI companion devices. Bustling crowds of people filled the floral pavilion, both human and Anthousai locals. An occasional alien inferior from one of the imperial colonies could be seen, too.

Alastriona found herself in a small boutique. Rather than racks full of clothing, there was a line of small canisters lining the shelves, decoratively placed of course. Feeling as if she had come into the wrong kind of store, she started to exit.

"May I assist you?

Instead of a robot salesperson, a petite woman was in the shop. She wore a skin-tight silver body suit that gave the impression that she was naked.

Alastriona was too stunned to respond.

"Are you new to Pegasus?"

"Yes," she said. "I've only just arrived this morning on the Tycho Brahe."

The woman tilted her head and smiled. "That is Captain Winters vessel, is it not?"

Alastriona found herself daydreaming of being in a relationship with the captain. She shook her head. *What am I thinking? He doesn't even like me.* She wasn't too sure she liked him, either. "Yes," she said. "You know him?"

"His wife, Eleanor used to shop here. May I assist you?"

Resisting an urge to look away, Alastriona said, "I was looking for an apparel shop."

"Yes, please come in. My name is Livia."

Alastriona, curious now, walked inside. "Where are the clothes?"

Livia laughed and reached over to take up one of the small canisters. "This is called, 'Slinxt.' It is liquid skin, programmable in an assortment of colors and textures. Would you like to try it?"

"Yes, all right."

Livia directed her to a changing room and said, "Remove your clothing and place this canister against your skin."

Alastriona went into the small room, removed her clothing and placed the canister against her shoulder. A liquid like substance flowed over her entire body. As it did so, Livia said, "Slinxt covers whatever portion of your body you desire. Simply think of what you want it to cover, along with the color you'd like it to be. It is capable of creating complex color patterns. If desired, you can also create textures such as leather, denim, or fur."

Alastriona stepped outside the changing room and found a large mirror. She imagined herself in a metallic turquoise body suit covering everything except her hands, feet and head. Moments later, she stood there, feeling quite naked still, covered in the substance. It felt like she wasn't wearing anything at all, but the reflection in a mirror showed that she was indeed covered. She whispered, "Wow!"

Livia giggled. "Slinxt has other properties." She picked up a feather which had been lying on a counter. Running it over Alastriona's shoulder, it sent tingling sensations over her skin, heightening the touch. "You may adjust the sensitivity with a simple thought. It can range from low levels of stimulation to—"

"I think I understand," said Alastriona. She turned towards the mirror and thought of another color. Moments later, she wore a hot pink body suit. She concentrated again and it changed to a white and gold checkered pattern. With another thought, she was wearing a black leather bodysuit. She couldn't wear Slinxt on duty or probably not at all while she was on the *Tycho Brahe*. But the idea of it fed a secret rebellious impulse inside. She ran a hand over her arm, fantasizing of running away somewhere, from all of her responsibilities. "I'll take two canisters."

As Livia was putting the Slinxt canisters into a bag, curiosity moved Alastriona to ask, "You knew Eleanor Winters?

"Yes. It's so sad they are parted from one another."

"What was she like?"

"Warm, friendly. She once came in to my shop with her son."

Alastriona thanked Livia and left the boutique.

Enchanting songs filled the air. One of the melodies, wild and passionate, was so enthralling that she found herself wandering towards it. The song carried her away and she forgot where she was going. She came down a green path lined with rocks and ferns. The path went through a  large field of colorful wildflowers. Each flower had it's own unique charm. She inhaled the sweet aroma of a thousand petals, none of them familiar.

A gentle wind brushed against the wildflowers and tiny seed pods rose into the air throughout the glade. Faint whispers swept along on the wind. She had the impression that she was being watched. Only a gentle noise at the edge of hearing, a soft fluttering as if it was a song, half-whispered, seemed to stir among the flowers.

Suddenly very tired, Alastriona picked up a flower and continued strolling. Each step forward became more reluctant than the last. Drowsiness seemed to be creeping out of the ground and up her legs. She followed a stream that led down a trail to a lake and sat down on a large rock, listening to the water flowing by. Her eyelids became heavy and she struggled to stay awake. Overwhelmed at last, she lay down and fell asleep.

*   *   *

The first thing she noticed when she awoke was the cold. It was a biting chill that pressed against her skin. With a sharp inhale of breath, Alastriona opened her eyes to darkness. A sliver of moonlight fell down onto the lake, which was frozen over. She sat up and breathed in the sweet aromas from the wildflowers surrounding her. The frozen lake had a large crack in the ice. Next to her hand, she found her Vajra Thunderbolt, though she did not remember bringing it here. She picked it up and looked at it, curiously.

A low moan slithered through the darkness. It was a sound devoid of humanity, a lamentation that crawled out from the depths of despair. Another haunting cry sent shivers down her spine. It came from the crack in the lake. The cry touched an emptiness deep inside her: The desolation of loneliness. An involuntary sob escaped her lips.

Something formless emerged out of the crack. It was an entity, wreathed in the forlorn darkness of despair. It crept towards her, reaching out with shadowy arms to embrace her.

Bright light appeared above, filling Alastriona with warmth and love. She looked up and saw the small ball of fire there. It pulsated with crimson flames.

The dark thing drew back from it.

It was like a breath of fresh air. Alastriona stood up and concentrated on her Vajra Thunderbolt. It transformed into a sword. She struck the dark entity with the sword and the thing screamed. She advanced upon it with her sword and the thing retreated, creeping back into the crack from whence it came. With a low moan, is seeped away into the crack and vanished. The crack faded away, too and the ice covering the lake turned back into water.

The little ball of fire winked out.

Alastriona took a deep breath, wondering what had just happened. She looked down at the Vajra Thunderbolt and it transformed back into a baton. She looked around the glade, peering into the faint moonlight.

A happy melody mingled with the sweet aromas of wildflowers. A woman emerged from the far end of the glade, humming a beautiful melody. The native Anthousai woman was tall and slender. White and purple flowers were woven into her long dark hair and she had luminous, jade-colored eyes.

In a lyrical voice, the woman spoke, and Alastriona's earring translated the words, "How did you find this place?"

"I don't know, exactly," said Alastriona. "I heard a song—"

The woman laughed.

Alastriona wondered why the Anthousai had laughed at her. "Who are you?"

"I am Meliae of the Anthousai."

"What happened?"

Meliae said, "This field is ancient, full of memories. No one comes here anymore. One of the Nameless Ones dwelt here once, long ago. Now, it's spirit lingers by the flowers, hoping to ensnare travelers. It would have dragged you into another world through a crack in our reality. At least that is what we believe. I am the guardian of this place. When I saw the light, I came to see."

Alastriona stared into the waters of the lake and shuddered. "Was that a Nameless One?"

"No, merely a weak, fragmented spirit," said Meliae. "Come, I will lead you away from this place."

*   *   *

Back on the *Tycho Brahe*, Alastriona sat in the officer's lounge, talking to Lieutenant Heikkinen. As soon as Saila heard about Alastriona falling asleep in the field of flowers, she laughed.

"What's so funny?"

"This planet if full of strange enchantments," she said. "Did you know? Songs from their enchantresses are famous all over the Imperium. I'm so glad you were found by one of the Anthousai. Didn't you read the report on this planet before you wandered out into the city?"

"Report?"

"Travel advisory reports from the Imperium."

"I just wanted to go to the mall," said Alastriona.

Saila shook her head and took a sip of coffee. Alastriona looked outside at the planet. Lights from the city glittered in the dark.

"By the way," said Saila, "Your equipment has arrived."

"My neutrino detector?"

"Yes," said Saila. Curiosity crept into her expression. "Did you buy anything at the mall?"

"Slinxt."

"Slinxt?"

"Yes, it's sort of a liquid garment." Alastriona reached into a bag, brought out two canisters, and handed one over to Saila. "I got one for you, too."

Saila smiled mischievously. "Where shall we wear this?"

Both of them giggled.

Alastriona caught sight of an elegant, impeccably groomed man who'd just walked into the lounge. He exuded confidence and magnetism. His dark, tousled hair framed a chiseled jawline, accentuating a piercing gaze that seemed to hold a thousand secrets. He was quite tall and had a slim athletic build that commanded attention with every stride. He had an undeniable charm that drew her in with irresistible allure. He wore a black suit, carried a Vajra Thunderbolt, which he had transformed into a cane with an ivory handle, carved into the image of a bloodhound, and wore a flat-topped fedora hat.

When their eyes met, she was surprised that the typical "doggy-dinner-bowl" look which she had seen countless times in the eyes of her admirers was absent. Instead, he met her gaze with a pompous smirk that matched her own superior demeanor. In his every movement, there was an unquestionable sense of entitlement, as if he knew he was a cut above everyone around him. His attitude ignited a silent challenge within her. A question surrounded him like a cloud of cologne, too much cologne. *Who does he think he is?*

She instantly hated him.

He walked over to their table and took off his hat. "Lieutenant Alastriona DeTroyes," he said. "Good evening."

Alastriona sensed a snake who'd been lying under the hot sun all day, ready to strike. She crossed her arms. "Who are you?"

He took off a pair of black calf-skin gloves. He examined everything with a probing gaze, as if he was taking part in an inquisition. "I am Chief Inspector Don Inocencio Maximo Navarro Ayala De Coronado."

When she was distracted she always dropped into her native French. "Excusez-moi?"

"You may call me, Maximo." His smile turned into a pretentious grin. "I am your prometido."

It felt like she had slipped off one of the platforms of a floating city over Scylanthia. She was falling down fast and had forgotten to put on her contra-gravity harness. "Que dites-vous?"

"We are under a legal contract, which I, at some length, have negotiated with your parents," he said. "We are to be married."

*　*　*

# SEVEN
## Perfect

Imperial Courier Drone: F1E8D7A5

Origin: Helvetios / Pegasus

Destination: Copernicus / Maria Celeste — HD 84117 / Scylanthia

April 8, 3235

*Dear Julie,*

*When we arrived at 51 Pegasi, I met my fiance. His name is Don Inocencio Maximo Navarre Aleya De Coronado. I am excited to learn that he has joined our expedition, and I am glad to finally get to know him while we are on this long journey into the night. We don't really need the time, though. We're perfect together, just as the computer simulations had predicted. I hope that our contentedness will demonstrate to you the proper way to conduct long-term attachments.*

*Love,*

*Alastriona*

Secure Data Transmission Encrypted

Imperial Regulations Compliant

*   *   *

## BLACK TORTOISE OF THE NORTH

## HELVETIOS / PEGASUS

Amid an occasional clink of glasses or silverware against china, the hum of conversation in the officer's lounge was like gentle rain. Soothing, but at the same time, cold. Now and then a laugh would break out.

Alastriona narrowed her eyes and tilted her head slightly. "You're Maximo?"

"I think I'm supposed to stand watch," said Saila. "Excuse me."

With a sly glance at Alastriona, she got up and slipped out the door of the lounge.

Resisting an urge to shout to her friend to remain here, Alastriona silently watched her departure. She picked up her cup of peppermint tea and took a diplomatic sip.

Maximo placed his cane against the table, sat down opposite her, leaned back and raised a hand without looking away from her eyes. The bloodhound handle of the cane was pointed at her, as if the dog had been hunting for her all day.

A slave came over, his polished chrome body glimmering in the candlelight. "May I help you, sir?"

"Chief Inspector," he said. It was a police rank equivalent to that of an officer, a tribune. He outranked everyone on the *Tycho Brahe* except for the reclusive leader of the expedition, Legatus Kevin Von Meyer.

"Apologies," said the slave with a slight bow. "May I help you, Chief Inspector?"

"Bring me a cup of Hausbrandt Espresso."

"I'm sorry, Chief Inspector," said the robot, "but that blend is not available on the Tycho Brahe."

"Indeed it is," he said. "I brought a consignment with me. It should be here by now."

The slave hesitated.

"Basta!" He waved a hand and then softened his voice, "Ve a buscarlo."

The slave bowed again and went back to the bar.

Though she wasn't wearing her translator earring, she understood what he had said. The way he treated slaves wasn't very important, though. They were only machines. But she wondered how he treated his inferiors and, even more, pondered about how he dealt with his peers. She resisted an urge to shake her head.

*No one is equal to him.*

Maximo gave Alastriona an appraising look up and down. His eyes roved over her white blouse, hesitated at her chest, for just a second, and finally swept up to her blue eyes. He nodded appreciatively. "A bit skinny for my taste," he said, "But you'll do."

She held her teacup in one hand, refusing to react to his discourtesies. *He's testing me.*

Silence stood between them.

The slave returned with a cup of espresso. He placed it down gently and went away. Maximo picked it up delicately and inhaled the aroma. "The secret of Italian roasting is to have much longer, slower roasts."

He sipped the espresso and returned it to rest upon the table with a soft click. It was as if he was trying to be as quiet as possible.

Alastriona lowered her teacup to the table and wrapped her hands around it, feeling the warmth spread into her fingers. The peppermint aroma was relaxing and stimulating at the same time. "I suppose we should get to know each other."

A rather charming smile slipped into his face. "If you don't object."

"Where are you from?"

"Salamanca, Spain," he said. "Earth."

She glanced over at the window of the lounge, which overlooked the Sky Palace. The forested city beyond the sky palace glowed with an otherworldly light, a mystical woodland metropolis illuminated by the soft gleam of moonlight. Hovercars flew through the air, lighting up the higher branches in the trees.

An urge to run away made her legs twitchy, so she leaned back in her chair and crossed them. She tilted her head, "How did you know I would be here?"

"Oh, that," he said. "It's quite simple. I read your scientific paper on IK Pegasi and heard that you were invited to speak at the Imperial Science Institute on Galileo. The seriousness of the situation demanded an investigation. I knew you would claim a ride on such a journey. The Imperial officer in charge of Galileo, what's his name—"

"Legatus Legionis Itoro Oliha."

"That is the one," he said. "These brainless fools who fancy themselves as competent officers are too numerous to count. I sometimes wonder how the Imperium has survived for so long with such inept leaders."

She had to resist smiling at his assessment, which she agreed with.

He put a hand on the ivory handle of his cane, which seemed to be for appearances only. He was not at all hobbled by any infirmity. In fact, he looked quite fit. "Oliho is a rather strict disciplinarian, but he isn't so moronic as to send off an expedition to study a supernova without one of the brightest minds in the Imperium."

Alastriona raised an eyebrow. *At least he appreciates my intellect.*

He finished his espresso. "The gateway to the Pegasus Constellation is through this star system, Helvetios. I have been waiting for your arrival here for several days."

"You wanted to meet me before I departed?"

"I'm joining your expedition." He leaned forward. "It's the perfect opportunity for us to get to know one another, don't you agree?"

She had an urge to run away into the forest, to lose herself among the trees. Instead, she simply nodded her head. "Yes, that is sensible."

He leaned back in his chair and glanced around the lounge. Maximo's face betrayed a murmur of relaxation, as if he had been nervous about their meeting. It was a look of relief.

*So he's as apprehensive as I am.* She put her teacup down. "I may not have much time for you on this journey. I have duties to attend to, and then there's my research."

"I'm not concerned," he said. "Now that I have met you face to face, I can see that you are like a rare gem, gleaming from afar with an irresistible allure. Your demeanor exudes an air of tranquility and authenticity that is uniquely yours. I am simply mesmerized by you."

Alastriona looked down at her tea, her face flushed.

He continued in his adoration. "I've been idolizing you, ever since I saw your holographic file. You're like a celestial angel, flawless and pure. You know, we're going to represent something great together. You and I and our accomplishments."

Her gaze went up to his face, but she didn't want to look at him, so her eyes traveled over to an ornate clock over the bar. An amusing thought came to mind: *I am intelligent and attractive. You are brilliant and beautiful, too. Let us be flawless together.* She whispered, "I don't want to be worshiped. I want to be loved."

"Semantics," he said. "I would never marry anyone beneath me, of course. You are my perfect counterpart."

*I am just a pretty ornament he wants to place at his side, but I will always be in his shadow. Glorified and admired and ignored and unloved.*

"Oh, that reminds me," he said in a dispassionate tone. He reached into his pocket, withdrew a small black box and placed it onto the table between them.

Alastriona picked it up and opened it. Inside, a beautiful diamond ring rested upon a little pillow of black velvet. The ring's intricate design reminded her of a bouquet of flowers. Several other smaller diamonds were mounted alongside the main princess cut stone. The band was white gold. She took it out of the box and held it up to the candlelight.

"Quite beautiful for lab grown stones, is it not?"

"These aren't natural diamonds?"

"Of course not," he said. "I wanted the best for you, so I had these diamonds manufactured in a laboratory on Earth. Like you, they are flawless, perfect."

"Oh." She put the ring back inside the box and shut it. "Thank you."

"Not going to wear it?"

"No, I can't wear rings while I'm on duty," she lied.

"What about that ring on your forefinger?"

"Oh, this?" She glanced at the silver ring. "I've had it since I was a child. I've never been able to take it off."

He stood, picked up his cane and put his hat back on. The bloodhound had been satiated for now. "Well, I'm sure you're tired. I shall bid you goodnight."

Before she could respond, he turned away and walked out of the lounge. She listened to his cane click against the deck as he walked down the corridor. Her parents were right. He was perfect. Alastriona leaned back in her chair with a sigh of resignation, feeling very alone.

*   *   *

Alastriona sat in front of her vanity, brushing her disheveled hair. It always seemed to defy order. Tonight, it was a mess of tangles. She glanced at the time and with a heavy sigh, she decided to put it up in a ponytail. *It'll have to do.* Standing up, she put on a white dress uniform jacket and stepped out of her cabin into the wardroom, where Saila Heikkinen stood, adjusting her uniform. Alastriona wore a white and blue uniform, trimmed in gold, while Saila's uniform was more conservative.

Every officer in the Imperial Star Force had unique uniforms. While they had to adhere to uniform regulations, there was extensive room for variation and personalization, allowing officers to showcase their social status, wealth and personal style. The highest ranking officers wore the most elaborate uniforms, with finer materials, custom tailoring, intricate embroidery, fancy embellishments and accoutrements. Pure Strain Humans often incorporated their family crests into their uniforms. Consul Leopold Voss, one of the two consuls ruling the Imperium, once said that members of the Imperial Star Force should always look like conquerors.

They made their way up to Legatus Kevin von Meyer's dining room, where all of the officers of the *Tycho Brahe* were attending a private dinner. The Marines guarding Von Meyer's private suite came to attention as they entered. All twenty officers were there.

Lieutenant Nils Ostergaard came over with glasses of champagne as they entered. He gave Alastriona a serious look. "Nobody believes your story about what happened down on Pegasus today," he said. "So I'd keep it to yourself for now, especially the part about that will-o'-the-wisp."

Saila said, "Will-o'-the-wisp?"

"Ignis Fatuus, Foolish Fire, Jack-o'-Lantern," said Alastriona. She picked up the glass of champagne and took a sip.

Saila frowned. "Jack-o'-Lantern?"

Alastriona explained, "It's an ancient term out of Earth folklore for a mischievous nature spirit who is shut out of both heaven and hell. They are said to lure travelers to their doom."

She saw Francois standing over by a stunning woman with long brown hair.

As he looked up, Alastriona felt a twinge of envy and turned her back on the pair to face Saila. "A Will-o'-the-wisp represents a misleading goal or hope."

Saila looked past Alastriona and smiled.

Francois' voice hummed a melody in soft, rhythmic tones, filling the room with a sense of mirth. A woman's voice joined in with a sweet, harmonious echo. Their voices intertwined for just a fleeting moment, a shared connection in the midst of the mundane, until they both stopped at once. But their melody lingered in the air like a gentle caress.

Francois and the beautiful woman had come over.

Alastriona's heart skipped a beat.

Francois had an irresistible smile. "Alastriona, this is the Tycho Brahe's second starsinger, Angelica Ricci."

Angelica had dark, lustrous hair that cascaded in loose waves around her shoulders, framing a face adorned with striking features —a strong Roman nose, full lips and piercing blue eyes. Every aspect of Angelica exuded the unmistakable allure of her Italian heritage, embodying both passion and sophistication in equal measure. As their eyes met, they simply stared at one another, neither willing to be the first to smile.

Saila interrupted their tug-of-war by giving the starsinger a hug. "Hi, Francois."

Alastriona gave the starsingers a shadow of a smile and turned back to the others.

Nils continued with their conversation, "Will-o'-the-wisps are caused by organic decay over swampy areas, where the oxidation of gasses produces spontaneous photon emissions."

"I read a book about that on my way to Galileo," said Alastriona. "It's all nonsense. Are there any swamps on the Tycho Brahe?"

"All right, I don't know what it was," said Nils. "Still, better not talk about it in front of the captain until we know more about it."

Saila asked, "It's not dangerous, is it?"

"No," said Alastriona. "Of course not."

Perhaps out of politeness, Francois didn't ask what they were talking about.

Maximo came over with a smile. "Good evening, Alastriona."

"Hi, Maximo," she said. Turning to Nils, she attempted an introduction. "Nils, this is Chief Inspector Maximo, um—"

Maximo laughed. "I am Chief Inspector Don Inocencio Maximo Navarre Ayala De Coronado. Alastriona is my fiancée."

Embarrassed, Alastriona said, "This here is Saila Heikkinen, this is Francois Chevalier  and this is our Chief Science Officer, Lieutenant Nils Ostergaard."

Nils didn't try to conceal his surprise. "How wonderful. Glad to meet you, sir."

Rather than react to Alastriona leaving her out of the introductions, Angelica smiled at Maximo and said, "I am Angelica Ricci, sir. I work with Mr. Chevalier on the Tycho Brahe as a starsinger."

"Oh?" Maximo smiled back. "You two must pair well together."

Angelica nodded. "Yes, sir. Francois sings baritone, and I'm a mezzo-soprano."

She started humming. Francois grinned and joined in, picking up on the harmonious melody they had sung together earlier.

Alastriona had an urge to run away.

As they stopped singing, they remained staring at each other, smiling together.

Alastriona looked away outside at the stars. It felt like Angelica was rubbing her nose in it, reveling in her ability to hold Francois' attention.

Angelica turned to Maximo and said, "I am surprised that a man of your status is engaged to a simple scientist."

Maximo nodded. "Yes, I had always thought I would marry someone appropriate to my  station. But the supercomputer matched my profile with Miss DeTroyes."

As Alastriona turned to look into Maximo's eyes, he smiled. But her smile in response was only illusive.

Angelica shook her head in mock astonishment. "May such wonders never cease."

"Yes, quite." Maximo's smile faded away. "I hear that you went down to the planet."

Alastriona nodded. "Yes."

Maximo sighed. "An entire planet full of mongrel aliens," he said. "I have always found inferiors tiresome."

"You don't like aliens?" asked Francois.

Maximo said, "They don't concern me at all. However, I do find it amazing that some of the creatures have the audacity to presume a level of intelligence higher than that of a rock slug. I am glad that the Imperium has banned the things from serving aboard our starships."

Alastriona bit her lip and glanced away from Maximo. Francois was looking at her with an amused expression. Saila asked Maximo a question, which brought Alastriona's attention back. "If you don't mind my asking, Chief Inspector, what are you doing here?"

Maximo said, "I have been ordered by Proconsul Sunita Das to accompany you on your quest. This mystery needs a great mind to decipher it, and I am the best investigator in the Imperium. I am also here to safeguard my beautiful queen."

*I wish he'd stop that.* Irritated, but unwilling to show it, Alastriona looked down into her glass of champagne. "We're just getting to know each other."

Francois raised a glass of champagne in a toast. "I think you two are made for each other," he said. "Congratulations."

Alastriona narrowed her eyes at him, annoyed.

Maximo cast his gaze over the room and proclaimed, "We have always been destined to reign together, don't you agree, Alastriona?"

She could only smile at him, politely, and wish he would shut up.

Angelica sighed, as if she was admiring a thing of beauty. "The perfect match."

The dinner bell rang and they all sat down at the large conference table. Maximo did not accompany her, opting to sit next to the leader of the expedition instead. Alastriona found herself sitting between Executive Officer Min Ji Ro, a petite Korean woman, and the captain of the contingent of Marines, Primus Helmand Muller. Sitting across from her was Lieutenant Cyril Ramaphosa, the Master Gunner in charge of the primary weapons on the *Tycho Brahe*. Feeling uncomfortable surrounded by warriors, she glanced down the long table to where the other science officers were sitting. Saila met her gaze and smiled.

Between Captain Winters and Maximo, Legatus Kevin Von Meyer sat at the head of the table. The incredibly wealthy CEO of Worldbuilders, Inc. possessed an aura of refined authority that spoke volumes about his status and experience in the realm of interstellar ventures. His well tailored suit of exquisite craftsmanship was made from the finest fabrics cut to perfection. He was a man of style and charm. He had piercing steel gray eyes that reflected a depth of knowledge and determination. His graying hair was meticulously styled and his smile captivating.

Moving with quiet confidence, a striking young woman approached Von Meyer, carrying a data pad. Her dark brown hair cascaded in gentle waves around her shoulders, and she wore a sophisticated charcoal pencil skirt and matching blazer. A woman of poise and charm, she exchanged smiles with Von Meyer, and said something to him just before she handed him the data pad. She retreated to the back of the room.

Alastriona leaned over to Min Ji Ro and asked, "Who is that, Ma'am?"

Lieutenant Ro glanced at the woman and said, "That's Von Meyer's Executive Assistant. I forgot her name."

"Elfriede Tischler," said Helmand Muller. "I heard that she is from Austria, on Earth."

Von Meyer stood up, raised a glass of champagne and said, "As the leader of our esteemed scientific expedition, I am honored to host this gathering in celebration of our collective achievements and in the spirit of discovery that unites us."

As he spoke, he cast his gaze around the officers seated at the table. When his eyes came to Alastriona, they stopped. For an instant, they regarded one another. He was obviously quite taken by her. A charming smile lit up his face.

Glad for the distraction from Francois' irksome comment, Alastriona returned Von Meyer's smile. They shared a moment together, in silence. Realizing that she had distracted him, she averted her gaze.

The interchange was only an instant, barely noticeable. It was merely a pause in his speech. Maximo either did not notice it or seemed not to care. Alastriona glared at Maximo. *He's so in love with himself, he can't believe anyone else is good enough for me*, she thought.

Her eyes dropped to the table. *Maybe he's right. Is anyone else here as brilliant as Maximo?* Out of sheer rebellion, her eyes went up to Francois. He didn't look back, which bothered her even more.

Von Meyer raised his glass. "Let us toast the success of our expedition."

Next to Von Meyer, Captain Winters stood up. He glanced over at Alastriona and raised his glass. "To our success in saving the galaxy."

Everyone stood up and gave a toast.

Alastriona returned her gaze to Von Meyer. Suddenly, an icy chill came over her. Shivering, she felt light-headed. Blackness encroached from the edges of her vision. As everyone returned to their seats, she closed her eyes, glad to sit, rather than faint.

Muller noticed her weakness. "Are you all right, Lieutenant?"

Opening her eyes, Alastriona nodded. "Yes, thank you, sir." She threw another glance at on Von Meyer, wondering how he could affect her so. Recovering from the woozy spell, she turned to Muller. "Can I ask you a question, Primus?"

"Certainly."

The dizziness was subsiding. "You and your men train with Vajra Thunderbolts?"

"Yes."

"Have you ever known one to appear from out of nowhere?"

"It happened once, a hundred years ago, during the Hymenopteran War," he said. "Vajras are connected to your soul."

Alastriona didn't understand. "How do they work?"

Muller chuckled. "You never studied at the academy, did you?"

"I mostly studied astrophysics."

"You qualified with the thunderbolt, didn't you?"

All officers were required to train with vajra thunderbolts. She had always considered it silly and useless to train with the primitive weapons. Nevertheless, she had done so. She nodded. "Yes, of course."

"What type of centurion are you?"

While training with a Vajra Thunderbolt, every student would discover which kind of centurion their soul was tuned to. There were three kinds: A Guardian, a Messenger of Love and the third type. "I am a Light-Bringer," she said. "But I never understood how thunderbolts function. The more I try to understand them, the less they work for me."

Muller explained, "There is an invisible webbing of sacred flow, an immaculate connection of all planetary realms of the life source. Apparent separations are actually connected through this webbing. When one steps into the flow of this with a vajra, we can step into our highest purpose. Vajras are pure neutrality. They are the essence of letting go and allowing this purification of communication to flow through your being. With a Vajra Thunderbolt operating in its highest harmonic form, one can touch infinity."

"That doesn't explain how it appeared," she said.

Muller's tone grew serious. "You're telling me that your thunderbolt appeared out of nowhere?"

She whispered, "Yes, I'm telling you that."

Perhaps out of disbelief, Muller did not respond.

*   *   *

After  everyone had finished eating, they all went into the conference room. Captain Winters waved a hand and a holographic star map of the Pegasus Constellation appeared. "Our mission is to travel to IK Pegasi to study the stars there. Does anyone have a suggestion?"

Sailing Master Dlamini said, "It is 109.11 light years to IK Pegasi from here. I can have us there in twenty-eight days."

Alastriona said, "No, sir. That would be a mistake. It is possible that the white dwarf has already reached the ignition temperature for carbon fusion in the core. It may have already exploded."

"We would know, wouldn't we?" asked Ethan Taylor, the centurion who was second in command of the Marine continent.

"As seen from this planet, the light from IK Pegasi is a hundred and nine years old," she said. "If the star has already turned into a supernova, we will arrive in a region soaked with gamma rays."

Taylor crossed his arms. "So?"

Primus Helmand Muller stared at his colleague and shook his head in disappointment.

Alastriona raised her eyebrows. "It would mean instant death for all of us."

First Officer Tinibu crossed his arms. "What do you advise?"

She pointed to the holographic controls. "May I, sir?"

Captain Winters nodded. "Go ahead."

With a wave of her hand, she brought up an image of their destination. "IK Pegasi is a binary star system. A red giant and a white dwarf. Neither have very strong astrospheres."

Dlamini said, "Yes, we'll have to run out the stuns'ls."

She brought up an image of the *Tycho Brahe* with solar sails deployed, including the stuns'ls. The technique of studding sails extended the booms which ran out along the yards, to dramatically increase the sail area. "Even at full sails, there isn't enough solar wind to propel us. We will be stranded there, becalmed with no wind."

Another wave of her hand brought up an image of a series of tethers extending out from the solar sails. "We will need to deploy an electrostatic tether system. This is a series of charged lines that extend out from the solar sails, electrifying them and giving us more propulsion."

Captain Winters turned to Francois. "Can you do this?"

"Yes, sir," said Francois. "These electrostatic tethering systems were once used to explore cool Class M stars in the past."

"Good," said the captain. He turned to Alastriona. "What else?"

Alastriona shrugged. " I suggest a cautious approach. We should travel to a star part way there, send a robot probe to IK Pegasi and wait for it's return. That way, we can travel there safely. I would suggest the star 41 G. Pegasi, which is 62.47 light years from here, about half way to IK Pegasi."

Captain Winters nodded. "Time to save the universe," he said. "Mr. Dlamini, plot a course for Sigma Pegasi."

Alastriona wasn't sure she heard him right. "Sigma Pegasi, sir?"

"Yes, Sigma Pegasi." Captain Winters smiled. "I'm taking your advice, Lieutenant. First we'll go to Sigma Pegasi and then we'll go to 34 Pegasi. Three steps instead of two."

*　　*　　*

The *Tycho Brahe* had sailed outside the stellar wind bubble—the astrosphere of 51 Pegasi. It passed through the termination shock and sailed through the astropause. It approached the final boundary to interstellar space known as the hydrogen wall, where invisible magnetic foam bubbles surrounded the starship. After it passed through the hydrogen wall, the *Tycho Brahe* retracted the solar sails and extended the hypersails.

Off duty, Alastriona sat in the officer's lounge on the upper gun deck. Over at the far end of the bar, Captain Winters sat by himself, drinking quietly. Realizing that he wanted to be left alone, she turned around and looked out at the stars.

She was waiting for the appearance of a mandala to whisk them away. This was a doorway which would take them through a hyperspace wormhole to their destination. The lonely stars would vanish while they were inside the wormhole. She imagined Francois standing inside the dark cathedral, focusing on their destination and singing. Resisting an urge to go up to the cathedral to watch, she took a sip of wine.

"You look tired, Lieutenant."

Alastriona turned to see Legatus Kevin Von Meyer standing next to her at the bar. She felt a flutter of excitement at seeing him, for the first time, in the officer's lounge. He wore an impeccably tailored suit, and was surrounded by an aura of confidence and charm. She shrugged. "I haven't been sleeping well."

He placed a tall box on top of the bar, raised a hand to get the slave's attention and took a seat next to her. "Spending all of your nights with your fiancé? You're far too good for him."

Despite the fact that it wasn't true, she blushed just the same. "No, no. That's not it. I haven't slept well ever since I came on board."

The robot came over. "What can I do for you, sir?"

"Two glasses."

The robot bartender's chrome exterior was blue tonight. He reached under the bar, brought out a pair of glasses and said, "Would you like anything else?"

"No."

The robot went over to another couple at the other end of the bar. Von Meyer opened the box and withdrew a very old bottle of whiskey. A unique hand painted design by an esteemed artist decorated the label. "Have a drink with me."

Alastriona had a hand resting on the stem of her wine glass. She withdrew it and looked at the bottle, curiously. "I don't drink hard liquor."

All charm, Von Meyer smiled. "Tonight, you do, just this once." He opened the bottle and poured. "This relic was recovered from the ruins of Old Earth. It was made in the year 3130 A.D., just before the Hymenopteran War. Only twenty bottles were ever produced, making this one of the oldest and most elusive vintages every produced by the distillery. It had been aged in sherry casks for six decades before the war."

She looked at the amber liquid in the glasses. "Expensive?"

"Indeed."

Alastriona raised her eyebrows in a silent question.

Von Meyer smiled but remained silent.

She turned away from him to face the bar. "Thank you, no."

"I always get what I want, Lieutenant."

As he slid the glass over to her, their hands touched. He held it there, fingers touching, for a moment. She looked into his eyes and then back to the glass. She picked it up and inhaled the aroma—a symphony of oak and spice.

He raised his glass, clinked it against hers and drank it all down.

She took a cautious sip. The first touch on her palate revealed layers of rich, velvety flavors that danced like stardust, hinting at centuries old secrets locked within each drop. She closed her eyes and was transported to realms of opulence, where time stood still. She heard him pouring another glass for himself and opened her eyes.

He picked up his glass and drank it down.

Alastriona squinted in curiosity as he did so, but did not take another drink. Von Meyer's charming facade melted away, revealing a sense of entitlement and arrogance that grated on her senses. *Is he trying to get me drunk?*

He leaned back and looked out of the window at the stars. "I make a great deal of money, building new colonies on the backs of dead worlds," he said. "It would be nice to have someone who I could share it all with."

He poured a third glass, drank it down and then poured another. "Won't you keep up with me?"

"I'm 1.75 meters tall, but I only weigh forty-nine kilos in 1G, Earth's gravity," she said. "I'm from a light gravity planet."

"Oh," he said. He admired the amber liquid in his glass, but his mind was elsewhere. "When we find inhabited planets, building a new colony is more complicated. The locals never like visitors."

He drank it all down and refilled his glass again. His speech slurred slightly. "The worlds I have discovered never have any locals to contend with," he said. "I am lucky that way."

He drank the fifth glass and then poured another one. He continued to hold onto the bottle.

"Are you all right, sir?"

"Call me Kevin, won't you?"

His attitude made her uncomfortable. Alastriona stood up. "I should get some sleep, sir. Thank you for the drink."

The bottle swayed in his hand slightly.

As politely as she could, she began to walk away. He reached out and grabbed her wrist. "No, stay a little while longer, won't you?"

"I'm sorry sir, but I'm on the morning watch tomorrow."

He stood up and stepped close to her. "No need to go to your cabin. You welcome to join me in my suite."

With a circular motion of her wrist, she broke his contact. She took a step back.

"Good evening, Legatus. Hello, Lieutenant."

Captain Winters had come over. Von Meyer sat down onto the stool, withering away under the captain's gaze. "Hello, captain. Have a drink with me, won't you?"

"Certainly, sir."

Captain Winters sat down next to Von Meyer, who poured the captain a glass. Winters  drank it down and his face filled with delight. "This is the best whiskey I've ever tasted."

"Yes, it is," said Von Meyer. He got up and stumbled out of the lounge, leaving the bottle behind on the bar.

Alastriona sat down next to the captain and placed her hand on top of his in silent thanks.

First Officer Tinibu's voice came over the intercom. "Now here this, now here this. We are entering hyperspace."

The darkness outside turned to light as the mandala appeared. Although the mandala wasn't visible from the stern of the starship, it's glow filled the lounge with illumination.

He withdrew his hand, stood up, picked up the bottle and went out.

Alastriona got up and left the lounge. As she went down the corridor, a chill followed after. Arctic storms were brewing.

*　*　*

**HYPERSPACE**

It was like swimming in a frozen lake and then trying to climb out. Frigid winds tormented her as she emerged from the nightmare. Alastriona awoke, trembling. Covered in sweat, she listened to her heart pounding against her chest. Unable to catch a breath, she wheezed and coughed. Sitting up, she brought her knees up to her chest and lay her head down on top of them. She brought her hands up to her face and concentrated. *Breathe, just breathe.* Slowly, her heart calmed down and her breath came easier. Lingering terrors still danced around her thoughts. Fleeting dread gave her a visceral reaction to a nightmare she couldn't recall. Her cabin was as frigid as a tent on the side of a mountain during a winter storm. She raised a hand and looked at her silver ring, which felt like a frozen band of ice. The ring steadied her.

Alastriona swung her legs out of bed and let the nightmare slip away into oblivion. Resisting an urge to wrap her blankets around her, she got up and went over to the sink. She turned on hot water and splashed it into her face.

During the entire journey though hyperspace, her restless dreams had gradually turned into nightmares. Tormenting ordeals out of the darkness, always forgotten. She hadn't had such nightmares since she was a child. *Why have they come back?*

* * *

Unable  or unwilling to sleep any longer, Alastriona went down the orlop deck above the hold. Electric blue lights filled the hallway, which was lined with a hundred warbots standing in recesses on either side. Like ancient tin soldiers, they stood quite still, frozen at attention. Deactivated for now, they were always on standby.

She entered the probe launch bay at the fore of the orlop deck and took a seat at a console. With a wave of her hand, she activated a holo display and began configuring a probe for it's upcoming mission to scout for a supernova explosion. An oddity appeared in the data.  The inventory of courier drones was low. *Strange. We just restocked everything on Pegasus, didn't we?* She  examined the data with more interest and found another anomaly.

A message had been received from deep space. She tapped the display, opening the communication. The data file was blank. Erased.

With a wave of her hand, she activated a search.

The message had come from one of the stars inside the Pegasus Constellation, where no Imperial starship had ever gone before. She ran another search for reports on the stars of Pegasus from the Watchers, Imperial scouts. There were no reports. The region was unexplored.

An alien message had been accepted from deep space and then it had been deleted.

Unable to recover the data file, she leaned back in her chair, dumbfounded.

*Whoever did this was an expert with high clearance.*

She stood up and went out, on her way to tell the captain. She was walking fast, turned round a corner, and ran into Maximo. Impulsively, he brought up his arms around her. He held her there for a moment. Surprised, Alastriona began to let herself sink into the warmth of his embrace. But there was a wall there, cold, irresolute, empty. She retreated back into herself just as he let her go. He stepped back a pace. "Where are you going in such a rush, my dear?"

Still startled, she took a step back. "Maximo? What are you doing here?"

"I like to walk the corridors of the starship. It helps me think," he said. "What is it?"

"I found something." Alastriona brushed a strand of hair out of her eyes and told him about the missing courier drones and the deleted alien message.

"It could be an error in the data," he said. "Best not tell anyone for now."

"Maximo, I have to report this."

"You have reported it," he said. "To me."

Alastriona wondered why he was asking her to remain silent. There was a strange look in his eyes that gave her the impression that she had better listen to him. She nodded. "All right, Maximo. I will keep it to myself for the time being."

The grave expression in his eyes went away and was replaced with a friendly grin. It was the first time she had liked his smile. She had the impression that she had just uncovered one of the layers he kept carefully hidden from the world. *Maybe he's letting me into his heart.*

He raised his arm, offering to lead her away. Alastriona glanced over her shoulder at the probe bay, letting her curiosity linger there still.

His voice brought her back. "Coffee?"

Smiling, she nodded her head and took his arm. They proceeded down the corridor towards one of the lifts that would take them up and away from the orlop deck.

*   *   *

# SIX
## Nightmares

**BLACK TORTOISE OF THE NORTH**

**SIGMA PEGASI**

The ship's bell rang out seven times, in sets of two dings each, followed by a final,  seventh ding. The sound echoed throughout the *Tycho Brahe* over the intercom.

Alastriona awoke, shivering.

Opening her eyes to her cabin, she peered into the dim illumination. There were no monsters lurking in the corners. She sat up and cradled her head in her hands. *It's getting worse.* She looked at her ring. The cold touch of it calmed her down.

A warm light appeared from above. She looked up and saw the

little ball of fire, hovering above her head. The little life form had followed her all the way from her homeworld, Scylanthia. In it's warm radiance, the icy terror in her heart gradually dissolved, like an ice cube melting under the heat of the sun, until the nightmare was completely forgotten.

She smiled. "Hello, little one."

She looked outside through her cabin porthole and saw the stars, realizing that they must have exited hyperspace after an eleven day journey inside the wormhole. She cupped a hand under the light and it settled down into her palm, not quite touching her skin. "So, you can't exist in hyperspace. Is that why you have been absent for so long?"

There was a knock at the door and the light blinked out.

Alastriona's hair fell into her face. "What is it?"

The door opened and Saila peered into the cabin. "Sorry to wake you, Alastriona."

She brushed the hair away. "I wasn't sleeping."

The light from the wardroom silhouetted Heikkinen in the doorway. "Lieutenant Tinibu wants us both up on the star deck in twenty minutes in our space-suits."

The star deck was the deck exposed to space, with a force field covering it. It included the forecastle, or "fo'c'sle, the waist, where the ship's boats rested, the quarterdeck and the poop deck. She nodded and replied, "I'll be there."

* * *

Alastriona walked out onto the star deck and strode over to where half of the junior officers, second lieutenants, stood in front of the thirty men and woman of the Larboard Watch.

Lieutenant Tinibu emerged from the captain's cabin at the aft of the quarterdeck and marched towards the crew. The Chief Deck Officer, William Davies, blew a whistle and called for everyone to come to attention.

Tinibu halted in front of the Larboard Watch. "Good morning."

They all replied in unison. "Good morning, sir."

Lieutenant Tinibu activated a small hologram from a device on his sleeve. The starship's log appeared and he began reading the updates which the executive officer had entered during the previous watch.

One bell sounded. It was the beginning of the Larboard Watch. The Starboard Watch came down from the rigging on the ratlines, emerged from openings inside the masts, walked out onto the star deck and went belowdecks. The brief activity faded away as quickly as it had begun.

Holding a smile on his face, which was a thin veil over a sneer, Lieutenant Tinibu glared at them with obvious disdain. He waited until the last of the Starboard Watch had gone before he spoke again. "At ease."

Everyone switched to parade rest with their feet apart and their hands clasped together behind their backs.

Executive Officer Min Ji Ro climbed down the shroud from the main mast, deactivated her helmet, which slid into a pocket dimension and walked over to Lieutenant Tinibu. She saluted. "Good morning, Mr. Tinibu."

Tinibu closed the log and returned her salute. "Good morning Miss Ro."

She gave her report. "The starship's current position is just past the ninth planet, an ice giant. We have just completed a starboard tack and are maintaining course towards the fourth planet at a quarter of light speed. We're sailing under tops'ls alone, except for a jib and a flying jib. No significant changes."

"Have any of the lookouts reported anything of note?"

"Yes, sir. Lookouts have reported that we are approaching a debris field on the port side. I've marked it on the chart for your review."

"Thank you, Miss Ro. I will assume the watch. You are relieved."

"I stand relieved, sir."

The first officer waited for her to depart before addressing the

Larboard Watch. He glared at them and said, "When we sailed out from Pegasus, I thought we had a crack crew, not this pitiful, witless bunch of stump-winged bilge rats. I shall leave it to fancy where your mothers were that let you come to the stars. So today, you shall all have the pleasure of your officers demonstrating their fine sailing skills alongside the rest of you. Perhaps you will learn how to sail a starship from them."

Alastriona glanced sideways at Saila, who didn't react at all.

Tinibu continued, "We're going in-system to the fourth planet, which is inhabited, or so the captain tells me. Get aloft now and crowd on sail. Dismissed."

Alastriona watched the crew climb up the ratlines into the rigging. She hadn't sailed a starship since she'd been at the academy. Everything on a modern starship was automated, but for some reason, the first officer wanted the junior officers to climb up into the rigging personally. She raised an eyebrow. "You want us up there, sir?"

Tinibu nodded. "I want the officers to know how to sail this starship even better than the rest of the crew." He grinned. "You're not afraid of heights, are you, DeTroyes?"

*What a silly notion.* Everyone on Scylanthia was as comfortable in the clouds as fish were in the sea. "Of course not, sir."

"Get to it, then."

There were nine masts, three rising from the quarterdeck and two other sets of three masts that went down and at an angle on either side of the hull. Alastriona activated her space helmet and it appeared from a pocket dimension to surround her head. She walked over to the lower starboard foremast, opened the door and got in, head-first.

As she climbed, she sensed the gravity switch direction so that it felt like she was climbing instead of going down at an angle of one hundred and twenty degrees from the star deck. Her ascent took her away from the starship, which felt like it was "down" because the gravity pulled her towards the starship. While climbing into the rigging, "down" went towards the center of the *Tycho Brahe*. She ascended all the way to the furthest point, the lower starboard fore top gallant sail, pronounced, "fore t'garns'l," and went out onto the yardarm next to an Able Bodied Starman. Together, they unfurled the sheet, which had already been tuned to match the frequency of the star, Sigma Pegasi, by the star singers inside the cathedral. As the material slid down, she watched the crystals lining the sheet glitter like a pool of jeweled milk.

A star rigger plugged into the yard arm holding the top gallant sail and he began singing to fine tune the solar sail. He was joined by all of the other star riggers on the *Tycho Brahe*, and the chorus rang out over the intercom. Alastriona joined in, singing along with the rest of the crew.

She tied off the solar sail and climbed down to the next one, the fore top sail, "fore tops'l," repeating the same sequence all over again, until all of the sails on the lower starboard foremast had been unfurled and fine-tuned. Though she knew the entire operation could have been conducted much faster with automation, she understood the need to do it manually.

After she was finished, she climbed back down the tube inside the foremast and emerged out onto the quarterdeck once again. Lieutenant Tinibu was standing there with a pocket watch in one hand. "Not good enough, Lieutenant."

*Of course not.*

She knew he was about to order her to do it all over again when the captain, emerging from his cabin, came over. "Post the lookouts, Mr. Tinibu."

"Yes, sir." Tinibu activated his intercom and gave the order. "Lookouts aloft."

ESPer lookouts went to the three main masts and went up to the crosstrees, platforms high up and away from all of the psychic "noise" which could interfere with their ability to sense starships or other objects beyond their immediate area. While the speed of light seemed instant around a planet, light could take several hours to reach the distant parts of a star system. So men and women, trained in Extra Sensory Perception, served as lookouts. They scanned the stars and discovered  objects and starships in real time which were not yet visible.

Chief Science Officer Ostergaard called the captain over the intercom. "Captain, you had better come see this."

"On my way," replied the captain. He turned to his first officer. "Have Lieutenant Heikkinen come away from up there and tell her to meet us on the poop deck. Take us to the fourth planet, Mr. Tinibu. Lively now."

"Yes, sir."

The captain turned a reluctant eye towards Alastriona. "De-Troyes, you'd better come along with me to see what the science chief wants."

Alastriona nodded and followed the captain. They ascended a flight of stairs leading to the poop deck. As she went up, she glanced at the star riggers still aloft and smiled.

* * *

As they stepped out onto the poop deck, Alastriona saw a holographic display of the Sigma Pegasi star system hovering in the center of the deck. A white F6V star and a cool red M3 star were surrounded by twelve planets. Two gas giants like Jupiter and four ice giants, similar to Uranus or Neptune dominated the star system and there were six other rocky planets. The fourth planet was supposed to be inhabited. They were approaching a large debris field, but it was far enough away that they didn't need to go through it.

Lieutenant Ostargaard stood next to a console in front of the holographic display. Maximo sat in a chair, observing everything, along with Von Meyer, who studiously ignored Alastriona. Von Meyer was speaking to his assistant, Elfriede, who was also present.

Alastriona stared at the woman. She was impeccably dressed, and had flawless skin. It was as if she was too confident. Too perfect. Just the kind of woman a trillionaire would want around him. She wondered if Von Meyer was sleeping with her.

"What is is, Nils?" asked the captain.

"Imperial scout drones analyzed this star system three years ago, during a survey of the ash worlds in this constellation," said Nils. He pointed to the fourth planet. "They found an inhabited planet, inside the orbit of the Ash World."

"Yes, I know."

Saila Heikkinen entered and approached the hologram.

Captain Winters glanced at Saila. "Lieutenant, I want you on our surface deployment force. As our contact scientist I will need your expertise."

Saila frowned. "Respectfully sir, this is highly irregular. An Imperial Watcher team should be the first to visit a new species. How we proceed with first contact is determined by their report."

"Never mind that," said Winters. "I don't believe in wasting time with bureaucratic processes."

"Respectfully, sir, they're not bureaucratic processes. It is military procedure, ordered by First Citizen Leopold Voss and confirmed by the senate."

"We're here now, so I'm authorizing a first contact mission."

"If I may ask, sir," said Saila, "Why are we even bothering with this world?"

"We are here to investigate anything which could prove a danger to the Imperium," he said. "Miss DeTroyes, how much time do you need to conduct your survey of IK Pegasi?"

Alastriona crossed her arms. "Thanks to my innovations in redesigning the Tycho Brahe's sensor suite back on Pegasus, I can do a more comprehensive study now. I have been collecting data on IK Pegasi ever since we arrived here, sir."

Nils crossed his arms. "Indeed?"

Alastriona walked up to a console and opened a holographic image of the distant binary star system. The red giant and the white dwarf swirled around each other in a stellar dance of death. A data readout appeared next to the stars. "I have compared my theoretical models of stellar evolution to our new direct observations of IK Pegasi."

Zooming into a closeup of the red giant, the image of the

star blinked a few times as the computer updated the data. The star shrank down slightly. Tilting her head, she muttered, "How intriguing."

Captain Winters looked at the image, not comprehending her comment. "Explain."

Raising her eyebrows, she said, "An analysis of the orbital motions of the two stars indicate an inexplicable mass loss in the red giant."

"So?"

The captain, obviously, had no idea why this was significant. She wondered how he had gained command of a science vessel with such mediocre talents in astronomy. She chose to acquiesce to his ignorance. "The red giant is losing mass at a rapid, inexplicable rate."

"So?

She closed her eyes for a second before replying. "It could go, 'boom' any day now."

"So, there is a danger?"

Alastriona checked the status of her neutrino detector. The device would detect the elusive particles that would prove a supernova was in progress. There were currently none. "Not at this time, sir."

Nils interrupted, "Captain, I think you had better look at this."

Nils waved a hand and the image focused in onto the fourth planet. Massive clouds covered the entire surface, obscuring the ground. Nils activated an instrument that was able to peer through the cloud cover. It revealed a nightmare. The world was pockmarked with massive craters. All of the cities lay in ruins.

Von Meyer stood up and approached the display. "Wonderful," he said.

Alastriona gave him a quizzical look. *What a thing to say about the death of an entire world.* A strand of hair fell into her eyes.

As if he had heard the accusing thought, he glared back at her. Perhaps out of defiance, he smiled.

Brushing the strand of hair away, Alastriona activated a BioSAR system to scan for biological life. "This planet is devoid of life, sir. No birds, no animals, nothing. Ground penetrating scanners have located several underground structures but there are no living inhabitants there either."

The expression on the face of the captain betrayed his shock and surprise. Bewilderment turned into apprehension. "No, it can't be," he muttered. "Run another scan. This is the fifth planet, isn't it? The Ash World?"

Nils shook his head and brought up the image of the fifth planet with the wave of his hand. It was a world of gray and white. A fine powder lay under the hot sun. No wind remained to disturb it's eternal rest. The entire planet had been cremated eons ago. Although there were rumors that the Imperium had recovered some ancient super weapons, no one really knew what powers the Archons had employed to turn a garden into a funeral pyre or why they had done so. Their judgment against this world had been final. It had been as fierce as the furies of hell and what little remained was still terrible to behold.

Alastriona wondered, *by what unholy art, grim and fearsome, had the Archons incinerated this garden paradise?*

Nils pointed at the new image. "This is the Ash World from our stellar surveys."

Alastriona had an impulse to ask for permission to land on the Ash World, where she could study it, but she pushed the thought away just as quickly as it had come. *Best not to trouble the dead.*

Nils switched back to the original display. "This is the fourth planet."

The captain wondered aloud, "What could have happened in the past three years to have done this?"

Nils said, "Unknown, sir."

The captain glanced at Saila. "It appears that our debate is meaningless, Lieutenant."

Saila was obviously relieved. She nodded in agreement. "Yes, sir."

Captain Winters spoke into his intercom. "Lieutenant Tinibu, report."

"We'll have to tack several times to get to the fourth planet sir, as we're sailing upwind."

He was referring to the stellar wind radiated outwards from the star. To approach the planet, which was closer to the star than where they had arrived, they had to sail against the wind. All stars were surrounded by the bubble of an astrosphere, caused by the stellar wind from the star. As stars spiraled around the center of the galaxy, their astrospheres became teardrops.

"Very good," said Winters. "Steady at the helm."

Alastriona activated the multispectral sensors, which were used to analyze the reflectance and the emission spectra of objects in space. She scanned the debris field and combined the multispectral sensors with the particle analyzer. The display lit up like a Christmas Tree. Silently, she congratulated herself. *Why is it that no one else thought of this?* She gave Chief Science Officer Ostergaard a disapproving look before informing the captain of her find. "Sir, I have detected the wreckage of hundreds of objects, which make up the debris field we're approaching. I recommend that we retrieve one of the best preserved items for study. It may give us an indication as to what occurred here."

"No, we'd have to slow down near the debris field," said Captain Winters. "It will take too much time."

A tapping sound came over the deck. Maximo had stood up

and was walking over to the holographic display with his cane. "May I suggest, captain, that I take out a space cutter. The skiff should be large enough. I can retrieve one of the objects and return here without us needing to slow down."

Captain Winters stared at Maximo for a moment, nonplussed.

Alastriona wondered if Maximo was just trying to get close to her, by offering to recover one of the objects. She looked at the captain, wondering what debate was going on in his mind. *It's simple enough. Why is he hesitating?*

The captain nodded in agreement. Maximo was, after all, his superior. "Very well, sir. If you think it is necessary, I'll authorize it."

Maximo placed both of his hands onto the top of his cane. "Excellent."

Alastriona continued to analyze the data from the debris field, holding back a smile of admiration. *He uses that cane for dramatic effect. What a showman. How can he be so annoying and admirable at the same time?*

Captain Winters activated the intercom. "Lieutenant Balina?"

Lieutenant Iveta Balina was the flight commander, in charge of the pilots for all of the ship's boats, including a pair of starfighters. A holographic image of the attractive brunette woman appeared. In anticipation of the captain's command, she already had her flight suit on. "Yes, sir?"

"Have Lieutenant Immelmann meet the Chief Inspector in the shuttle bay. He will give your pilot further instructions."

"Yes, sir."

Maximo picked up his cane and tapped the bloodhound handle to his forehead in a salute. "I shall take my leave, now."

Captain Winters nodded. "Good hunting, sir."

Maximo went down below on his way to the hangar bay.

The captain seemed anxious. "Prepare a longboat. I'm taking a surface deployment force down to the planet, once we've established orbit."

"Yes, sir," said Balina. "Shall I inform Primus Muller?"

"Yes."

Alastriona looked up from her display. Muller was the captain of the Marine contingent. Though there were only twenty-five Marines on board, the *Tycho Brahe* also carried a hundred warbots. The robotic war machines would be more than enough protection.

"Aye, aye, sir." Lieutenant Balina nodded and her image winked out.

Captain Winters adjusted the holographic display and it swept over the surface of the dead world, as if he was scouring the planet for something. A red targeting reticule accompanied the image like a lost puppy, wandering outside, unattended. Eventually, the view flew over a domed building next to the ocean by one of the ruined cities. The image halted and came back to the odd looking building, followed by the targeting reticule, which settled on top of it. The image zoomed in. The uneasiness in the captain's demeanor melted away. He activated the intercom. "Lieutenant Tinibu?"

The Nigerian's scarred face appeared in a hologram. "Yes, captain?"

"What is the ETA to the fourth planet?"

"From our position, ten hours, more or less, sir."

The captain nodded and closed the channel.

Von Meyer said, "I'd like to go down there, too, if you don't mind. I want to see if this planet will be a good site to establish a colony."

"By all means, sir." Winters glanced at Ostergaard. "Who is our best archeologist?"

Nils said, "Warrant Officer Yize Taichi, sir."

Captain winters nodded. "He'll be joining us," he said. Then he turned towards Alastriona. "You're coming, too, Lieutenant."

* * *

**BLACK TORTOISE OF THE NORTH**

**SIGMA PEGASI / DEAD WORLD**

The surface deployment force approached the domed structure they had identified from orbit. It was a symphony of stone, water and the subtle play of reflected light. The silvery dome appeared to float over the rest of the building. The whole effect was accomplished with clever construction methods. The dome was made out of a complex of geometric structures, repeated at various sizes and angles in several layers. As the local star, Sigma Pegasi, passed overhead, it's light filtered through the geometric openings in the dome to create an enchanting effect. Dappled patterns moved slowly over the ground beneath it.

Wind blew Alastriona's hair into her face. The faint aroma of death still lingered over the planet. The city just up the coastline had tumbled into ruins. Pausing, she raised a hand scanner and surveyed the horizon. No life at all was detected by the scanner.

Unlike the Ash Worlds, this planet had been obliterated in a storm of crude violence. Compared to the work of the Archons, whatever had destroyed this civilization had the mark of a brute. Whereas the Archons had incinerated their enemies in an elegant display of annihilation, whoever or whatever had done this was both clumsy and primitive by comparison.

A squad of Marines accompanied them, along with twenty warbots. The machines glided through the air silently, floating on anti-gravity mechanisms, their sensor arrays fully activated. They were armed with a variety of weapons: Particle beams, lasers, and electromagnetic railguns.

The archeologist, Lieutenant Taichi, had trouble containing

his excitement. He picked through the local ruins like a happy ghoul digging up corpses. All of the alien bodies they had found had decayed to bones. As he came out of a nearby building, his eager voice resounded over the communicator, "Captain, this species would have towered over us. At twice our size, their skeletons suggest a robust physiology adapted to the slightly heavier gravity on the world. Intriguingly, the artifacts we have found alongside their bodies suggest an advanced, open society with a sophisticated understanding of technology and artistry."

They came to a halt by the domed structure. Alastriona noticed Von Meyer's secretary, Miss Tischler, with him. *Why bring his secretary?*

Captain Winters waved for them all to remain outside while he and Von Meyer went in with a couple of warbots. Over the communicator, he asked, "What happened here?"

Taichi said, "I don't know yet, sir. There are no signs of war on this world. Yet, they had extensive underground military installations, which were not used. This was a fortress world with no wars. What a tantalizing puzzle."

Alastriona was looking through the feed of one of their survey drones when the display went black. She checked the transmission, but it had stopped. It was the tenth drone to fail over the planet. She checked for atmospheric interference which could have interrupted their signals, but found none. She glanced at Primus Muller. "Lost another one."

The Marine captain stopped and looked into her eyes. Alertness swam with caution through a sea of blue. "Cause?"

She shrugged. "Unknown."

"Have you finished your survey?"

"Yes, sir."

"Recall the rest of the drones."

Alastriona nodded. She sent out a withdrawal order to all of the drones crisscrossing over the planet. They activated their anti-gravity mechanisms and ascended up to space where the *Tycho Brahe* would recover them.

"This building appears to be just a local museum," said the captain. "Nothing interesting, really." He said, "Mr. Taichi, how long have they been dead?"

Taichi replied, "The native inhabitants probably died one or two years ago, by Sol's calendar."

Alastriona's scanner beeped. She made an adjustment to analyze a new signal. It was a power source, which had just come on like a light switch. She turned towards the direction it had come from.

Accompanied by the warbots, Von Meyer emerged from the museum, carrying a small package, wrapped in what appeared to be gold silk. He placed the package inside a hyperspatial bag, which he folded into a small cloth. He put it into his pocket and walked over to Alastriona. She forgot all about the power source and tilted her head in curiosity, wondering what he had found. Presumably, the museum held ancient artifacts. *Archonian artifacts?*

Von Meyer said, "Didn't I tell you, Lieutenant? I'm lucky. This is another perfect site where the Imperium can build a new colony."

Alastriona lowered her scanner and regarded the man. "How can this tomb of a planet be lucky for anyone?"

He put his hand onto her shoulder and smiled. "Without locals to resist our presence, building a colony will be easy. My company will make a fortune again."

As he dropped his hand, Alastriona turned away from him so that he couldn't see the disgust on her face. She looked over at the domed structure, admiring it's beauty and wondering what kind of people had made it. She saw the captain walk outside and he came over to where she was standing. A wintry gale picked up, causing her to shiver.

The captain looked directly into her eyes. "Report."

Alastriona raised her eyebrows. "Whatever happened here, it's all over now, sir. Our drones have completed their survey of the entire planet. I've studied the various craters spread out over the surface. The largest one is over 300 kilometers in diameter. The planet appears to have been struck by dozens of asteroids."

Winters walked over to a low wall and raised a pair of binoculars to scan the horizon. "So it was a natural disaster?"

Alastriona nodded. "Yes, sir, in all probability. Though I would like to continue my research."

He nodded. "Put it all in your report. I will file it with the Interstellar Survey Department when we return to the Imperium."

Her scanner beeped again.

The captain lowered his binoculars. "What is it?"

Raising the device, Alastriona examined the readout. "A power source. It just appeared, like a light switch coming on. I make it a hundred and twenty meters in that direction."

The captain raised his binoculars and scanned the horizon.

Alastriona saw a dozen objects come into view. They were fast approaching their position.

The captain lowered his binoculars. "Drones," he muttered.

"I see them," said Primus Muller over the communicator. "Attention Marines, listen up! We're moving to defensive positions. Naidu, Schneider, Tremblay and Petrov, take cover behind that wall on the left flank. Sokolov, Rossi and Mensah, set up a firing line behind those trees on the right. Traore, Cho and Iyer, secure the perimeter and watch our backs. Shields on. Move out!"

The Marines raised their shields and took up their positions while the warbots moved to surround the surface deployment force in a protective circle.

"I thought you said this planet was uninhabited," said Von Meyer.

Alastriona shrugged. "They're robots."

A laser beam flashed out from the horizon and struck one of the warbots as it was moving into position. It's shield erupted into an intense orange flame and collapsed. The warbot exploded.

In the distance, little puffs of smoke appeared around the approaching drones. Trails of vapor followed dozens of objects, fast approaching.

Muller shouted over the communicator, "Incoming!"

All at once the area erupted with explosions.

Captain Winters grabbed Alastriona and pulled her down to the ground just as a laser beam shot past where she had been standing. Covering her body with his own, the captain called into the communicator, "Muller, report!"

Primus Muller's voice was calm. "The drones have opened fire with rockets and lasers. We've lost one of our warbots. We'll take care of it, sir."

Captain Winters moved away and activated his personal force field. "Activate your force field, Lieutenant."

With trembling hands, Alastriona turned on her force field. A nearly invisible bubble of protection surrounded her. Sitting against a wall, she brought her knees up and put her arms around them, still shivering in a chill that would not go away.

Satisfied that she had her force field turned on, the captain crept away to a low wall. He raised his binoculars to scan the field. "Everyone, stay down until the Marines have cleared out the area."

The warbots and Marines returned fire.

Another explosion landed close by. Shrapnel and debris thumped against her personal force field. She was glad for its protection. Nevertheless, she scrambled over to a better hiding area with more cover, next to the wall of the domed building. She remained there for some time, listening to her rapid heartbeat.

Eventually, Muller called out, "All clear."

All of the alien drones had been destroyed, one at a time. Captain Winters got up and held out his hand. Alastriona took it and got to her feet. Though their sheilds were on, an encrypted IFF system was active. It transmitted coded signals that identified friendly forces and differentiated others as potential threats. This allowed them to touch each other.

"Come on," he said. Over the communicator, the captain asked, "What's your assessment, Muller?"

"Automated robotic defenses," said the Marine commander. "They were probably triggered by all of our activity."

They made their way around the domed building, towards the

longboat.

As they went around the structure, a mechanical monstrosity came into view. It was a towering mechanical behemoth. It's metallic frame gleamed in the light of the star, Sigma Pegasi. It's design was imposing, with six massive, angular limbs. It's body was covered with sleek, armor plating adorned with intricate patterns and symbols. In the center of its head was a single, glowing eye that pulsated with energy. It scanned the surroundings with eerie intensity. Though it was a hundred meters away, Alastriona could still feel the ground tremble beneath it's colossal weight.

A warbot came around the building and fired a particle beam weapon, burning a hole in the armor covering the machine.

It seemed not to even notice the damage. The behemoth fired a beam weapon and the warbot was atomized in a blinding flash.

Everyone dove for cover.

Alastriona darted for the entrance to the domed building, running into the courtyard. She ran across the stone floor, which was awash with shifting shadows. She leaned against the stone wall, catching her breath. Shadows danced over the courtyard from flashes of the explosions outside. She could feel her heart racing.

She saw two warbots advancing into position just outside the courtyard. They both fired railguns. A moment later, they were obliterated in a blinding explosion that sent debris and rock chips flying over the courtyard. Rock chips struck against her force field and shattered.

Alastriona drew her blaster and looked at it. *This won't do me any good.* Still, it felt comforting to hold it while the battle raged outside. She had an urge to run into the building. At that moment, there was another explosion and the building entrance collapsed. Smoke swept over the courtyard, covering the dancing shadows. She coughed.

The Marine squad fired lasers and blasters at the machine from their hidden positions, unleashing a massive barrage of energy. She heard energized atomic particles from blaster rifles detonate against the armored monstrosity. The sound was deafening. She closed her eyes and put her hands over her ears.

Someone was screaming.

When the noise died down, Alastriona holstered her weapon and crept to the edge of the courtyard. Peering outside, she saw the behemoth far off in the adjoining field. It's red eye darted back and forth, in search of targets. She raised her scanner and analyzed the machine. It's eye was an infrared sensor, combined with a motion detector. She activated her communicator. "Target the eye."

She heard Muller's voice over the communicator, "Acknowl-edged. Send me your analysis, if you have it."

Alastriona realized that he was asking her to send him a detailed study of the type of sensors being used by the machine, so that he could customize a formula to block it most effectively. All of their equipment could be customized right on the battlefield, if necessary.

She leaned against a broken wall and pointed her scanner at the machine, which lumbered towards the building, shooting weapons at anything that moved. She held it there, impatiently waiting for it to finish the analysis.

The eye in the behemoth turned directly towards her and halted. A plume of smoke appeared from a pod attached to the machine.

Her scanner beeped and she dropped down to the floor.

An explosion turned the wall into rock chips and fire that collapsed her force field.

Alastriona threw herself to the side just as the wall crumbled. She rolled onto her back and looked at the scanner, which had a green light. With a smile and a wave of her hand, the data was sent over to Muller.

There was another round of detonations nearby. A warbot rumbled into view and crashed against the entry to the courtyard. The tip of it's blaster rifle glowed ruby red. She could see a light from its command module grow dim and wink out.

At last, Muller gave the order. "Deploy IR smoke, bearing zero-nine-zero, distance, seventy-five meters."

The infrared smoke was composed of carbon particles, which

would absorb and scatter infrared radiation, metal oxides such as zinc oxide or titanium dioxide to enhance the smoke's infrared blocking capabilities, and various obscurants, such as graphite or silica. The mixture also contained combustible materials and binder agents to facilitate its dispersal. The specific formulation could vary, depending on atmospheric conditions on the planet, and the type of infrared detectors it was being deployed against.

Captain Winters gave a command, "When Muller gives the order, everyone retreat back to the longboat."

There came a thumping sound in the distance.

Several seconds later, Muller shouted, "Go, go, go!"

Alastriona watched everyone in the surface deployment force running towards the longboat, which rested in a field just over a nearby hillside. Von Meyer came into the courtyard, followed by his secretary. Staring at the woman, Alastriona whispered, "Why aren't you afraid?"

Von Meyer put his hand on Alastriona's shoulder. "Let's go, Lieutenant."

The behemoth fired randomly through the smoke and the ground erupted with explosions. Somehow, they made it back to the longboat. Captain Winters stood outside the door, making sure everyone got back.

Out in the field, the remaining warbots set up a defensive line and fired at the machine.

From inside the longboat, Alastriona watched as each warbot, one by one, exploded or vanished in a flash of intense light. The behemoth came over the crest of the hill, it's giant eye scanning back and forth. It halted and gazed down at the longboat just as the last person stepped inside. Captain Winters jumped in. He slammed the door shut and shouted to the pilot, "Go, go."

The behemoth rotated a turret holding an immense beam weapon until it was pointing at the longboat. At that moment, the pair of fighters from the *Tycho Brahe* swept over the field, firing ordinance at the machine, and it was obliterated in a fiery cloud of smoke.

As the longboat rose up into the atmosphere, Alastriona switched on a view of the giant machine, now immobile, as dead as the world that had given it mechanical life. She looked at the rest of the dead planet, wondering what had happened there. Nothing remained now, except the bones of the giants who had once lived there, along with their deadly machines.

*   *   *

The longboat passed into the shadow side of the planet. Darkness profound covered the dead world below. After they had returned to the *Tycho Brahe*, Alastriona learned that several of the Marines had been injured, and three of them had been killed. Only two of the warbots which had gone down to the planet were intact.

Étienne Leclerc, the priest on board, held a funeral service for their fallen comrades. Throughout the ceremony, the captain had a determined look in his eyes, mingled with a hint of defiance. After the funeral service, he gave orders to set sail. They were leaving the star system.

Though Alastriona was shaken by the experience, she didn't want to bother the healers because they were busy helping the injured Marines. Healers could eliminate post traumatic stress syndrome within a few minutes but something much darker threatened to emerge from the shadows of her dreams. Over the course of the journey, a chill had come over her which she was unable to shake off.

Alastriona went up to the star deck. Since her watch was over, she went over to the fo'c'sle. She sat down onto the deck overlooking the stem of the *Tycho Brahe* and gazed up at the stars. She peered into the dark, immeasurable abyss while the starship raised sails and headed away from the doomed world. Why had her nightmares returned?

She got up and was instinctively drawn to the entrance to the cathedral, seeking the darkness within. She opened the hatch and entered. The black passage was comforting. She walked several paces to the archway that led into the cathedral and went in.

The only light inside the cathedral was a dim, reddish glow.

An energy dome covered the chamber, which kept out the vacuum of space. Solar sails were arrayed throughout the chamber, their pale silver surfaces tinted red. Francois stood in the center of the cathedral, at a console. With the wave of one hand, he activated the controls to raise the sails high, until he was surrounded by the silvery sheets.

Alastriona walked over to him, letting the hidden terrors from her dreams slip away into the blackness. She had always sought re-assurance from the dark. It was like curling up into a warm blanket.

Francois greeted her in French, which brought a smile to her heart. "Bonsoir."

"Bonsoir," she said. She looked up into the darkness. "This is the first time I've come into the cathedral on this starship. I have always been curious. Why the red light?"

"We have only found a few inhabited planets around red stars, so we rarely travel to such places." He looked up into the darkness covering the cathedral. "So, like in a darkroom, the crystals lining our solar sails are not affected by that frequency."

"You work in the darkness."

"Yes," he laughed. The sound of it was like a burst of sunshine "Before I joined the Imperial Star Force, I was a photographer and an artist."

She smiled, though he couldn't see it very well. "You paint?"

"Yes," he said. "I have always been fascinated by the play of light against dark to create moods and emotions. We are defined by light. Light brings a painting to life. Light is where the beauty in a painting comes from."

He brushed a strand of hair out of her face.

Alastriona whispered, "Sing me a song."

Francois sat down, closed his eyes and took a deep breath, focusing on the star Sigma Pegasi. Silence filled the chamber for some time. Then, as if it was a slight breeze, a hum emerged from deep inside his chest. He let it drift in the air for a moment until it was caught up, like a kite catching the wind.

The humming turned into a melody and the melody became a song. The ballad came out of the darkness. Something lonely, empty, and far away lingered there for a time. The crystals covering the solar sails tingled like a fluttering wind chime.

Alastriona felt herself slipping into the stream of music and before she realized it, she was singing too. With a voice as pure as the night itself, she joined his song, her harmonies weaving seamlessly with his, creating a tapestry of sound that transcended time. Two ballads  danced together in the darkness. Alastriona and Francois smiled at one another, bound together by the symphony of their shared longing.

All of the crystals lining the solar sails vibrated to the stream of music until they had been tuned to the light frequency of the star, Sigma Pegasi. A red light flashed on the computer console to indicate the sails were ready for deployment.

When Francois and Alastriona stopped singing, they realized they were holding hands.

Alastriona took her hand away and stood up, dropping her gaze to the floor. "I'm sorry. I have ruined your project."

"No," he said. "This is my best work."

Francois stood up and faced his console. He waved a hand and the set of solar sails rose up beyond the energy barrier protecting the chamber and they went out to the rest of the crew, who took them up into the rigging.

Alastriona ran out of the cathedral. No longer shaken by the trauma of the day's events, she was unsettled in much a different way. She went down to her cabin and cast herself onto her bed, falling fast asleep.

*　*　*

## 3220 A.D. — YEAR OF THE METAL RAT  (TEN YEARS AGO)
## THE REQUIEM

Alastriona awoke.

She was in a cold dark room full of shadows and whispering voices. She spoke in her native French, "Maman? Papa?"

Alastriona didn't see her parents anywhere. She stood up, holding a rag doll in her hands.

A cold breeze brought a murmur with it.

Alastriona giggled. It was a game. She shouted, "Vous êtes le Épouvantail!"

Devouring all the light in the room, a shadow approached. It was a being of pure hatred. The body that once gave it form had faded away, leaving only a twisted thing wrapped in centuries of loneliness. The creature whispered, calling out for her to come closer.

Alastriona began to get cold.

A man and a woman walked into the room. They held small batons that glowed in the darkness. The shadow receded back into the corners. Surprised at the sight of the little girl, the woman stopped and smiled. "Hello, what's your name?"

"Alastriona."

The shadow waited.

The woman murmured to herself, "What are you doing here, all alone in the Requiem?"

The man's voice was harsh. "Leave her."

The woman was insistent. "No! We can't do that. They'll devour her soul as soon as we are gone!"

The man was tired. "Those Who Wait are always at the gateway. There is no way out. Like the rest of us, she can never go back.

Maybe it's a better thing that her soul is devoured, rather than to live out an eternity in this place."

"How can you—"

The woman stopped and looked around.

There was movement in the darkness.

She hissed, "They're here, now, with us!"

The man's face shifted into an expression of terror. He raised his baton and it transformed into a sword that glowed in the dark. "Let's get out of here! Bring her, I don't care."

The shadows whispered.

Alastriona giggled as she felt the woman pick her up.

The man and woman ran out of the chamber, carrying Alastriona away.

They were pursued by shadows.

*   *   *

# FIVE
## Traitor

Imperial Courier Drone: B43F9E2C

Origin: Externum Imperium — Sigma Pegasi / Ash World

Destination: Copernicus / Maria Celeste — HD 84117 / Scylanthia

April 23, 3235

*Dear Julie,*

*We have just sailed away from Sigma Pegasi, a star system that contained an Ash World. Even after tens of thousands of years, the devastation there is complete. It was quite frightening to see. I hope we never discover what weapons the Archons used in their ancient wars. Hopefully, whoever killed IK Pegasi isn't using rediscovered Archonian technology. As for myself, everything is fine. I have not met with any kind of disaster like you keep dreaming about. I know that they have classified you as an ESPer, but do all of your psychic visions really come true? Seriously sis, did you think I was sailing away to my doom? Unlike you, I am managing my life quite well. On the other hand, you are most certainly headed for tragedy. You think you can live in your romantic fairy tale forever? Let mom and dad find you a proper match, like they have done for me.*

*Love,*

*Alastriona*

Secure Data Transmission Encrypted

Imperial Regulations Compliant

*   *   *

## HYPERSPACE

Alastriona entered a circular chamber where blue lights flickered off the walls from instrument panels. A ring-shaped bench rested on the floor of the science lab. Mist floated in the middle of the ring, concealing the cavity that lay beneath it.

She looked at Nils Ostergaard, who was standing in the domed room next to a window that looked out onto space to the fore of the starship. The *Tycho Brahe* slipped through the blackness of hyperspace like a mystical dragon swimming downriver.

She stepped up to a console next to Nils and with a wave of her hand, activated a control hologram. She flipped a switch and, like a pearl rising from the depths, a glistening white sphere emerged from the cavity in the center of the ring, rising into view. White vapor licked its surface and drifted into the air around it. She studied the readouts on the holographic instrument panel.

Nils looked into her tired face and down at her hand, which was trembling. "Your face is as white as a sheet. Trouble sleeping again?"

Alastriona closed her eyes. With the onset of darkness, she could feel a tremor in her soul. With a heavy sigh to steady herself, she nodded, not willing to voice her troubles out loud.

Nils stopped entering data into his console. "There's something else this time, isn't there?

Opening her eyes again, she whispered, "Yes."

Throughout her childhood, when she had encountered the nightmares, she had never recalled any of them. This time, she had remembered the horrid land of shadows. It filled her with a desire to run away into the darkness where she could hide. Alastriona looked up at the giant pearl hovering inside the chamber, wishing she could forget the night terrors.

Before Nils could ask another question, Legatus Kevin Von Meyer appeared in the hallway outside the arched opening to the chamber. His secretary, Miss Tischler, was one step behind him with a data pad in her hand. She had an impatient look. Von Meyer turned to Nils and said, "Lieutenant, may I speak to Miss DeTroyes in private?"

"Certainly, Legatus."

Nils walked out of the chamber and went aft to the science department towards his office.

"Miss Tischler, why don't you go with Lieutenant Ostergaard?"

Her voice had a melodious, captivating tone that resonated with warmth and clarity, carrying a gentle cadence that was both soothing and enchanting. "Sir, my role includes maintaining real-time data synchronization and security protocols. Is there anything I can help you with during your conversation?"

He shook his head. "No, Elfriede. Go get a coffee or some-thing."

A slight smile touched the secretary's face and she turned to gaze into Alastriona's eyes for a moment. Coming to a decision, she looked at Von Meyer and nodded. "Very well, sir."

Hearing the woman walk away, Alastriona turned away from him and examined the readout in front of her, wishing that Von Meyer would go away.

He didn't. Instead, he put a hand on the doorway without coming in. Blue light reflected off his finely tailored suit. He was surrounded by some of the misty vapor that had drifted into the hallway, making him look like a visiting deity. His voice held a trace of concern. "Are you all right?"

"Yes," she said. "I didn't sleep well, that's all."

He gave off a nervous chuckle. "After Sigma Pegasi, I've had a few sleepless nights myself."

"Your secretary is an android, isn't she?"

"How did you know?"

"She wasn't terrified when we were attacked. She's not just a secretary, though, is she?"

"No, Elfriede is my bodyguard."

Alastriona didn't respond. *How can I be jealous of a machine?*

He changed the subject. "What are you doing?"

Alastriona didn't look at him but she was glad to get her mind off the nightmares. She replied, "I'm testing for neutrino decoherence as a result of small fluctuations in spacetime, caused by quantum gravity."

She heard him chuckle. "I have no idea what you just said." Von Meyer looked up at the giant pearl. "What is this thing?"

Alastriona decided to deal with him quickly, so that he would go away. She turned to face him and was instantly captivated by his charming smile. His steel gray eyes held a taste of reluctance, but he didn't turn away from her gaze. Their eyes locked for an instant. Like a drowning child searching for something to hold onto, she took refuge in his strength. The feelings were as surprising as they were annoying.

She casually tucked a loose strand of hair behind her ear and realized that her hands had stopped shaking. "This is a large-scale, high light yield liquid scintillator detector. It's used to test for neutrino emissions, which will arrive just before the blast of the supernova. This is our early warning system."

He took his eyes away from hers and for a moment, she felt adrift in a sea of shadows. He inspected the device and asked, "How does it work?"

Alastriona paused and looked up at the giant sphere hovering in the chamber.

The particle-physics detector featured an onion-like design, with its innermost layers boasting the highest radio-purity. At its core lay a pseudocumene scintillator fluid infused with diphenyloxazole, enhancing the emission light to optimize the sensitivity of the instruments. Surrounding this inner vessel was a stainless-steel sphere housing thousands of photomultipliers. The steel sphere sat within a tank of highly purified water. Along with a precisely calibrated force-field, it shielded the instruments from environmental radioactivity. It was designed to detect and locate the source of neutrinos.

*He doesn't really care about this.*

Alastriona turned towards him and crossed her arms. "I didn't realize you were interested in particle physics, tribune."

Von Meyer grinned and walked into the chamber.

She had an urge to step back but stood her ground.

His grin faded away. "I wanted to apologize to you, Lieutenant, for my behavior the other night. I was rude towards you. I'm sorry."

Alastriona narrowed her eyes and bit her lip, not knowing what to say to him.

A shy smile slipped into his face. "Desire can drive a man to do some crazy things sometimes."

"Ah, love." Turning back to the console, she started sifting through the data once again. She muttered, "So you were overcome by the greatest force in the universe."

"I'm not so sure what you're—"

"What a powerful man you are. Are you overcome often, around women?"

"Of course not."

She laughed softly. "I bet it happens all the time."

"All individuals merit the opportunity for absolution."

Frowning, she glanced at him. "What?"

"Everyone deserves forgiveness."

Alastriona shook her head and sighed, refusing to give him any more attention. "Respectfully, sir, I have a great deal of work to do."

*　*　*

Bright light poured into the hangar bay from the ceiling, shining down upon several small cutters and longboats, along with a pair of imperial starfighters. Alastriona saw Lieutenant Iveta Balina with her arms crossed on the other side of the hangar. The flight leader was supervising a mechanic and a pair of robots as they conducted maintenance on one of the starfighters.

Alastriona walked across the main deck towards the object which Maximo had recovered while they were away on the planet. Maximo was there already, next to a pair of maintenance robots, studying the device.

It was a missile, fifteen meters long.

With a wave of her hand, she activated a scanning probe, which hovered next to the missile. She glanced at Maximo and said, "You found this in the debris field?"

Maximo rested both of his hands on the handle of his cane. "Yes. There were hundreds of them. Their remains were spread out in an area of space inside an immense cloud of sand. Unlike the rest, I found this one mostly intact. It's motor, no doubt, is burnt out."

"Sand?"

"Sand."

Alastriona tilted her head and read over the results of the scan. "I would classify this object as a Relativistic Kill Vehicle, an RKV."

"A missile," he said. "What kind of warhead does it have?"

"There is none. This is essentially an interstellar ballistic missile, meant to travel at near light speed. As you get closer to the speed of light, the kinetic energy no longer rises with the square of velocity, but it goes up even more sharply."

Maximo nodded. "So this thing carries an unbelievable punch."

Alastriona gave him a look of admiration. It was rare to encounter someone who knew what she was talking about. *Maybe we are right for each other.* She continued with her explanation of the missile. "What's more, a RKV is extremely difficult to see because it moves so fast. Even if you could locate it, you would have little time to react because the light from it would only reach you just ahead of the missile."

He remained silent, taking in her words.

She went on, "The only real way to detect this would be from the slight glow of collision radiation with the interstellar medium, which becomes brighter the faster it travels."

He whispered, "The faster something is moving, the less time you have to react to it and the more energy it has to inflict damage. Yet, they stopped hundreds of them by deploying a massive cloud of sand."

She nodded. "A tiny grain of sand would destroy anything moving so fast."

"They knew where to deploy the sand," he said. "They knew

their enemy."

Alastriona activated a hologram of Sigma Pegasi. Little planets whirled around the star system. A white light and a red light indicated the position of the two stars. The other planets were tiny pinpoints of light, barely discernible. She expanded the size of the planets so she could see them better. After some study, she located the debris field and began entering data.

"What are you doing?"

Her hand instinctively moved to remove a stray hair obstructing her view. "I'm calculating the location of the mandala wormhole opening of the RKVs, based on the position of the debris field in relation to the planet, taking into account the celestial movements of the rest of the planetary bodies over time."

"You're trying to figure out where it came from."

"That's what I said."

Maximo walked down the length of the missile, went around the rear and proceeded to walk around the other side. She could hear his cane clicking as he walked.

Alastriona activated a communicator.

A hologram of Captain Winters appeared. He looked tired. "Yes, Lieutenant?"

*Does he have nightmares of his own?*

With a wave of her hand, she sent him the data on the RKV.

"Sir, I have been examining the object which we  recovered from Sigma Pegasi. It's a weapon. It was part of an armada of such weapons, deployed against the planet in a massive assault."

He activated a hologram of his own. She could see a duplicate of the missile in miniature next to him. He took a deep, pained breath and closed his eyes. "So this is how the planet was destroyed."

"Yes, sir. An interplanetary war was fought here. This planet lost."

A beep came from the computer and she paused to read it. She frowned in disbelief.

"Something else?"

"Yes, sir. This missile came from 34 Pegasi."

"What?"

"I have run the calculations several times, sir." Alastriona wasn't able to keep the surprise out of her voice. "This weapon came from 34 Pegasi, the star system we are traveling to now."

Winters crossed his arms. "That's a crazy coincidence, if it's true."

"I agree," she said. "If I may ask, why did you choose this destination, sir?"

Annoyance slipped into his voice. "It was a random choice, Lieutenant. Thank you for the report. Good work."

His hologram winked out.

Alastriona raised her eyebrows. *I wonder what's wrong with the captain?* A light indicated that the communication channel was still open. She considered turning on the hologram again, but decided against it. With a shrug, she gave her attention to the data readout. Maximo walked around to the front of the missile and came to a stop close to her.

Flight Lieutenant Balina walked up to the RKV and halted next to them. She was listening to a communication channel from one of the maintenance staff. "Both repairs and maintenance of the damage to the starfighters have been performed, Ma'am. As well as full replacement of the disabled subassemblies."

"Thank you, Dmitry."

Balina cleaned her hands with a rag while she examined the missile. "I see you've captured a Relativistic Kinetic Missile. It's rare to find one so intact. Most have a self-destruct mechanism."

Both Maximo and Alastriona stared at Balina.

Maximo was the first to speak. "You recognize this?"

"Yes, sir." Balina tossed the rag onto a workbench. She raised an arm and activated a hologram from the wrist computer built into her flight suit. Blueprints appeared in front of them. She waved her hand to cycle through hundreds of designs and finally came to a stop. The blueprints perfectly matched the missile in front of them. With another wave of her hand, she sent the image to the main console. A duplicate hologram now floated in front of them.

Alastriona frowned. "Wait, this can't be right."

Balina said, "A few hundred years ago, the Imperium used stars to fuel our war machine. They used mega-lasers to shove missiles with high tech guidance systems up to relativistic velocities. They fired volleys of hundreds of missiles at distant star systems. The trickiest part was the timing."

Alastriona raised an eyebrow. "Timing?"

"Yes," said. Balina. "So that they all hit their target at the same time."

Alastriona took a step back and stared up at the missile, as if it was a ghost. "This RKV was constructed from our blueprints. This is imperial technology?"

Balina laughed softly. "It's old technology, but yes, it's ours. We don't use these anymore."

Alastriona noticed a slight difference. She pointed at a slot along its surface. "This one has been modified slightly."

Balina nodded. "Yes. Though it has been retracted, this looks like an extendable mast for a mini-hypersail. So it came here through a hyperspace wormhole. With the original design, it would still have taken years to get here. Hyperspace cuts the time down to days."

Alastriona frowned. "So whoever destroyed Sigma Pegasi could pose a serious threat to the Imperium."

"That's right," said Balina.

Alastriona looked at Maximo, but he didn't seem surprised at all. Rather than looking at the missile, he was studying her face.

There came a loud crash from the other side of the launch bay. Smoke came from a damaged maintenance robot. Lieutenant Balina sighed audibly. She went over to the other side of the launch bay and began shouting at Dmitry.

Alastriona rechecked the data. "51 Pegasi is at the edge of the Imperium, just over fifty light years from the Forbidden Planet, Earth."

Maximo nodded. "It is."

"34 Pegasi is just over a hundred and thirty-one light years away from Sol," she said. "It's far away, in unexplored space."

Maximo nodded. "34 Pegasi is our destination. We're headed there now."

She peered into his eyes, which contained a knowing look. She frowned. "How could aliens obtain our technology?"

"I have a confession to make," he said. "I have another reason for being here."

She raised an eyebrow. "Another reason?"

"I have come here to investigate a series of crimes which have been committed by someone on board the Tycho Brahe. Someone has been communicating with and giving technology away to aliens."

She stared at him in silence for a moment. Afraid to say it aloud, she finally whispered, "That's treason."

"Yes, it is."

"How do you know this traitor even exists?"

"That is why I am here."

Beyond the crimes he was describing, there was something else that irritated her even more. Aggravation ignited into fire. A flash of heat swept through her body. Angry, she looked away from him, up at the missile, avoiding his eyes. In a carefully controlled voice, she asked, "So, you used me to get on board without anyone knowing why you were really here."

"Yes," he chuckled. "How convenient of you to be on board."

She turned to face him, eyes narrowing. "You have informed the captain, of course?"

"No. Just you."

"Why me?"

Maximo laughed. "My dear, you are almost as intelligent as I am."

*What a pompous jerk. How can Francois compare me to him?* She brushed away the thought. "What has that got to do with anything?"

"You can assist me."

She turned away from him, shut off the hologram containing the imperial blueprints and closed down the scanning equipment next to the missile. *I'm nobody's assistant.* She looked up at him and crossed her arms. "You lied to me."

"Don't be irrational," he said. "It's beneath you. I did not lie to you."

Narrowing eyes, she remained silent.

He seemed not to even notice. He studied the imperial missile. "Could it have come from an imperial starship?"

Letting it go for the moment, Alastriona turned her eyes back to the RKV and uncrossed her arms. "Unlikely. According to Lieutenant Balina, there are no similar weapons in our current arsenal. They're outdated."

Maximo swept their relationship issues aside as easily as erasing an incorrect equation off a chalkboard. It was infuriating. "Have you noticed anything else unusual while you've been on board the Tycho Brahe, aside from the record of the alien transmissions you found?"

She had forgotten about the messages. She shook her head. "No, nothing unusual. But why would someone give aliens imperial technology?"

Maximo gave her an condescending look. "You spend too much time with your cold equations." He pointed at her head. "Stop using this," he pointed at her heart and continued, "and start using this.

Whoever our culprit is, they will have a strong emotional reason for betraying humanity."

With a  sigh, she considered his question.

After a moment, it finally dawned on her. *Von Meyer. He had said that he was lucky. He bragged about making a fortune from building colonies on dead worlds.* In a superior tone, she said, "I know who it is."

"You do?"

With a smirk on her face, Alastriona turned to look into his eyes. "You used me to get on board. Make it up to me and I'll tell you."

"How?"

She turned away from him and looked down at the scanner readouts for the RKV. "That's just another mystery you will have to solve."

"This is serious, Alastriona. If you know something you should tell me."

"I know who it is."

Maximo chuckled. "That's cute. No you don't."

"I guess you will never know."

"So you're an astrophysicist and also a detective?" He laughed out loud and said in a condescending tone, "You don't know anything. Perhaps I was mistaken in telling you about this."

Angry at his remark, Alastriona shook her head. "I have to analyze all the data that I have collected from the new observations of IK Pegasi before we arrive at 34 Pegasi."

"My inquiry has priority."

"So investigate it."

Furious, she walked out of the landing bay.

*　*　*

Alastriona didn't know if she was shaking from anger or from something else. She went up to the quarterdeck where star sailors were busy adjusting the hypersails. The hypersails were much larger than the solar sails. The Executive Officer, Lieutenant Min Je Ro, shouted her orders up at the star riggers. "Hands to the halyards, sheet home! Ho, sheets and tacks!"

Thinking that the quarterdeck would have been relatively quiet, she was surprised by all of the activity. She looked up into the rigging and saw the massive hypersails sparkling in the darkness. Then she remembered that the *Tycho Brahe* needed to continually adjust the hypersails against the turbulence inside the wormhole. Without such vigilance, a starship could lose it's hypersails while navigating through the vortex. Such starships were never seen again.

Lieutenant Ro turned around and walked over to the helmsman at the wheel. In a much calmer voice, she said, "Steady as she is."

Turning away, Alastriona sought refuge inside the cathedral.

180

She entered the dark passage at the foredeck. A sign at the entrance warned against carrying any kind of light source inside the cathedral that was not red. The domed chamber housed the solar sails. An errant stream of photons would propel the solar sails at a massive velocity. So a security checkpoint stood inside the passage. It was designed to detect light sources that a crewman might have on. She walked through it without triggering an alarm and entered the chamber.

Bathed in red light, the cathedral was empty. She walked over to the center of the room and sat down on the floor. Shuddering at dark memories, she brought her legs up and hugged them tight. Closing her eyes, she waited for the quivering to subside. Like leaves blown out of a tree, the tremors gradually blew away into the darkness.

Breathing easy again, she fell asleep.

*   *   *

## 3220 A.D. – YEAR OF THE METAL RAT  (TEN YEARS AGO)
## THE REQUIEM

It was safer in the darkness. They could not reach her there. Light always seemed to bring out the creatures that sought to devour them. Always on the move, they were continually searching for something they called the "Gateway." After a year in the Requiem, she had forgotten what it was like to eat or drink, but she never seemed to be hungry. The only thing she felt was terror from those who were hunting them. Fear seemed to devour her entire existence, while they sought the shadowy recesses of the labyrinth inside the Requiem.

There was suddenly a low, mournful wailing that arose out of the darkness.

*   *   *

## 3230 A.D. — YEAR OF THE METAL DOG (PRESENT)
## HYPERSPACE

A gentle touch on one arm made her jump. Alastriona opened her eyes to a red night. Her heart was pounding.

A voice came from the darkness. "You shouldn't sleep in here."

Though the voice sounded familiar, she didn't recognize it. Part of her mind was still running through the shadowy labyrinth inside the Requiem. Disorientation turned to surprise. *Another nightmare remembered.*

She blinked her eyes against the dim glare of red light. "Who's there?"

Laughter. "Lieutenant Chevalier."

"Francois?"

"Yes."

She felt him take her hand into his and he tugged. She stood up and swayed a little bit. He brought her close and held her there. "Are you all right?"

His warm arms had naturally slipped around her waist. Alastriona had an irresistible urge to hold onto him. He was an island in a sea of darkness. But she let go and stepped away. "I came in here to be alone," she muttered. "I must have fallen asleep."

Francois laughed again. He brought up his hand and tousled her hair playfully. "A starsinger's first rule is no sleeping inside the cathedral."

He took her hand into his. "Come, I will lead you out of here."

Though he took a step and pulled gently at her hand, she didn't move.

He stopped. "What is it?"

"Its just that, the Tycho Brahe isn't known for privacy."

"Of course not. There are two hundred people on board," he said. "Why did you really come here?"

Alastriona shrugged, though he probably couldn't see it. "Maximo used me."

She told him all about Maximo's secret investigation.

"Why would you tell me that?" he asked.

She shook her head. "I don't know. I guess I'm mad at him for using me."

"You're furious that he will never really love you."

Alastriona peered into the darkness. The dim red light provided some illumination, but it wasn't much. *Like in a tomb*, she thought. A lonely whisper escaped her lips, "Yes."

Francois didn't probe deeper. He chose a different path. "So, there are two mysteries to solve. First, you have your exploding star. Second, he is looking for a traitor."

"I suppose so, yes."

Francois laughed playfully. "It's a competition. Dueling detectives. If he solves his crime first, you will marry him. But if you solve yours first—"

He paused.

Alastriona looked at him and she smiled. The idea of it was reckless, misguided, childish even. Her sister would be proud. Her parents would react poorly, of course.

A pretty voice emerged out of the darkness. Angelica hummed a happy melody as she strode into the cathedral. She came over to where they were standing and halted. The music died. "Why, hello."

Francois turned to Angelica. "Hello, Angelica."

Angelica adopted a patronizing attitude. "You shouldn't be in here, DeTroyes. We have to retune some of the hypersails."

Though they were all surrounded by red light, Alastriona's eyes had finally adjusted and she could see that Francois had turned to gaze into Angelica's eyes.

He asked, "Which set of sheets is it this time?"

Angelica said, "The Fore Course, the Fore Tops'l and the Fore T'garns'l."

"All three sets?"

"Of course. You know that," she said. "What is the condition of the current hypersails?"

His voice grew weary. "Unpredictable, like sunlight, like the Tycho Brahe, like the Imperium."

Alastriona stared at the two of them. They seemed to be engaged in some kind of silent duel. She wondered how long the two starsingers had served together on the *Tycho Brahe*.

Francois never took his eyes away from Angelica's. "I've come to a decision. I'm resigning my commission after this voyage."

Angelica frowned. "Why?"

Dissatisfaction mingled with resentment. "I'm tired of helping the Imperium conquer alien worlds."

Angelica adopted a patronizing tone, "So you think it's better to let aliens destroy humanity?"

"I'm just tired of it all."

Angelica's voice dropped down to an intimate whisper. "Where will you go?"

Light came back into his voice. "Someplace where there's more sunshine for artists, all year round."

"Where's that?" asked Angelica.

"The Vermilion Bird of the South," he said. "HD 84117. Scylanthia."

Alastriona's lips parted in surprise.

Angelica's whisper grew quieter. "Whatever for?"

"Can't you see that I'm in love with this woman?" said Francois. "I want to tell her so. I want her to come with me, back to her homeworld."

Angelica finally broke eye contact with Francois. She turned to face Alastriona. Curiosity mingled there with a trace of sadness, but her smile was kind. "I need to go find a robot. I'll be back with the hypersails in a few minutes."

Alastriona and Francois looked into each other's eyes. They stood there in silence for a moment while Angelica went out.

After she was gone, Alastriona said, "You don't even know me."

"What?"

"You don't even know me."

"I don't know Scylanthia either."

* * *

The tiny robotic bee hovered over a flower. Its metallic body was adorned with intricate sensors. The bee's body shimmered under the sunlight while its antenna sensors twitched and adjusted, surveying the surroundings with meticulous accuracy. While collecting nectar from the flower, grains of pollen adhered to its mechanical body. With a tiny hum, the bee flew over to another flower and transferred the pollen to it, fertilizing the plant.

As part of her workout routine every morning, Alastriona was required to practice with her Vajra Thunderbolt in a martial arts session led by either Primus Helmand Muller or Centurion Ethan Taylor, who were the Marine officers on board. Occasionally, one of the other Marines would lead the workout. After this, she liked to run a few kilometers on the racetrack that encircled the arboretum.

On one tranquil morning, simulated sunlight filtered through the swaying leaves of the trees in the arboretum, casting intricate patterns on the racetrack as she ran along the winding path. Greenery covered the grounds, punctuated by flowers of all kinds. The air was always as fresh as it would have been after a rainstorm. The sound of birds and other wildlife filled the air. She knew they were all robots, even the bees and butterflies, but it didn't matter. The arboretum was designed to get you to forget that you were on a starship.

Her heart was burdened by the weight of conflicting emotions. So she tried to run it out. Even so, she couldn't shake the image of Francois, who had ignited a wildfire of passion. *What a ridiculous notion.* She didn't permit her mind to complete the thought, knowing that she could never go there. Every step she took seemed to echo his name and she wanted to run away from it as fast as she could. As she passed another runner, she thought of Maximus. He checked every box on the list of what she would ever want. He was brilliant, reliable and committed  to being with her. Since he had been born on Earth, he was a Pure Strain Human, too. Francois was from the planet Sakura, which orbited the star Beta Hydri. He was only a Provincial Citizen.

*Like me.*

Maximo was so annoying, and yet he was invariably correct in his assessments. She both admired and disliked him. How could he use her like that?  Would he use her again and again in the future? Traversing around the curved track at one end of the garden, she realized that his ruse was the best way to get on board without anyone suspecting why he had come here.

Still, she hated him for it.

She came to a stop and bent over to catch her breath. Walking over to the entrance to the gym, she went inside to take a shower and change into her uniform. But while standing under the hot water, all she could think about was Francois. As she got dressed, she muttered, "He's just not good enough."

* * *

Alastriona walked into the science lab and dropped into a chair with a huff. Waving a hand, she turned on her computer. A hologram full of data appeared and she began to read through it.

IK Pegasi had a slight dimming in a predictable pattern. Most likely, it was caused by  the orbiting planets they had detected. But this time it was different. Using advanced data analytics from the computer, she analyzed the vast datasets collected over the past two thousand years. Subtle patterns in the stellar data revealed something new.  Then she examined the quantum sensor data from the observations made while they were at Sigma Pegasi and compared it to the historical data.

Something was there, orbiting the red star.

Something big.

*Is it something the Archons built?*

If the ancient race of god-like beings had built something around the star, it could explain a great deal. Unless someone else had built whatever it was. She rather hoped it was built by the Archons.

She manipulated the display to focus on what it could be. Though too blurry to make out clearly, it appeared to be a series of objects orbiting the red star. Since Sigma Pegasi was far closer than any observatory in the Imperium, the images and data collected were more accurate.

She adjusted the image so she could look at the second star in the binary system. The white dwarf didn't appear to have any objects around it. It was, however, surrounded by an accretion disk of hydrogen and helium, which it siphoned off from the red star.

She switched back to examine the object, wondering what it could be.

Saila Heikkinen walked in. "Who sent you flowers?"

Alastriona turned around in her seat. A bouquet of red roses sat in a vase on top of her desk. She stood up and walked over to the flowers. Their aroma perfumed the air.

She read the note attached:

*Amongst riches untold, I seek the priceless treasure of your companionship.*

*With hope,*

*Von Meyer.*

Alastriona sighed and muttered, "I really don't have time for this."

Saila walked over to the vase, picked up the card and read it. "Oh, my God! Von Meyer has the hots for you?"

Alastriona pulled the bouquet out of the vase, sat down in her chair and swiveled back around to look at the data. Absentmindedly, she began to pull off the rose buds, one at a time and she dropped them onto the floor.

With a perplexed expression on her face, Saila took another seat at the adjacent desk. "What are you going to do?"

"What?" Alastriona glanced at her friend and then back at the data. "Nothing."

With a smile, Saila leaned back in her chair. In a teasing voice, she said, "Does Maximo know you're having a tryst with Von Meyer?"

"I'm not having a—" Alastriona stopped and looked into Saila's amused eyes. "Don't you have something to do?"

"No." Saila leaned forward, dropping her voice to a conspiratorial whisper. "You can tell me. What's he like?"

"Who?"

"Von Meyer!"

"I wouldn't know," said Alastriona. "Don't you remember? I'm engaged to Maximo Navarro Ayala—something or other."

"You don't even know his name."

"It's a long one. Anyway, I'm already taken."

By that time, all of the flowers were on the floor. Alastriona took the remaining bunch of thorny stems, placed them back into the vase and set it back onto the table.

"What's wrong with you? Von Meyer is really good looking, and he's one of the richest men in the Imperium. Who wouldn't—"

"I wouldn't."

* * *

Over tthe rest of the days while they were in hyperspace, Alastriona couldn't resist the impulse to spend time inside the cathedral, where it was dark and quiet. The chamber wasn't needed much while they were still in hyperspace, but once they had arrived at 34 Pegasi, both of the starsingers would be quite busy tuning the solar sails to match the frequency of the trinary star system. Francois often joined her there, and they spent much of their time together, sometimes talking, but more often in silence. She never felt the need to talk around him. He was there to sing, of course, and to focus on the stars.

*   *   *

On the day they were to leave hyperspace, Alastriona went into the cathedral. She walked over to the control area and took a seat, waiting for Francois to arrive. Her gaze rose up towards the top of the dome. Several of the solar sails were there already, awaiting the music from the starsingers. Their jewelled surfaces glinted in the red light of the chamber. For some reason, she wondered why they were not fluttering. There was usually a slight breeze in the cathedral. Today, all was a still as a tomb.

She picked up her Vajra Thunderbolt, which hung from her uniform belt, and started twirling it like a drumstick out of boredom. She looked towards the closed door leading outside onto the star deck, wondering why Francois was late today. She put the Vajra Thunderbolt back onto her belt and leaned back into her seat. Inhaling deeply, she looked up at the solar sails again. The jewelled surface had begun to dance and sway in a gentle breeze. She tilted her head, wondering at the sudden movement. A gust of wind caught them, causing the solar sails to flap and ripple. A swift gust of wind came up and they shivered and swayed.

Alastriona's ears and sinuses throbbed with pain, and each breath felt like a struggle against the frigid air that enveloped the cathedral. Rising to her feet, she reached out to the control console, but to her dismay, her gestures yielded no response—the console lay dormant, it's functions disabled.

She activated her communicator. "This is Lieutenant DeTroyes. I'm in the cathedral and it's venting atmosphere into space."

There was no response.

Her communicator had also been deactivated.

Alastriona strode over to the door, which was closed. Resisting an urge to pound on the door, she tried to open it, but it had been locked from the other side. She brought a hand up to her chest involuntarily, as she struggled to breathe.

Pins and needles rippled all over her skin and she realized that the gases dissolving in her blood were coming out of solution from the decrease in pressure. She was getting lightheaded as her body struggled to cope with the sudden change in pressure and lack of oxygen.

Alastriona closed her eyes to focus.

*Think! How do I get out of here?*

Intuitively, her hand reached down to touch her Vajra Thunderbolt.

Opening her eyes, she ran over to one of the solar sails. With a thought, she transformed the Vajra Thunderbolt into a sword and she cut out a section from the solar sail. She ran over to the door and placed the shiny fabric against it.

The dizziness became overwhelming. She felt herself falling to the floor and she dropped the Vajra Thunderbolt. Blackness washed out her vision. The red glow from the cathedral was fading away as she began to lose consciousness. She reached out and probed the darkness with her hands. Pins and needles made it hard to tell if she was touching it, but she thought she felt the edge of the sword. She picked it up, and focused on transforming the Vajra Thunderbolt into a baton. Not even knowing if it would work, pointed it towards the solar sail patch propped up against the door. With the last bit consciousness remaining, she concentrated on turning the Vajra Thunderbolt into a flashlight.

A bright beam of light emerged from the tip of the Vajra Thunderbolt. The piece of the solar sail shot towards the door at the speed of light. There was an explosion, followed by darkness.

* * *

# FOUR
## The Child

**BLACK TORTOISE OF THE NORTH**

**34 PEGASI**

Adrift in an endless sea of shadows, Alastriona was surrounded by numbing cold. She struggled to breathe. Unable to move, she swirled through the gloom. Untroubled by dreams or even nightmares to keep her company, she was utterly alone.

A distant star flared, pushing away the darkness. It brought warmth and light—and something else that touched her heart. She had never felt such a gentle caress before. All of a sudden, she began to rise out of the gloom and into the light.

Alastriona opened her eyes.

A bright light made her blink. The illumination came from her little companion, the tiny ball of fire. Like an anxious puppy, the little flame which hovered above her flared happily when she opened her eyes. But just as she smiled at it, the flickering orb flared brightly and vanished.

Peering into the sudden darkness, she noticed a glass canopy arching overhead. She was lying in a medbed. Monitors hummed with quiet vigilance, tracking her vital signs and orchestrating the intricate dance of bio-regeneration. A cool, soothing mist enveloped her body, numbing the remnants of pain and trauma that lingered in the recesses of her memory.

Turning her head to the side, she saw Francois sitting next to her with his head resting on his arms, asleep. But he was a star that she could never really visit. She turned to look the other way. *Where is Maximo?* She closed her eyes. *There is no reason for him to be here.* Either she would recover, in which case, there was no need for him to visit, or she would not. His attitude was quite sensible.

She was a solitary star, lost in the infinite expanse of the universe.

Soft tendrils of luminescent light gently pulsed around the edges of the medbed, bathing the chamber in an ethereal glow. Alastriona turned her head to look at Francois again. A part of her was surprised by his presence. *Is he putting on a show for me?* She had an urge to tell him to go away. *He's just a mere provincial. He will only drag me down.* She tried to move one of her arms to wake him up, to tell him to leave. But she was still too weak to do anything but lay there. She closed her eyes and fell back into a deep slumber.

*   *   *

In a dream, she found herself immersed in the frigid waters of an arctic ocean, surrounded by a vast expanse of ice that stretched endlessly in every direction. The chill of the water seeped into her bones as she navigated through the crystalline depths. Intense cold turned into numbing pain. Gradually, the biting cold started to dissipate, and it was replaced by a gentle warmth that gradually melted the chill away.

When she woke up, Healer Leonardo Silva was standing there with his arms outstretched over her body. The cold had gone. Tingling sensations spread throughout her body while he moved his hands back and forth. He finished the energy healing treatment and opened his eyes. "Do you remember what happened to you?"

"Some of it, yes."

Silva made some adjustments to the medbed controls. "You were caught in an explosive decompression event," he said. "You had a traumatic brain injury, a broken leg, and injuries to the ears, sinuses and lungs due to the rapid change in pressure. You nearly died from decompression sickness."

Alastriona frowned. "I don't feel so terrible."

Silva laughed and gave her a warm smile. "No, you're all better now. The regeneration of your body is complete. However, you'll need a few more energy treatments for a full recovery. How do you feel?"

Inhaling a breath of cool air, she smiled back. "I feel fine. How long?"

"Twenty-eight solar days."

She glanced around the medical bay and the fog began to clear from her head. "I woke up once. Francois was here."

Silva brought up a hand scanner and ran it over her body. "Lieutenant Chevalier? Yes, he's been at your side every day, when he wasn't on duty," said Silva. "I sent him away to get some sleep."

Alastriona had trouble believing the healer. *No one really cares that much.* Still, the thought of it brought warmth to her heart. A tear came, but she wiped it away. She took a deep breath to steady herself against an irrational display of emotion.

"Did Maximo come by?"

"Who?"

She searched her memory to recall his long name, but only remembered part of it. "Chief Inspector Maximo Navarro Ayala De Coronado."

"No. He hasn't come by."

"Not even once?"

"No."

*Well, Maximo is a practical man.*

A musty odor tickled her nose. A vase full of of forsaken flowers sat on top of a stand next to the medbed. Its once vibrant blooms were now withered and lifeless. Petals, once soft and delicate, now curled and drooped. Their colors had faded into muted shades of brown. The water in the vase had turned murky. Faint traces of a foul odor came from it. A card lay against the neglected vase. Curiosity was too much to bear. Alastriona picked up the card and read it:

*Miss DeTroyes,*

*I hear you're not feeling your best. I wanted to extend my well wishes during this time. Don't worry about me, though. I'm not losing any sleep over it. In fact, I'm confident that your recovery will be swift and soon you will return to your usual self. I've got some exciting plans in mind for us once you're back on your feet and I'm looking forward to our post-recovery rendezvous.*

*Von Meyer*

Alastriona looked up at the dead flowers and back down at the card. *I'm going to get this framed.* She tossed the card back onto the table.

Silva turned off the medbed. The canopy overhead retracted

just as Lieutenant Ostergaard entered the medical bay. Blue lights from instruments lining the walls glinted off his white uniform. As Silva elevated the bed so that she could sit up, Nils came over. Silva nodded to him and went out.

Nils glanced at the dead flowers for a second and then turned his attention back to her. "How do you feel, Lieutenant?"

Alastriona shrugged. "I'm very tired, sir."

"You wrecked the cathedral," he said. "The captain is furious."

She closed her eyes for a moment. *Is that what happened?* Shaking her head, she looked up into his gray eyes. "Where are we?"

He walked around to the other side of the medbed to glance at the indicator lights from  the instruments. "We're in orbit around an ice giant in the 34 Pegasi star system. We're waiting for your probe to come back."

They had intended to send a probe out to scan their final destination, just in case the supernova had already exploded. If the *Tycho Brahe* had gone directly there after a supernova deflagration had occurred, they would all have emerged inside the shock wave. If the *Tycho Brahe* wasn't crushed immediately, they would have been killed instantly from intense radiation. The probe was a safety precaution.

She sat up a little bit in bed. "You sent my probe to IK Pegasi already?"

He nodded. "Of course. It's the first thing we did after we arrived here. It takes twelve days to get there through hyperspace, several days for it to explore, and another twelve days to return here through a wormhole. So, we wait. We've sailed to all of the planets in this star system to conduct detailed surveys of the worlds here. We found an alien civilization on one of them. You slept through most of it."

Alastriona felt an urge to rush down to the science lab. She closed her eyes and dropped back down against her pillow, wishing she could have prepped the device before it had been launched. *I bet they screwed up the configuration of the probe. These so-called, "colleagues" can't possibly comprehend the intricacies of my work.* When she opened her eyes again, she saw the captain standing next to Nils.

Captain Winters was a bit pale. He gave her a hollow smile. There was a touch of something else there, too.

Alastriona realized what it was. *He's heartbroken over whatever happened to his wife.*

The captain rubbed his arm and glanced at Nils before speaking. "Healer Silva tells me that you'll make a full recovery."

She nodded.

"Good."

Alastriona tilted her head in curiosity, hoping he was more open to talking about his past. "Captain, is it true that you're from

Pleione?"

Caught off guard by her question, he crossed his arms. "Yes. I'm from Metis. My wife was an archeologist at Eurynome University. She was excavating the ancient ruins we found just outside Dysis. She hoped to discover if the prehistoric city was established by the Archons or by one of the races that fought against them."

Alastriona smiled. "I'm from Pleione, too. Calypso."

"I thought you were from Lisieux on Scylanthia," he said, uncrossing his arms. "That's what your service record states."

The medical bay was cold. She shivered. "I was born on Pleione, but I moved to Scylanthia after my parents were killed in the catastrophe."

For a moment, Captain Winters had a faraway look in his eyes. "Luckily, my family and I were off-planet when that happened. The historian, Lulu Vasquez had invited my wife to speak at the Imperial Library on Alexandria. Eleanor was presenting a lecture on the Archons when the comet struck Pleione. When we came home, everyone was gone."

"Gone," she repeated. It wasn't really a question.

"Dead," he explained. "Though they never found all of the casualties. A hundred thousand people are still unaccounted for."

Alastriona didn't think about her parents much. "Yes, I know."

"You were there?"

She nodded.

Captain Winters couldn't keep the surprise out of his voice. "How did you survive?"

The temperature seemed to have dropped even more. She pulled a blanket up over her chest and shrugged. "I don't know. All I remember is the cold."

There was a trace of admiration in his eyes. His voice dropped to a whisper. "You're a survivor, Lieutenant. Quite hard to kill."

Alastriona wondered if the Archons had something to do with prematurely destroying the star IK Pegasi. But before she could ask another question, he changed the topic.

The captain grew serious. He walked around the medbed like a shark circling its prey. "So, what were you doing in the cathedral just before we came out of hyperspace?"

Alastriona didn't want to tell him about her irrational fascination with Francois. It was embarrassing. The captain was too close to Maximo, too, and she dreaded trying to explain her behavior to her fiancé. So, she repeated the reason she had been telling herself.

"I like the dark."

"Pardon?"

"I like the darkness inside the cathedral. I go there to think."

Captain Winters put his hands on his hips and glanced over at Nils. "This is just the kind of accident that a new officer, fresh out of the academy might make. I want you to re-read the Starship Operations Handbook, Lieutenant. The cathedral vents atmosphere just before we exit hyperspace and enter a star system. All experienced officers know that."

"Yes, sir."

A medical robot came in with a container of supplies. It opened an empty cabinet and began placing items inside. As Captain Winters turned to leave, he looked at his chief science officer. "Mr. Ostergaard has convinced me not to order an official inquiry, so your record will remain clean for now."

"Thank you, sir."

It looked like he was considering saying something else. Instead, he simply went out.

Warmth returned to the medical bay. Nils looked at the doorway as if he were watching the captain walk down the corridors of the *Tycho Brahe*. He was about to say something when the little ball of fire reappeared.

It hovered over her like a glowing Will-o'-the-Wisp.

Alastriona raised her hand. The little sphere dropped down into her open palm, but didn't quite touch it. She felt it's heat against her skin and the chill in her bones faded away. Old Earth legends about the Will-o'-the-Wisp came to mind. *Is this a dangerous nature spirit?* She smiled and whispered playfully, "Hello. Are you leading us to our doom?"

Nils laughed. "Have you figured out a way to communicate with our little friend?"

She shook her head.

"We have a few days to wait for that probe to return," he said. "Figure it out, if you can."

She smiled. "It's cute that you think this is beyond me."

As if it realized they were talking about it, the little ball of fire vanished.

For a moment, Nils stared at the air where the tiny flame had been. He gave her a grin and went out, muttering to himself, "Where does it go, I wonder?"

Chief Medical Officer Nikolina Felinski came in to examine the readouts of her medbed. She gave Alastriona an appraising look. "Are you ready to return to duty, Lieutenant?"

Alastriona nodded. "I think so, yes."

*   *   *

Communicating with an intelligent alien entity that took the form of a small ball of fire presented a unique challenge. It required an innovative approach rooted in understanding both the nature of the being and the properties of its environment. Alastriona stood in one of the science labs, making adjustments to a device which she had just finished constructing. The little ball of fire hovered nearby, perhaps curious.

Saila came in and sat down. Raising her hand, she opened her palm. The tiny sphere moved to float over it, and this brought a smile to her face.

"Careful," said Alastriona. "It took me all day to entice our little friend out of wherever it was hiding. I'm almost done with this."

"You forget," said Saila. "I'm a contact scientist."

The little flame darted away from Saila and returned to hover just over Alastriona's shoulder. It seemed to be observing her work.

Saila crossed her arms. "So, have you figured out a way to talk to it?"

Alastriona stopped working and sat down. "I'm going to harness the electromagnetic spectrum to establish a form of communication. By modulating and encoding signals within specific frequencies of light, I can transmit messages to the entity, exploiting the medium through which it exists."

She didn't continue, knowing that Saila wouldn't understand it anyway. The device would encode information within the fluctuations of the entity's energy emissions, and would serve as a method of establishing a dialogue.

Saila examined the device resting on the workbench. It was a small, bowl-shaped object with a holographic projector. "I should think that by employing mathematical principles and universal constants as a common language, one might facilitate comprehension, allowing for the exchange of concepts and ideas transcending linguistic barriers."

*This one isn't as witless as the others.* Raising her eyebrows, Alastriona stood up and went back to work on the device. "Indeed, that seems to align with my expectations."

Saila grinned. "You don't know it's going to work, though."

Alastriona huffed. She made one final adjustment and sat down. She brandished her eyes as sharp swords of disdain, aiming them squarely at Saila. "Sometimes, I surprise even myself. It'll work."

With the wave of her hand, she turned on the device. There came a bright flash, blindingly bright, in fact, followed by the acrid stench of burning metal. It had a distinct odor reminiscent of molten metal. Thick plumes billowed into the air, enveloping the lab in swirling tendrils of smoke like ghostly tendrils, veiling the once-clear space in a murky haze.

They coughed.

The atmospheric controls automatically cleared the air. In just a few moments, the puffs of opaque smoke had gone.

The little ball of fire had vanished, too.

They looked at each other, defeated. Alastriona sighed audibly. "It appears your initial assessment was flawed."

* * *

A holographic model derived from spectral modeling analysis of the IK Pegasi star system floated in the center of the main science laboratory. It was only a preliminary model from observations made inside the Imperium, over a hundred and fifty light years away. It had been updated with observational data they had acquired from Sigma Pegasi and 34 Pegasi. But their probe would bring back the best data they could acquire.

Alastriona couldn't hide her excitement. The probe had returned. It was resting in the launch bay. Most of the science staff sat or stood impatiently around the science lab, waiting for the data retrieval process to complete. She glanced around the room, wondering if Francois was there, but he was absent. *Forget about him.*

Assistant Chief Science Officer Thando Mthembu stood watching the data transfer from the probe. He asked, "Lieutenant DeTroyes, I'm not an astrophysicist. How does a supernova work?"

Alastriona said, "There are different kinds of supernovas. In this case, we have a Type 1a Supernova. IK Pegasi is a binary star system. The primary used to be a Class A blue star. It has evolved into a red giant. The secondary is the white dwarf. This is called a single-degenerate scenario, where the white dwarf—the degenerate star—accretes matter from the nondegenerate companion star until it reaches the Chandrasekhar mass limit and explodes."

Tilting her head curiously, Lieutenant Heikkinen grinned. "A degenerate star?"

"It's not a psychological term." Alastriona said. "A nondegenerate star is a type of star that has not exhausted its nuclear fuel and has not undergone gravitational collapse to the point where quantum mechanical degeneracy pressure becomes significant in supporting its structure against gravitational collapse."

With a shy smile, Saila shrugged. "Okay."

For a moment, Alastriona grew silent. *Why do I waste my time explaining myself to those who lack the intellect to comprehend my work?* With a loud sigh, she explained, "This is a binary system, so there are two stars. One is a red giant star and the other is a white dwarf. The white dwarf is pulling hydrogen gas off the red giant. When the white dwarf gets too big, it will ignite into a supernova explosion because it can't handle the extra mass."

Out of the sixty scientists on board the *Tycho Brahe*, some were physicists, and astronomers. Alastriona was irritated by their presence. They were constantly deriding her work. *Their lack of understanding only highlights their inferiority.*

Pascal Reist, an annoying man from Switzerland, was the first to complain. "A problem with many single-degenerate scenarios is that it rarely results in a supernova explosion. The white dwarf has to pull matter from the companion star while also growing in size. Mass can be lost through helium flashes, disk winds or nova eruptions."

True, if the accretion rate was too low, the hydrogen-rich material would be burnt at the same rate it was accreted, resulting in no mass growth. If the accretion rate was too high, the accreted material would build up in an expanded red giant-like configuration, which would engulf the donor star and halt further accretion. Therefore, theoretically there was only a narrow range of mass accretion rates where the white dwarf could accrete the companion star material in a stable configuration.

Reist proclaimed, "I doubt IK Pegasi will ever become a supernova."

Alastriona resisted an urge to roll her eyes. *His lack of aptitude is truly astounding.* She crossed her arms. "Look at the historical data. IK Pegasi B has never exhibited recurrent nova flashes. It has steadily accumulated mass and is now a close-binary supersoft x-ray source. Quite ripe for an explosion into a supernova."

Reist was insistent. "Most likely, the white dwarf will undergo an accretion-induced collapse and evolve into a neutron star."

Closing her eyes, Alastriona shook her head. *How can he be so stupid with the data right in front of him?*

She glanced over at Lieutenant Ostergaard, who sat nearby with a smile on his face. He was obviously enjoying her reactions. She never understood why Nils was proud of his science department. *It's so exhausting, dealing with these intellectual lightweights.*

First Officer Tinibu walked in, accompanied by the captain. They took a seat at the conference table and waited. Captain Winters seemed distracted, though. He sat there, reading a report on a tablet whilst the science team conducted their investigation of IK Pegasi.

With only a momentary glance at the captain, Alastriona was glad at their distance. Their input was unnecessary and only served to hinder her progress. She watched a light bar complete its cycle on the data readout. A chime sounded and she smiled. With a wave of her hand, a new hologram of the IK Pegasi star system appeared.

A pair of stars hovered before them. An immense gaseous accretion disk had formed around the white dwarf, which sucked hydrogen off the red giant like an immense vampire. Alastriona checked the data as it came in. The white dwarf was currently at 1.43 solar masses. It had nearly reached the Chandrasekhar limit. She whispered, "So, carbon burning will begin soon."

Lieutenant Tinibu asked, "Is it safe to travel there?"

When the white dwarf began to burn its carbon, it would ignite a subsonic deflagration flame front that would propagate through the ejecta of a rapidly forming supernova. Alastriona nodded and then shrugged. "Yes, sir. Though it could explode at any moment."

What were the chances, of finding a star on the brink of turning into the brightest object in the galaxy? Her calculations had born fruit. *They should be grateful for the opportunity to witness my ground-breaking research firsthand.* For the first time in human history, they would have an opportunity to witness the death of a star. Alastriona couldn't resist smiling.

Captain Winters stood up. "We need to land on a planet here, before we can make the journey to IK Pegasi."

Saila said, "Sir, the only planet in this system with a breathable atmosphere is inhabited."

"We'll have to break the Imperium's First Contact Protocols," he said. "Have you deciphered any of their languages, Lieutenant Heikkinen?"

With a smug glance at Alastriona, Saila nodded. "Yes, sir. I have programmed three of their primary languages into our translator earrings."

"Good work." The captain turned flinty eyes towards Alastriona. "We need to make repairs to our cathedral."

Alastriona felt his intense gaze and looked away.

"Mr. Tinibu, set a course for the sixth planet."

"Aye, aye, sir."

*  *  *

While the *Tycho Brahe* sailed towards the sixth planet, Alastriona remained in the observatory, sitting at her desk, studying the photometric data points of IK Pegasi A and B, which were obtained from broadband optical filters on the probe. The trip to the sixth planet would take several solar days because, without the cathedral, they were unable to tune the solar sails to match the frequencies of the three stars that made up the trinary star system, 34 Pegasi.

Some on the *Tycho Brahe* might have thought she was hiding in the lab out of a sense of guilt, but the notion was nonsense. She had work to do. *Those with menial minds cannot comprehend the magnitude of my work.*

A chime sounded from the computer. She stopped reading. "What is it?"

The computer announced a discovery. "I have found an anomaly around IK Pegasi A."

"Specify."

"Would you like me to show you?"

"Certainly."

The hologram of IK Pegasi appeared in the center of the room. Wreathed in a swirling disk of hydrogen, the white dwarf was nestled inside the envelope of the massive red giant star. It was the same image she had been staring at for hours. "I don't see it."

Rather than give a verbal reply, the computer zoomed in on the red giant star.

Before the image had come into focus, she heard a soft, melodic humming coming from outside. She couldn't help but smile.

*Francois.* She turned just as the door opened. But instead of Francois, Angelica Ricci came in. Her voice was a cascade of honeyed tones, weaving through the air like a gentle breeze, carrying with it a sense of sadness. Alastriona was momentarily lost in a world where only the music mattered.

The song on Angelica's lips died just as she halted. She looked directly into Alastriona's eyes. For a brief moment, they remained there, staring at one another. Then, as if a spell had been broken, they both turned away and went back to work. Angelica walked over to a console and entered readings into a data pad.

Unable to concentrate, Alastriona swiveled around in her chair.

Angelica studiously ignored her and continued to enter data into her device.

"Was it you?" asked Alastriona. "Did you try to kill me?"

Not deigning to respond directly to the accusation, Angelica said, "Do you think that if you act crazy, people will think you're a genius?"

Alastriona crossed her arms. "I am a genius."

Angelica shook her head. "That's right. You're an eccentric genius. Just like Nikola Tesla. Are you obsessed with pigeons, too?"

"Why all the hostility?"

The starsinger turned to glare at Alastriona. "How could you?"

Surprised, Alastriona dropped into French. "Quoi?"

"How could you send your boyfriend to beat up Francois?" Angelica broke into angry tears and rushed out of the room.

Perplexed, Alastriona stared at the door. "Computer, where is Francois Chevalier?"

The computer's voice responded in a calm tone. "Lieutenant Chevalier is in Medical."

Her work now forgotten, Alastriona ran out the door.

After she had gone, the image came into focus. Millions of giant satellites orbited the red giant, forming a cloud surrounding the star. No one was there to see it.

Noticing that the room was empty, the computer shut off the display.

*   *   *

Soft illumination cast a serene glow over the Medical Bay. Alastriona entered and looked around. Though most of the medbeds were not occupied, there were a few being used. The light glinted off of the chrome and white body of a passing robot nurse, whose body was made to look like a female. The robot had a human appearing face though. Alastriona waved at the robot and it halted. Its voice sounded like any other young woman. "May I help you?"

"Is Lieutenant Chevalier here?"

The robot motioned towards a medbed with a curtain around

it and then departed.

Healer Silva came out from behind the curtain and made his way towards another door. Noticing Alastriona, he walked over to her. "Hello."

Alastriona bit her lip and nodded towards the medbed.

Silva glanced over his shoulder at the chamber housing the medbed. It was illuminated by soft blue light. "Its just a broken arm and a black eye. He'll be all right."

"May I?"

Silva smiled. "Of course."

Francois was sitting on the edge of the bed. He winced slightly as he adjusted  the sling supporting his injured arm, but he smiled at her as she came over. She sat down next to him and they looked into each other's eyes. He said, "I came to see you here, but you had already been discharged."

Alastriona glanced around the room and wrinkled her nose. She teased, "You shouldn't get into fights with the doctors."

"Yeah. Healer Silva has a strong right hook."

A medical robot hovered next to Francois, finishing its work. In a soothing feminine voice, the robot said, "If you have pain, dizziness or vision disturbances, please contact us immediately."

With that, the medical bot retracted its mechanical arms and it went away.

The smile on her face faded. She took his hand into his. "What happened?"

"I was going to ask you the same thing."

"I don't know what happened to me," she said. "I was waiting for you in the cathedral and someone vented the atmosphere."

"I was called away by the first officer," he explained. "I'm sorry I wasn't—"

He didn't finish.

"Did Maximo do this?"

He shook his head. "Forget it. I'll be all right."

Assault by a senior officer was a serious offence. *He won't say anything against my fiancé.* A fiery rage simmered within her heart and threatened to ignite. Alastriona took a deep breath and let it out.

Healer Silva approached. "I'm sorry, Miss DeTroyes, but you'll have to leave. He needs another treatment and then some rest."

Alastriona squeezed his hand gently.

He didn't squeeze back. Francois lay back down in the medbed.

Standing up, Alastriona took a step back to let the healer in. She didn't know what to say or do. Biting her lip, she just stood there for a moment. She wasn't ready to let him go. She was a dog waiting for him to toss a ball, but he didn't want to play.

Silva activated the medbed. As it came to life, a soft, melodic hum filled the air. The surface of the bed pulsed with a gentle luminescence. Intricate panels and monitors embedded within the bed's frame flickered to life, casting a mesmerizing turquoise glow across the room.

Alastriona turned away and walked out, not willing to let anyone see her tears.

* * *

Making her way up to the star deck, Alastriona stepped out onto the quarterdeck. She had an urge to run away and this was as far as she could go on a starship without climbing up into the rigging. The Starboard Watch was up there, adjusting the solar sails. Though the *Tycho Brahe* sailed through the stars with ease, she knew it wasn't going as fast as it should have. She looked forward and winced when she saw that the cathedral had collapsed. Makeshift repairs had been done, but it was inoperative. Her dark refuge was gone. With nowhere to go for privacy, she turned away from the cathedral and went aft. Executive Officer Min Ji Ro was one level up on the poop deck, holding an electronic spyglass.

Desperate for solitude, Alastriona avoided climbing up to the poop deck and she walked by the binnacle, which was currently active. A hologram of the star system hovered above it. A pair of stars were encircled by thirteen planets, and the third star, a red dwarf, circumnavigated the entire system. The *Tycho Brahe* had arrived near the inner asteroid field, and was sailing past it to the sixth planet. A helmsman stood behind the binnacle with his hand on the wheel. He nodded to her but remained silent.

No one else seemed to be around, so she went past the helmsman and entered the hallway leading to the captain's cabin. Finding an empty place, she stopped, leaned against the wall and lowered herself down to sit in the hallway. Putting her head in her hands, she let out her feelings in a torrent of silent tears.

After a few minutes, her tears were joined by another voice. Startled into silence, she heard sorrowful cries coming from an adjacent room. The mournful sounds pierced through her despair, igniting a flicker of empathy. With a trembling hand, Alastriona wiped the tears from her face and strained to hear.

It was a child.

Alastriona stood up. She was just outside the captain's cabin. She put her ear to the door and clearly heard pitiful weeping, tinged with innocence and anguish. Desperate pleas of a child, enveloped in fear, penetrated the silence in the hallway.

It sent shivers down her spine.

It reminded her of something, too. Something horrible.

An arctic breeze seemed to have come out of nowhere. In a wintry chill, each exhale sent forth a misty plume, a delicate dance of translucent vapor swirling in the frigid air. It was ephemeral and fleeting, like the whisper of a secret. Shivering, she hugged herself just as the door to the hallway opened.

Footsteps approached.

Alastriona straightened up and ran a hand through her hair.

The captain came around the corner and stopped.

She gave him a shadow of a smile.

The captain recovered from his surprise. "Hello, DeTroyes. Are you feeling better?"

"Yes, thank you for asking, sir."

"Can I help you?"

"Have you seen Maximo, sir?"

"I think he went down to the orlop deck."

"Thank you, sir."

Before he could say anything more, she went away from him.

* * *

The soft glow of status indicators illuminated the shadows, casting a cold ambiance into the passageway. In the dim corridor of the orlop deck, a line of silent guardians stood inside alcoves, immobile as stone. Each warbot bristled with weaponry. Although the sleek machines exuded an aura of formidable power, three of the alcoves were empty.

Alastriona made her way forward, towards the stem of the *Tycho Brahe*. As she went by cabins for the midshipmen recruits, she looked around, searching for Maximo. Cold terrors swam in the waters of her memory, threatening to break free. Unable to shake the chill which had engulfed her, she leaned against the wall of the corridor next to a warbot. She looked at it, wishing it could give its strength to banish her nightmares.

Shaking her head, she muttered, "Why don't I simply ask the computer where he is?"

Footsteps approached.

Shaking away the shadows, she straightened up, hoping it was Maximo. She walked towards whoever it was.

Von Meyer rounded a corner and stopped in front of her. He wore a classic white t-shirt that hugged his toned physique in all the right places, perfectly fitted leather pants and a pair of custom leather boots. An elegant leather jacket completed the look and added a hint of rebellion to his otherwise polished appearance.

Like a deer caught in the lights of a speeding hovercar, Alastriona blinked in surprise. In the past, she had only seen him in business attire, or in a uniform. This change was enticing, though she hated to admit it to herself. *Why are all the worst kinds of men so attractive?*

For once, he was not accompanied by his secretary, Elfriede Tischler, who was always at his side. He turned on his confident, charismatic smile and she was instantly charmed. "Miss DeTroyes!"

Resisting an impulse to return his smile, she chose a formal response. "Legatus."

As if she had been posing at a fashion show, he looked her up and down, admiring her beauty. "How wonderful to see you so fit and fine."

A tinge of jealousy touched her heart. "Where is your secretary?"

"Elfriede isn't feeling well today."

Alastriona wrinkled her nose. "What are you doing down here, sir?"

"Just sending a courier drone," he said. "I still need to evaluate this system before I can make any recommendations to the board."

"The board?"

He crossed his arms. "If you remember, I'm in the business of building new colonies for the Imperium. This system may not be viable, though, especially since it's so close to IK Pegasi. That's what you're for."

"Pardon?"

He took a step closer and lowered his arms. "If that little white dwarf turns into a fiery ball of destruction, will it destroy this star system?"

Alastriona shrugged. "IK Pegasi is 56.68 light years from here. Supernovas typically destroy everything within about thirty light years, but there could still be harmful effects. It could drastically alter the climate of the habitable planets here."

"So," he moved his head back and forth, playfully. "Is that a yes or a no?"

Finally, she couldn't resist giving him a smile. "Unfortunately, there's no way to know for sure. It may be best to wait until after the supernova explodes."

He glanced at one of the warbots. "How soon will the blast wave strike this system?"

"Nearly fifty-seven solar years."

"Quite a long time to wait." He lowered his voice to a sensuous whisper. "Did you get my message?"

Alastriona held back a laugh. "Yes, I got your dead flowers."

"They were alive when I had them delivered."

With a huff, she started to walk past him, but he grabbed her shoulders and spun her around to face him. He pressed her against the wall of the corridor. As her back slammed against the control panel, the warbot inside the alcove came online with a beep. Its optics scanned the corridor with a cold, calculating gaze.

Von Meyer leaned in for a kiss.

"Stop."

"No."

His lips touched hers, but she turned her head to the side.

With a finger, he gently touched her cheek and turned her head back so that he could press his lips against hers.

Desire flickered within, tempting her to let him prevail. She pushed the impulse away. Thinking quickly, she said, "Robot, Guard Mode: Activate!"

In a flash of movement, the warbot stepped out of the alcove, grabbed Von Meyer and threw him to the floor. It drew a blaster rifle and pointed it at him.

Von Meyer rolled onto his back. He raised his arm to ward off a blow from the machine, and shouted, "Countermanded!"

The warbot did not lower the rifle.

He lowered his voice and said in a calmer tone, "Robot, though I am wearing civilian clothing, I hold the rank of Legatus. Disregard your previous order and return to your alcove."

The robot directed its optical sensors at Von Meyer. There was a slight whirring sound, followed by a beep. The robot lowered the blaster rifle and stepped back into its recess, though it did not deactivate just yet.

Von Meyer got to his feet, brushing off his leather jacket. Rather than displaying anger, he laughed. "I see. But feigning disinterest only goes so far, my dear. As I've said, I always get what I want."

He went away.

After he had gone, she allowed herself to relax.

Alastriona trembled in shock, her heart racing as adrenaline surged through her veins. She rushed down the corridor, desperate to put some distance between herself and the danger she had just narrowly evaded.  A tapping sound brought her to a halt. She stopped and took a few deep breaths to steady herself.

Maximo entered the corridor and strolled up to her, his cane tapping a tranquil rhythm. "Forgive my curiosity, but could you enlighten me on what you have discovered?"

"How did you know?"

"How do you think?"

Alastriona nodded in realization. As a trained investigator, not much would ever escape his attention. "Von Meyer sent a courier drone out," she said. "He's the one you're looking for."

He put both hands on top of his cane. "I highly doubt that. May I inquire as to the purpose of your presence here?"

"I was looking for you."

Maximo smiled. "Yes?"

"You shouldn't have assaulted Francois."

"I was only questioning him."

"Is that what you call it?"

Maximo looked into her eyes. There was no anger there. Only cool logic. "After you were attacked, I realized that Mr. Chevalier could be the traitor. When he isn't singing in the cathedral, he often comes down to the orlop deck. He works with courier drones."

"What?"

"It would be easy for him to lure you into the cathedral," he said. "He knew you were on to him."

Alastriona raised a hand to keep him from saying more. *That's ridiculous. Francois is no traitor.* "I don't believe you."

"No one harms my property."

"What?"

"As my fiancée, you are part of my family," he said. "I protect what's mine."

She glared at him. "You didn't have to hurt him."

Maximo laughed. "I am no criminal. I always obey the law. After the interrogation, I released him."

She crossed her arms. "Then why is he in medical with a broken arm?"

He shrugged. "I did not harm him. Perhaps he offended someone. These provincials are so unpredictable."

He offered his arm. "Come now. Let's sit down and discuss our future together in more pleasant surroundings.

All of the heat drained out of her heart. Not knowing what else to do, she took his arm and they went up to the officer's lounge. On the way there, she looked at the warbots standing inside their niches. The lights in the hallway flickered and faded into darkness, leaving a cold and empty place.

* * *

# THREE

## The Sorcerer

Imperial Courier Drone: 8A5D6B1F

Origin: Externum Imperium — 34 Pegasi / Kishtatu

Destination: Copernicus / Maria Celeste —HD 84117 / Scylanthia

June 3, 3235

*Dear Julie,*

*For the first time, I fully realize just what you have been dealing with. I was tempted away from Maximo by another man I met here on the Tycho Brahe. It led to a disaster that nearly cost me my life. I understand how you feel, but I really need to caution you again about getting into wild entanglements. We have encountered a planet inhabited by primitive savages here and the captain has decided to make first contact. I feel he may be acting as reckless as you are because of the feelings he had for his late wife. I think it's best to leave romantic desires untouched, no?*

*Love,*

*Alastriona*

Secure Data Transmission Encrypted

Imperial Regulations Compliant

* * *

## BLACK TORTOISE OF THE NORTH
## 34 PEGASI

The starship's bell rang out six times, in three sets of two dings. The tone rang out over the *Tycho Brahe's* intercom. It was chilly up on the poop deck. Shivering, Alastriona stood at the stern, next to the captain, feeling the shadow of his loneliness. His sadness was a dark cloud that stretched out to engulf every corner of her heart. She felt a silent kinship with him and wondered if a life full of love was worth it. She had never had the courage to ask him what had happened to his wife, but knew he suffered from her loss keenly. *Love is pain.*

She walked away to the other side of the deck and looked down at the quarterdeck. The path her parents had chosen for her was better. With a glance over the star deck, she saw that neither Maximo nor Von Meyer were there, and she was glad for it.

Down on the quarterdeck, Sailing Master Jabulani Dlamini, called out commands to the starboard watch, who were high up in the rigging. "Ho, sheets and tacks! Shorten sail." Although they had been sailing under topsails alone, the crew worked to reduce the area of sail even more as the *Tycho Brahe* approached the sixth planet. They sailed into the night side of the planet and tiny lights covered the surface from hundreds of cities there. She heard Dlamini give orders to the helmsman. "Starboard a little—starboard yet—steady, so—that's it. Port a little—steady."

The captain peered through his electronic spyglass at the planet and called over his shoulder, "So Lieutenant, what do you think?"

Alastriona had been studying a holographic display. "There are dozens of communication satellites over this world, but I detect no weapon systems in orbit. Ground penetrating radar reveals that they have a large network of cities underground, connected by tunnels. They use underground trains powered by magnetic levitation. I'd say they are still in the early stages of interplanetary travel, sir."

The captain took in her report silently, while continuing to peer through his spyglass at the planet. "How strange," he muttered. "Have you ever seen this, Lieutenant?"

As Alastriona walked over to the captain, he handed her the spyglass. She looked at it curiously. The ancient tool was still used on

starships. She wondered why the military put up with such anach-
ronisms. She looked through the device at the continent sliding
underneath. Thousands of city lights covered the nightside of the
world. A strange thing happened. Some of the lights blinked out,
while others came on suddenly in different areas. It was as if entire
cities were vanishing in an instant, while other cities appeared out
of nowhere. The uncanny sight sent shivers up her spine.

"Lieutenant?"

Lowering the spyglass, she shook her head. "No, sir. I've never
seen anything like it."

"What do you think is causing it?"

"It is a mystery to me, sir."

Captain Winters laughed. "One of the most brilliant minds in
the Imperium, that's what Oliha said."

At the mention of Legatus Legionis Itoro Oliha, the commander of the Imperial Star Force on Galileo, Alastriona narrowed her
eyes, irritated. She handed the spyglass back to the captain. "I shall
require more data before I can formulate a hypothesis, sir."

As the *Tycho Brahe* slowed down, the captain continued surveying the world. After they had settled into orbit, he closed his
spyglass gently and used it to point down at the day side of one of
the continents. "It's happening all over the planet. Entire cities, gone
in an instant, while other sites appear just as quickly."

Activating another console, Alastriona engaged the *Tycho Brahe's* full sensor suite to gather more data. She used multispectral imaging systems, super-quantum sensors, gravitational wave instruments, nanotech swarm scanners, and the dimensional phase shift analyzers. With a wave of her hand, she gathered all of the data into a file for further analysis.

Saila climbed the stairs leading up to the poop deck. She walked up to the captain and saluted. "Lieutenant Heikkinen, reporting as ordered, sir."

The captain returned her salute and waved his hand over a console, activating a holographic image of what appeared to be some kind of lizard. It had a slender body, four short legs and a long tail. Its moist, velvety black skin was spotted with translucent turquoise spots. A cloth necklace held a gold medallion. It stood in an underground grotto that had bands of luminous stripes along the walls. Strange, alien furniture rested in the cave. A wall of illuminated glass stood behind him, and scrolling data slid across it. A few elegant gold items of unknown purpose decorated the room, too. An odd array of ambient noises came from the creature. It was a strange collection of hissing, rasping, and thrumming noises, interspersed with water drop sounds.

Without thinking, Alastriona smiled and blurted out, "How cute."

With a glance in her direction, Captain Winters shook his head slightly. He crossed his arms and turned to gaze at Saila, dubiously. "You said you've managed to translate this deluge of noise?"

Saila nodded. "Yes, sir. I have identified over a hundred separate dialects on this world. With the help of our quantum computer, I have interpreted three of them and have downloaded the linguistic references to our translator earrings."

"Fine work, Lieutenant," he said. He looked at the hologram expectantly.

Saila stepped forward and waved her hand to activate a console. She operated the controls and the creature's speech patterns became clear. "Pleasantries, celestial wanderers. I am the Ascendant One, Shar-Kali-Sharri of the Kishtatu."

The captain replied, "Hello. I am Captain Karl Winters of the Imperial starship, Tycho Brahe. We're explorers from a distant part of the galaxy. Although we come in peace, we are here to investigate a crime. A planet in a neighboring star system has been destroyed by interstellar missiles, which came from here."

A rasping sound, interspersed with thrumming, came from Shar-Kali-Sharri. The computer translated it. "No. This is not possible. We are a peaceful people."

"We can discuss it further when I get there," said Winters.

A single water drop sound came from Shar-Kali-Sharri. The

translator said, "Yes."

"Where shall I land my starship?"

Shar-Kali-Sharri nodded to an assistant.

A chime sounded as a data packet was received from the planet. Alastriona opened it with a wave of her hand. A holographic image of Kishtatu appeared. One of their cities in the hologram pulsated with a turquoise glow. A readout next to the city suggested the atmospheric entry velocity and the descent rate, along with the latitude and longitude numbers of a targeted landing site. "Captain, they have sent us entry, descent and landing parameters."

He nodded and turned to Shar-Kali-Sharri. "Very well. I will bring my starship down."

After he shut off the communication, Saila shook her head and sighed audibly. "I can't believe you did that."

"What?"

"Respectfully sir, you broke every diplomatic protocol we have," grumbled Saila. "You don't want to start a war, do you?"

The captain laughed. "First contact isn't that difficult."

Alastriona and Saila exchanged a quick glance. The same thought was on both of their minds: *Quite reckless for a starship captain.*

The landing specifications assumed they would conduct a de-orbit burn, reentry into the atmosphere like a primitive ball of fire, some limited atmospheric maneuvering and then a landing. Alastriona withheld a grin. *We haven't used these type of procedures in over two thousand solar years.* "Sir, their landing parameters indicate a primitive form of space travel. They don't even have anti-gravity."

He sighed and muttered, "Another world of savages."

He activated the intercom and a hologram of the first officer appeared. Alastriona had never gotten used to the scar on the African's face. Lieutenant Tinibu spoke first, "Yes, sir?"

The captain said, "Mr. Tinibu, after we have established orbit, take us down to the planet. Land us in the water of the local harbor."

The first officer crossed his arms but didn't complain. "Aye, aye, sir."

Captain Winters turned to face them. "You two will be joining the surface deployment force. Lieutenant Heikkinen, I expect you to keep me in line, diplomatically speaking."

It was like diving into a moonlit lagoon, anticipating crystal clear waters, only to encounter a murky, stagnant pool. Alastriona had hoped to study the new probe data while the *Tycho Brahe* was being repaired. Instead, she would have to slog her way through a planet full of uncivilized troglodytes. "Sir, may I ask why I am needed?"

"What's wrong, Lieutenant? Aren't you tired of staring at the stars?" Before she could respond, he added, "Although this is only a temporary assignment, I think the experience will make you a better officer."

*What am I supposed to do there?* "Sir, perhaps—"

"That's an order, Lieutenant."

*Hierarchy and obedience. Trademarks of the rigid, senseless, military mind.* Irritated, but unwilling to show it, Alastriona simply nodded. "Aye, sir."

*   *   *

The bouquet of dead flowers stood in a vase on the table in the ward room. Alastriona sat next to it, checking her equipment. Aside from her anti-gravity belt, she had a personal force field, a hand laser in a holster, her Vajra Thunderbolt and an omniscope. The standard Imperial multi-functional device was used for data collection, analysis and diagnostics. It could analyze a wide range of substances, environments and conditions with precision and versatility.

Saila was checking her equipment, too, which included emergency supplies, a first aid kit and communications gear. She unholstered her psi-beamer, sat down and stared at the weapon. "It's always a bit tricky, programming my psychotronic pistol to work on aliens. Some inferiors are too dull-witted to be susceptible to mind control."

"Why not bring a regular sidearm?"

"I'm a diplomat, not a soldier." Saila gave Alastriona a probing look. "So is Maximo coming to meet our alien friends?"

Alastriona shook her head and imitated his voice, "Inferior mongrels are of little interest to me. I shall remain here, away from the disgusting creatures."

They both giggled.

"Where is he?" asked Saila.

"He's down in the hangar bay, studying the RKV," said Alastriona. "I think he's going to stay there until he uncovers another clue."

"Are you still going to marry him?"

Alastriona shrugged. "Probably."

Alastriona finished downloading the navigational data for Kishtatu onto her hand computer so that it would sync up with the mapping data they had created for the planet. An imperial GPS satellite was launched just before they headed in for a landing.

"Von Meyer is a better catch."

"Yeah, but he's obnoxious."

Saila glanced at the dead flowers in the vase. "Why don't you toss those?"

With a glance at the withered blooms, Alastriona adopted a sarcastic tone. "Why, they're a symbol of our love."

Saila didn't laugh. "You know he saved you, right?"

"Whatever are you talking about?"

Saila holstered her psi-beamer. "Von Meyer was on the star deck when it happened. After the explosion, he went into the airless cathedral and brought you out. He carried you down to medical. He had severe injuries himself, but he wouldn't let them treat him until they had helped you. He nearly died."

Unbelieving, Alastriona stared at Saila. "He didn't say anything about it."

Saila crossed her arms. "Oh."

The little ball of light appeared and drifted closer until it hovered over Alastriona's shoulder. She picked up the omniscope, pointed it at the fiery sphere and took a reading. "Just as I suspected. You're a little ball of energized plasma." She whispered to herself, "But how do you move? How are you conscious? Where do you go when you vanish?"

Saila giggled. "Still trying to talk to it?"

Alastriona put the omniscope away and frowned. "I'm curious, Saila. How did you figure out the Kishtatu languages so fast?"

Lieutenant Heikkinen didn't answer.

Alastriona stopped what she was doing and stared at her friend. "Saila?"

Saila dropped her voice to a conspiratorial whisper. "I cheated. I found an extensive linguistic database on this planet. It was hidden inside an encrypted folder on the computer connected to our courier drones."

"Someone has been talking to them."

Saila nodded. "Yes. I found several messages back and forth between Shar-Kali-Sharri and someone on the Tycho Brahe."

"Someone?"

The contact scientist shook her head. "There wasn't a name. I don't know who it was."

"What did they say?"

"I couldn't decrypt them. As soon as the computer noticed my presence, all of the messages were automatically deleted."

* * *

## BLACK TORTOISE OF THE NORTH
## 34 PEGASI / KISHTATU

With the lower six of the nine masts retracted into the hull, the *Tycho Brahe* activated it's contra-gravity engines and floated down to the planet. The bottom of the cylindrical hull of the starship transformed into the sleek, curved hull of a sailing ship. As they descended, they were joined by an escort of primitive space fighters.

This region of Kishtatu was surrounded by a hot jungle. Nestled in the dense foliage, the city was part of the natural landscape, with structures intertwining with towering trees and lush foliage. Beautiful buildings made from timber and black marble were arranged around the central plaza. Suspended skyways crisscrossed the city, connecting the various levels and allowing the residents to walk under the cool canopy of dense foliage that covered the sidewalks. A beautiful harbor next to the jungle served as their landing area. The *Tycho Brahe* came down gently and settled into the water of the harbor. Three of the masts remained and the starship now resembled an ancient sailing ship.

As Alastriona emerged from the *Tycho Brahe*, she heard the chittering and whistling of birds. She inhaled the hot, muggy air, which was scented with aromas from exotic flowers. Noticing the slightly heavier gravity, she made an adjustment to her personal anti-gravity belt to compensate, so that a bubble of lighter gravity surrounded her. In the trees, she noticed several monkey-like creatures, sitting in the branches, watching them.

A pleasant melody came from a group of natives striking metallic percussion instruments. The music was haunting, soothing and deeply resonant, evoking a sense of tranquility and contemplation. Each note lingered in the air long after it was played and it gave the impression of enveloping the listener in a cocoon of enchanting sound.

A security contingent of warbots and Marines formed a protective circle around the starship. Down on the shore, Alastriona saw the captain talking with the boatswain, Lieutenant William Davies. The deck boss was responsible for the day to day operations aboard the *Tycho Brahe*. The captain gave an order and Davies directed the robot maintenance crew to go to work on the cathedral. Dozens of robots emerged from the starship and began to clear away the debris in preparation for the new construction.

Saila emerged from the starship and joined Alastriona. They walked out to the dock and onto the shore where the captain and first officer were standing. A convoy of alien vehicles approached. The sleek black vehicles drove up and parked at a discrete distance from the harbor. For a brief moment, Alastriona wondered what the vehicles contained, since they had too low a profile for human occupants. To her surprise, openings appeared in the vehicles and the Kishtatu people slithered out.

The music from the percussion instruments stopped. Silence was only interrupted by the sound of the wind and the birds in the trees. The Kishtatu crawled forward like a group of snakes slithering through the grass.

The aliens looked like giant salamanders. Each one had different colored skin and they came in an assortment of colors. Orange, yellow, white, black, green, gray and even purple. They also bore different kinds of markings, some striped, others spotted and still others with no markings at all. Though they were only two meters high, they were considerably longer, with bodies as long as five meters from snout to the tip of their tails.

Shar-Kali-Sharri crawled up to Captain Winters with a slow, undulating motion. When he was close, he rose up into a sitting position like a cobra. It was unsettling. While he sat on his tail, he was still considerably taller than any of the humans. He spoke with his peculiar form of water drop sounds mixed with rasping and thrumming noises. Alastriona's translator earring interpreted the alien's speech. "Pleasantries, celestial wanderers. I am the Ascendant One, Shar-Kali-Sharri. We are delighted that you have come to Kishtatu."

The captain replied, "Hello. I am Captain Karl Winters. This here is my first officer, Lieutenant Salisu Tinibu and two scientists from my crew, Second Lieutenant Saila Heikkinen and Second Lieutenant Alastriona DeTroyes."

The alien took great interest in the two scientists. His globular eyes blinked a few times while he stared at them in curiosity. Alastriona felt like a lab animal under observation. A shy smile slipped into her face. "Hello."

Shar-Kali-Sharri made a motion. Another Kishtatu with gold skin and black stripes approached with an ornate white box, a reliquary. He slithered up and placed it at the captain's feet. At the same time, all of the musicians began to strike their convex steel percussion instruments again, filling the air with a harmonic, peaceful melody.

While the music played, Alastriona looked down and noticed that the reliquary was decorated with carvings of sacred geometry. The most dominant symbol on the reliquary was the Vesica Piscis, formed by the intersection of two circles. "How interesting," she whispered.

Saila glanced at Alastriona. "What?"

Alastriona shook her head, "I'll tell you later."

The monkey-like creatures came closer to watch. The music faded into silence and Shar-Kali-Shari spoke. Several water drops, followed by a single thrumming sound came from him. Their translator earrings whispered his words into their ears. "May this gift prepare you for your journey into the realms of night."

Captain Winters bowed his head slightly.

With a smooth motion, he signaled a robot to come forward. Though the machine was made to resemble a human, its body was constructed from silver chrome that glittered in the light of the three stars that illuminated the planet.

The Kishtatu stared at it, perhaps in wonder or curiosity. It was hard to tell what they were thinking. Alastriona noticed that Saila was studying their reactions.

The captain gave an order to the robot. "Take this to my cabin."

The robot picked up the reliquary and took it over to the *Tycho Brahe*.

Bowing his head, Shar-Kali-Sharri addressed the captain. "Hear our plea. Today, we stand on the precipice of annihilation. Our astronomers have detected ominous signs of a star which will soon explode into an immense ball of fire. This cataclysmic event threatens to destroy our planet. When we discovered your approach, we were overjoyed. Your arrival offers a glimmer of hope. We beseech you, to grant us the secrets of interstellar travel, so that we may construct vessels like yours to escape. Save us."

Alastriona couldn't help but feel a pang of empathy for the Kishtatu. A whisper of a memory returned, where she had been abandoned to darkness by her parents. She looked into Shar-Kali-Sharri's eyes, sensing the struggles he would face when the supernova shock front arrived here. A fierce determination settled in her heart. She resolved to do whatever she could to help the Kishtatu.

Blindsided by the appeal, the captain was silent. He glanced at Saila, who whispered, "Diplomacy, captain."

Captain Winters returned his gaze to the leader of the Kishtatu. "I shall consider it."

Shar-Kali-Sharri withdrew a cylindrical object from his belt, turned around and waved the baton in an arc through the air. All at once, a beautiful palace appeared. Carved out of black marble, streaked in silver and turquoise, it looked like it had been there for a hundred years.

They all stared in wonder at the sudden appearance of the palace.

"Tonight, I invite you and your officers to come to a banquet, prepared for your pleasure," said Shar-Kali-Sharri.

The captain bowed again. "I accept."

"Come to the palace tonight," said Shar-Kali-Sharri. "All will be prepared."

Shar-Kali-Sharri dropped down onto all fours, scurried over to his vehicle, slithered in, and was driven away.

They stared at the palace. Saila was the first to speak. "How?"

Alastriona considered for a moment before replying. "It's the reason we saw so many of their buildings disappear and reappear when we were in orbit. They have mastered the mystical arts of the spirit realms and have combined it with high-technology, creating a fusion of the two. They're techno-sorcerers. Their entire culture must be based on it."

*  *  *

When they returned to the *Tycho Brahe*, they went up to the star deck. Von Meyer and Maximo were on the deck, looking out over the planet. Francois and Angelica were standing in the cathedral, overseeing the repairs. Captain Winters went over to talk to them.

Not wanting to think about Francois, Alastriona turned away from the starsingers, and watched the robot carry the reliquary up to the star deck.

Saila took one look at it and crossed her arms. "So tell me about that box."

The robot carried the reliquary to the aft of the star deck, past the quarterdeck and into the hallway leading to the captain's cabin. Alastriona watched it go before replying. "That container is covered in sacred geometry. The Vesica Piscis is the most prominent symbol."

"So?"

She explained, "The mathematics of the cosmos are present in symbols. You begin with a single point, representing infinity. Expand infinity equally in all directions to create a sphere or circle. The circle then casts its own shadow, a reflection of itself. This is the first movement of creation. The intersecting circles are linked across their centers. The two circles represent two realms. The overlapping space is the Vesica Piscis. This is the harmonizing, balancing, mediating force between the two. It's a portal from consciousness into physical reality."

"I see," said Saila. "The intersection represents a common ground of mutual understanding between two equals. How appropriate for a diplomatic gift."

The thought of portals to other dimensions touched a forgotten memory. Alastriona shrugged. "Yes, that's probably what it means."

As Captain Winters came aft from the cathedral towards his

cabin, Alastriona asked, "Sir, what do you intend to do about Shar-Kali-Sharri's request for aid?"

He came to a halt and rubbed his chin. "Nothing."

"You're not going to help them?"

He crossed his arms. "I thought you said this star system isn't in any real danger from the supernova."

Alastriona shrugged. "We do not have any definitive evidence of the effects at this distance from a supernova."

Captain Winters tilted his head slightly while he frowned. The expression made him look all the more attractive. *Irresistible.* Alastriona pushed her feelings aside. *What are you thinking?*

He said, "You said there was no danger to planets beyond thirty light years. IK Pegasi is fifty light years away, isn't it?"

"Fifty-six point six eight light years."

"Then what's the problem?"

Alastriona crossed her arms. "Supernovae emit intense bursts of radiation across the electromagnetic spectrum, including x-rays and gamma rays. Even at this distance, the high-energy particles could have significant effects on this planet's atmosphere and surface. Cosmic rays could cause genetic mutations, the ozone layer could be depleted or destroyed, and the shock wave could trigger seismic activity."

"But nothing that would kill off everyone here?"

"Probably not, sir, but that doesn't mean they wouldn't suffer from it."

Uncrossing his arms, he shrugged. "The Imperium has a policy of non-interference with alien cultures. We are especially prohibited from transferring high-technology to them."

She was insistent. "We could give them a means to open a wormhole, and more advanced hypersail technology so they could traverse wormholes safely."

He shook his head. "We still don't know if they were responsible for destroying the planet in Sigma Pegasus."

"What about the law of the stars?"

The Law of the Stars was like the ancient Law of the Sea, where there was a duty to provide aid to anyone who was endangered, in distress or otherwise in need of assistance. The obligation to help applied to everyone, regardless of who they were, aliens, humans, enemies, anyone.

"This isn't a derelict starship in space," he said. "This is a planet."

"That's right, sir. An entire planet full of people who will suffer if we don't help them."

He shook his head. "No way."

Captain Winters went into his cabin.

Saila muttered, "I'm going down to the lab to analyze my linguistic data."

Irritated, Alastriona watched Saila depart. *Thanks for the words of support.* She went over to the edge of the quarterdeck and looked out onto the world. The two stars were going down and night was coming. The third, a distant red star, was still high up in the sky, but it was too far away to give much illumination to the world. She could hear the monkey-like creatures chattering, whistling and howling from the trees.

She closed her eyes, remembering the cold and the darkness after she had been abandoned as a child. She didn't know where it was, but she couldn't shake the darkness covering her heart.

A voice brought her back to the present. "You're not going to do anything stupid, are you, Alastriona?"

Maximo had never spoken her first name before. Alastriona opened her eyes. "Why would you ask me that?"

He didn't reply. Just past Maximo, she saw Francois walking by. The starsinger looked into her eyes. She turned around to avoid looking at either of them.

The Kishtatu crept through the tall foliage outside the energy shield that protected the *Tycho Brahe*. Lights came on in the palace, inviting them to come over to the soiree. She felt obligated to do something. *How can the captain be so cold?*

Maximo raised a hand computer and activated a hologram that showed the interior of the RKV. A violaceous fire stirred there, emanating from a crystal. "What do you think?"

Alastriona examined the hologram. The crystal looked like a miniature sunstone, which were used to power the starships of the Imperium. The one in the engine room of the *Tycho Brahe* was five meters tall, though. This one was only about half a meter in size. "This is the precurser of a sunstone crystal," she said. "Not nearly as efficient, and too small to power a starship, but it's strong enough to propel the RKV at relativistic velocities."

"How fast?"

Alastriona calculated for a moment. She brushed a strand of hair out of her eyes and looked into his cool gaze. "A significant fraction of the speed of light."

"This is Imperial technology," he declared.

"Where did they get it?" she asked.

"That's why I'm here," said Maximo. "I'm going to examine that missile in more detail."

With some time remaining before they were to leave for the banquet, Alastriona went down to the communications center. Usually, there was always someone from the crew manning a station here, but no was was present. She sat down at a console and brought up the blueprints for a hypersail, along with the means to open a wormhole. She brought up a command to transmit the information to the Kishtatu. She paused with her hand in the air, considering what she was doing. She closed her eyes, but all she could see were nightmares coming out of the shadows. Her spine tingled.

Von Meyer's voice brought her back to the present. "Don't do it."

"What?"

"Let them die," he said. "This planet is the perfect place to build a new colony, after the radiation subsides."

Alastriona glared at him. "Don't you have something better to do, Legatus?"

Von Meyer flashed a charming smile that threatened to ignite a flutter in her heart. "I will be up in my cabin, in case you'd like to visit. I have a bottle of Champagne Rosé de Saignée on ice. Join me, won't you?"

She watched him go with a mixture of revulsion and incredulity over what he had suggested. She was haunted by Saila's words. *You know he saved you, right?*

After he had gone, she closed her eyes. The fate of an entire world rested in her hands. *I must abandon them to their fate, just as my parents had to abandon me.* She waved her hand to delete the message.

*   *   *

The palace entrance led to a series of interconnected waterways, slides and crawl spaces. It was like going into an exotic cave. Each chamber transitioned seamlessly between terrestrial and aquatic environments. The central chamber had a retractable roof and adjustable humidity controls, ostensibly to accommodate the needs of the different types of Kishtatu from various societies on the planet. The palace was constructed from rock, marble, logs and vegetation, incorporating intricately carved woodwork, stone sculptures and foliage. Bioluminescent passageways and illumination gave the area an ethereal quality.

A dozen members of the *Tycho Brahe* came to the banquet. Most of them were scientists, but there were a few officers present as well. They all had to crawl through tunnels and swim through different areas to get to the banquet hall. Alastriona used her omniscope to create a map of the passages and tunnels in and out of the palace. With the wave of her hand, she transferred the data to rest of the crew. Salisu Tinibu took notice on his device and gave her an approving nod, which made her smile. He rarely gave recognition to anyone.

The banquet hall was like an underground swimming pool, with stone terraces rising out of the warm turquoise water. A large circular opening in the roof held greenery and flowers that perfumed the air. A waterfall cascaded down from the opening. The area was illuminated by candles, bioluminescent lanterns and even by some of the Kishtatu. Groups of the salamander-like aliens peered out of dark recesses while their glowing stripes or spots cast blue or pink lights onto the walls of their dining chambers. The banquet itself was an exotic affair, with brightly colored dishes of native fruit and vegetables, and several kinds of fish.

Alastriona noticed that the Kishtatu were wearing the batons like the one Shar-Kali-Sharri had used to transform boulders into the palace. She noticed one of the natives point a baton at a pile of rocks. A light beam struck the stones and they changed into gems. Another Kishtatu brought a vessel full of mud up from the pool. He deposited the mud into an enclosed pit, pointed his baton at it and the mud transformed into coal. He built a fire and proceeded to cook fish over a grill. Another Kishtatu dipped a large vessel into the pool, brought out water and turned it into a beverage. The Kishtatu brought over a cup and handed it to Alastriona. She took a sip of the fruity drink.

Surreptitiously, she picked up her omniscope and pointed it at one of the devices so she could analyze it. The baton used an energy beam capable of penetrating matter at the subatomic level, a quantum entanglement matrix to hold predefined templates of different objects, and molecular resequencing to transfer quantum information between the target and the template. She was surprised by the sophistication of the device.

She overheard Boatswain Davies speaking to Captain Winters

over the intercom. "Sir, the cathedral has been repaired. We can leave whenever you wish."

"Good work," said the captain. "We will return soon."

Alastriona's phone chimed, and she saw the Chief Inspector's face. "Maximo, If you wanted to talk you should have come to the banquet."

"I found a transponder in the Relativistic Kill Vehicle."

The banquet forgotten now, Alastriona lowered her voice. "Really?"

"I used the transponder to locate the launch sites for the RKVs," he said. "They're all on the surface of the planet."

Alastriona was relieved that she hadn't sent the Kishtatu any of their technology. "So they're definitely responsible for the destruction of the planet in Sigma Pegasi."

"Yes."

There came a deafening roar from the phone, followed by a crackling sound. The receiver vibrated and went dead as the signal was cut off. Silence remained. Alastriona felt a sinking sensation. A palpable sense of dread came over her.

"Captain?"

But Captain Winters was engaged in a conversation with Shar-Kali-Sharri, who was sitting next to him. "I appreciate the friendliness you have shown my people."

Water drops mixed with thrumming sounds, which were translated by their earrings. "Have you considered my request?"

"Yes."

Shar-Kali-Shari asked, "Will you help us?"

The captain shook his head. "I am sorry. Our laws prohibit us from aiding you. But my scientists assure me that your world will not be destroyed if the star explodes."

Shar-Kali-Sharri flicked his tongue out and in a few times. He lowered himself to all fours and gave out a raspy sound. The translator earrings whispered a simple phrase. "Your cooperation is not necessary."

Shar-Kali-Sharri dove into the water of the pool and swam away into an underwater passage. The crew looked at each other, wondering.

"Everything is fine," said Saila. "I have a good feeling about this."

Alastriona motioned at the captain to get his attention, but she was interrupted by one of the Kishtatu, who crawled over, pointed his baton at Warrant Officer Louis Rodriguez. A beam of light shot out, striking him. He screamed and fell to the floor, writhing in pain. His body rapidly transformed into one of the monkey creatures they had seen that afternoon. All at once, the Kishtatu attacked the crew of the *Tycho Brahe*. They used their batons and several crewmen were transformed into the monkey-like animals. Chaos erupted. She saw the captain activate his personal force field just as one of the Marines was struck. His screams turned into the howling of the animal he had been turned into. Primus Muller and another Marine escorted the captain out.

Alastriona sat there, dumbfounded. A Kishtatu slithered up the stone tiers from the water, and rose up to a sitting position in front of her. He pointed his baton at her heart.

Thinking quickly, she knocked the device out if its hand.

The Kishtatu swung his tail around and struck her in the head, knocking her to the stone ground. She closed her eyes in pain. Blackness tugged at the corner of her vision. Disoriented, Alastriona reached up to touch her head and found that her hand was covered in blood.

The Kishtatu picked up his baton and pointed it at her again.

Alastriona dove into the pool of water next to the banquet table. Swimming down, she found a tunnel leading out of the central area. She came up for air in a low tunnel, illuminated by the turquoise glow of bioluminescent fungi. For a moment, she tread water, gazing up at the magnificent light show. Taking a deep breath, she shook her head but the motion only made her feel dizzier. The side of her head throbbed in pain.

Alastriona crawled out of the water and onto the stone floor of the tunnel. She sat up and leaned against the cold stone. Activating her holographic map, she prompted the computer to plot an exit route. A little arrow appeared at one side of the hologram.

She managed to get up and walk a few paces but had to lean against the wall to keep from falling. Dizzy and disoriented, she followed the map route until she came to another low tunnel, full of water. With no other way to go, she slid into the water and swam through another low passage. The computer route brought her to a muddy tunnel with a low hanging roof, no more than a few meters over her head.

Alastriona struggled to drag herself through the muddy, cramped tunnel, desperate to escape the palace. Each painful meter she crawled was a blur of disorientation. The darkness pressed in around her and mixed with the earthy scent of damp soil, confusing her further. Distant echoes of the strange alien language reverberated in her throbbing head, amplifying her urgency to flee. Fueled by a primal need for survival, she pressed on. Each movement was a battle against pain and the murky confusion clouding her thoughts.

Covered in mud, she emerged from the palace, crawling on all fours. Relieved, she rolled onto her back and inhaled the cool night air, catching her breath. A single moon illuminated the jungle in silver. Closing her eyes, she summoned what strength she had left. Darkness threatened to pull her into unconsciousness. She shook her head and the pain woke her up a little. Rising onto all fours, she surveyed the area.

The *Tycho Brahe* sat in the water, silent. Recovering her senses, Alastriona activated her force-field and tried to get up. Dizziness overwhelmed her and she fell down into the mud again.

Like a dragon rising from slumber, the *Tycho Brahe* came alive. Warbots surrounding the starship fired laser pulses into the jungle. Alastriona lay there in the mud, unable to move. Through the fogginess in her head, she heard Primus Muller's command over the communicator. "All hands, fall back to the *Tycho Brahe*. We're leaving!"

Alastriona fumbled with her communicator and dropped it into the mud. She closed her eyes, hoping the dizziness would go away, but it only got worse. It reminded her of falling into the the clouds on Scylanthia. Once she had jumped off one of the city platforms and had let herself drop for a long time. Her entire body felt the pull of gravity as she plunged down towards the surface. It was exhilarating. Instinctively, she reached down and touched her anti-gravity belt. She twisted the dial to completely neutralize the gravity. She hovered in place for a moment, peering over at the *Tycho Brahe*. More pulses of laser light shot out from the starship. She smiled. It was like a box of fireworks which had caught fire. Shaking her head, she pressed a control on her belt and flew through the darkness towards the starship, but her hand slipped on the gravity dial and she plunged down into the jungle.

*   *   *

## BLACK TORTOISE OF THE NORTH
## 34 PEGASI / ASTROSPHERE

Cold. So cold that there was no need for shivering, no attempt to regain any kind of warmth. Cloaked inside a blanket of paralysis, Alastriona lay still, unable to do anything except try to endure the icy touch of whatever lay beyond, inside the shadows.

All at once, light penetrated the cold. It melted away the frozen shroud. Alastriona opened her eyes. Turquoise lights gave a sense of serene warmth to an otherwise cold place. To the right of the bed, a window looked out onto a vast region of impenetrable night. Stars lay quietly in their places.

With eyes closed, Healer Leonardo Silva stood next to her, one hand suspended over her head. A warm, tingling sensation touched her brow, banishing the pain there. The dizziness faded away to a tiny dot that itched slightly and then finally went away. He opened his eyes and lowered his hand. "Feeling better?"

Alastriona nodded. "Yes, thank you doctor."

"I'm a healer, not a simple medical mechanic," he grumbled.

Medical robots performed physical repairs to the body. They did the work that ancient doctors would have done. Doctors were primitive, compared to a modern energy healer. The remark brought a smile to her face. She sat up and looked around. The medical bay was full of patients. Over to one side, several of the monkey-like animals sat complacently on beds. In the adjacent room, she saw a biobed regenerating a Marine's arm. She recognized the man. It was Centurion Ethan Taylor, the second in command of the Marine detachment. She turned to Silva and raised her eyebrows.

"You were brought in by that Marine," he said. "Three of our warbots were transformed into stone while they got you and the others out. They hit his arm with a transformation beam and I had to amputate it to prevent him from turning into one of those." He nodded towards the monkeys. "He'll be all right in a few hours after we regrow his arm."

"How many of us were turned into those animals?"

"Ten. They're all here, though."

Alastriona wondered if Saila was among them or if she had made her way out.

Silva said, "You're fine now. Just a concussion. You can leave."

Maximo appeared in the entryway, tapping his cane to the floor as he walked in. "Feeling better, I presume?"

"Yes," she said. "What happened? I heard an explosion."

"While I was examining the RKV, someone sent it a self-de-struct code."

"I thought you were dead," she whispered.

But he wasn't listening. He examined one of the readouts over her biobed. "When I noticed the data signal, I realized someone wanted the RKV destroyed," he said. "I activated a force-field around the missile, containing the explosion." He smiled. "No harm done."

Alastriona had felt nothing when she thought Maximo might have been killed. No remorse, no sadness, no worry. Nothing. She shook her head. "I don't think I can marry you, Maximo."

He ignored her remark. "That's what I admire so much about you. You have always exuded an aura of majestic elegance, an effortless grace and independence that's truly beautiful."

Alastriona whispered, "That's because I don't have any feelings for you."

Maximo was too caught up in his own words to hear what she had said. He continued, "Your purity is captivating. Together, our charms will command esteem and reverence from everyone."

She shook her head. "I don't want a loveless marriage."

Maximo shrugged. "It doesn't matter that you don't love me. All marriages start off like that. Trust the scientific process. Let the computers do the heavy lifting."

Alastriona wasn't sure if she should say it. She didn't want to hurt him. But she had to tell him the truth. She shrugged. "I'm not sure if I will ever love you."

Maximo chuckled. "You're still light-headed from your concussion," he said. "You'll feel better once you're back on your feet. Do you want a silly romantic like that starsinger—what's his name—Francois? Those kind of sentimental fairy tales never last long. I can offer you much more."

He held out his hand and helped her get to her feet.

She stepped over to the window and looked out onto the stars. "Where are we?"

He joined her at the window. The lights in the darkness were motionless. The planet had already fallen away. It had become a tiny light among the rest of the stars. "Sailing away from here, pursued by the entire Kishtatu star fleet. Their technology is inferior to ours, of course. I suppose mediocrity is their specialty."

A pang of concern touched her heart. "What about the Kishtatu? Did the captain bombard their planet?"

Maximo shook his head. "No. The captain said to let the supernova deal with them."

The Kishtatu were desperate. Once they realized that Captain Winters was not going to help them, they had tried to take what they had needed by force. She wondered if they would have attacked if she had sent out the data file. Despite what Shar-Kali-Sharri had done, she understood them. Now, their future was in doubt. The Kishtatu civilization could face extinction when the shock wave arrived. Would their planet become just another speck of lifeless dust in the universe?

Alastriona closed her eyes to the stars, unwilling to look at the lights. Silently, she reassured herself. *They're too far away. They will survive.*

The scientist inside her considered sending a probe to watch what would happen here when the shock wave hit. Just as quickly, she brushed the cold-hearted thought away. *What a horrid idea.*

When she opened her eyes again, Maximo was watching her. He held out his hand.

She took his hand into hers.

It wasn't too cold but it would always be there.

*   *   *

# TWO
## The Final Key

**HYPERSPACE**

Alastriona was sitting in her office, staring at a computer data readout. She was in the middle of analyzing a multidimensional hydrodynamical simulation of thermonuclear supernova explosions when a knock at the door brought her back to the present. Not wanting to take her eyes off the data, she didn't bother to look up. "Yes?"

Nils came in and leaned against the wall. "Theory establishes two distinct modes of propagation for combustion fronts in a supernova: Subsonic deflagrations and supersonic detonations."

His understanding of supernovae was like a flickering candle in a cavernous abyss—dim, feeble, and utterly inadequate. *Why do I waste my precious time engaging with intellectual inferiors?* Resisting an urge to shake her head, Alastriona brushed a strand of hair out of her eyes. "Yes, but neither the combustion waves nor their interaction with fluid flow and instabilities can be directly resolved in my simulations."

Nils grew silent. Neither of them wanted to talk about what happened on the planet. She had buried herself in her work. But he decided to broach the subject anyway. "Saila was transformed into one of those monkey creatures. How horrible."

Alastriona didn't want to try to imagine it. Too sensitive to bear the pain of it, she had wrapped up her feelings into a little ball, which she hid somewhere deep inside. Her only response was a single, numb word. "Yes."

"You don't seem very concerned about it."

Unwilling to come out of her study trance, she raised her eyebrows. "Should I be?"

Nils crossed his arms. "I thought you two were friends."

He was trying to get her to open the little ball, to bring her pain out into the light. She wouldn't let him. In a matter of fact tone, she said, "With respect, sir, I should think it was obvious, to any competent scientist."

Dropping his arms down to his sides, Nils laughed softly. "Not everyone is as smart as you are. Nor as conceited."

"No, they aren't." Alastriona smiled at him.

Nils didn't return the smile. "You need to stop it."

"Stop what?"

"Pushing people away from you."

Alastriona looked away from his probing eyes. "What did the captain say about it?"

Nils shook his head. "He made a strange remark. 'Not my monkeys, not my circus.'"

*The circus the captain is referring to is mine.* If she hadn't damaged the cathedral, they would never have landed on Kishtatu. *He blames me for what happened.* Stone cold determination settled into her heart.  She let out an impatient sigh. "Sir, I really do have to prepare for our arrival at IK Pegasi."

Anger drifted into his countenance like the onrush of a thunderstorm. Nils put his hands on his hips. "Always the cold scientist, you are. A woman's life has just been changed, forever."

"Ten people, if you count the others," she said, "and don't forget the three Marines that died on Sigma Pegasi."

His storm clouds faded to white and began to blow away.

Alastriona continued, "They're merely the first of billions of people if this isn't stopped.  Imagine the power to engineer a supernova! Such might is too terrible to contemplate. It's the most serious threat that humanity will ever face."

The storm in Nils face faded to annoyance. "Your work will have to wait. The captain wants to see us both in his cabin."

*   *   *

Standing next to Nils, Alastriona stood outside the captain's cabin and knocked.

"Come in."

They both walked in. Though the wood table in the center of the room had nothing on it, the captain's desk to one side of the room was cluttered with books and star charts. His wife's image in the silver frame had been moved to one of the cabinets, along with the little crystal sphere. She paused to look at it, curiously. She had the sense that it was full of secret whisperings.

Nils saluted. "Lieutenant Nils Ostergaard reporting as ordered, sir."

She saluted, too. "Second Lieutenant Alastriona DeTroyes, reporting as ordered, sir."

Returning their salutes, Captain Winters said, "At ease."

Alastriona noticed the reliquary from Kishtatu sitting on a shelf, unopened and forgotten. Two circles had been carved into the lid of the stone box. Two realms, meeting, with the Vesica Piscis in-between them. A thought drifted into her mind. *Is it a doorway?*

The captain led them through his dining room, which doubled

266

as an office, to his day cabin at the  stern of the *Tycho Brahe.* The windows looking out onto the blackness of hyperspace were curtained off. Electronic lanterns illuminated the room, casting a warm glow onto the assembled officers.

In addition to Chief Science Officer Nils Ostergaard, the Assistant Chief Science Officer, Thando Mthembu was present. First Officer Tinibu, Executive Officer Ro and the Marine commander, Primus Helmand Muller sat at the conference table. Sailing Master Dlamini occupied a seat next to the captain's.

Von Meyer moved through the room with the effortless grace of a prince, his tailored suit accentuated the chiseled lines of his physique, while his piercing eyes captured her attention like jewels gleaming in the sunlight. He went over to a cabinet behind the captain to mix a drink.

It would have been be easier to ignore him if he wasn't so gorgeous. Despite Alastriona's annoyance with him, part of her couldn't resist dreaming of the life he could give her. But she felt an uncomfortable, penetrating iciness in the room.

*Why am I always cold around Von Meyer?*

Chief Inspector Maximo stood on the other side of the room from Von Meyer, leaning on his cane and observing the meeting with his calm calculating eyes.

The aroma of coffee touched her nose. Chrome-plated human-shaped robots were present, serving drinks to the seated officers. Sometimes she forgot about the slaves on board the *Tycho Brahe*. They were so unobtrusive that they might as well have been invisible. *Perhaps that's why they are made to shine so brightly.* One of the machines walked up. "Coffee, Lieutenant?"

She shook her head. "No, thank you. Could you bring me some peppermint tea?"

The gleaming robot went to retrieve the beverage.

Alastriona sat down and folded her hands on the conference table. Directly across from her sat the two starsingers, Francois and Angelica. Francois smiled at Alastriona, but she didn't return it, choosing to look away, down the length of the table towards Maximo.

The robot returned and placed the cup of tea onto the table.

"Thank you," she murmured, before taking a sip.

With a cup of coffee in his hand, Captain Winters sat down and turned to Tinibu. "How long until we arrive at IK Pegasi?"

"It's a fifteen day journey through hyperspace, captain," said Dlamini. "We will arrive tomorrow."

Lieutenant Min Ji Ro had a dark expression on her face. Her mind, no doubt, swirled around a relentless whirlpool, threatening to pull her into its depths. She asked, "How many casualties did we accrue while we were on that mudhole of a planet?"

Primus Muller said, "Technically, no one lost their lives. My Marines brought everyone back to the Tycho Brahe."

Tinibu crossed his arms. "What do I enter into the log? That they were all turned into monkeys?"

Ro stated the obvious question on everyone's mind. "What should we do with them?"

Chief Medical Officer Nikolina Felinski held both her hands around a cup of coffee. "They don't appear to realize what's happened to them. Otherwise they're perfectly healthy."

Alastriona resisted an urge to shake her head. Watching them struggle was almost painful. Almost. *I am a visionary in a sea of mediocrity. They simply can't keep up.* She proclaimed in an untroubled tone, "I wouldn't worry about them."

Maximo sat down at the table. "Why not?"

Alastriona placed her hand computer onto the conference table. With the wave of her hand, a holographic image was projected overhead. The display showed one of the Kishtatu transformation batons. "I analyzed their devices while we were on Kishtatu. They operate by exploiting the principles of both energy-based transmutation and quantum entanglement."

As she spoke, the display changed to show a human transforming into one of the monkey creatures. "When directed at a target, the device emits a concentrated beam of exotic energy that permeates the body, disrupting molecular bonds and initiating a cascade of quantum-level changes. As the energy beam interacts with the target's biology, it establishes a quantum entanglement between the target and a predefined template, which is stored within the device's memory. As a result, the target's molecular composition begins to resequence itself according to the genetic blueprint of the chosen form."

"That's right." Felinski nodded in agreement. "Over the course of seconds or minutes, the target would undergo a rapid and comprehensive transformation as it's cellular structure realigns itself to match that of the template. Organs, tissues, and physiological features would shift and morph, giving rise to an entirely new biological entity."

It was like hearing a symphony from a broken music box. *Finally, a glimmer of intelligence among these geniuses.*

Noticing the expression on Alastriona's face, Von Meyer smiled.

Captain Winters crossed his arms. "So?"

Alastriona shrugged. "Despite the radical transformation, the process is temporary in nature. At some point, the quantum entanglement will be severed, causing the target's molecular structure to revert to it's original state."

This caught the healer's attention. Felinski leaned forward. "It's temporary?"

Alastriona nodded.

Tinibu asked, "Why haven't they changed back since we left Kishtatu?"

"Presumably, the hyperspace vortex is preventing their reversion," she said. "They will most likely return to normal some time after we arrive at IK Pegasi."

The thunderstorm had returned to Nils. "We've been in hyperspace for two weeks and you're just now telling us this?"

*Their lack of aptitude is truly astounding.* Alastriona shrugged. "As I said, don't worry about them. They'll be fine."

Like storm clouds dissipating at the break of dawn, all of his anger slipped away. A grin broke out onto his face. Alastriona had to resist smiling back at him. Though she realized he wasn't as smart as she was, she had great fondness for Nils.

The captain sighed. "Very well. When we arrive at our destination, I want us prepared to exit the star system rapidly, if we need to." He turned to look at the two starsingers. "After you tune the solar sails to this star system, I want you to prepare the hypersails for a rapid departure."

Angelica turned to Francois and they exchanged a smile.

The familiarity and affection between the two twisted around Alastriona's heart like a thorny vine. *I don't deserve him.* Angelica possessed an ethereal beauty that seemed to defy description; her dark locks fell like a silk waterfall around her face, accentuating her captivating features—delicate yet defined, with high cheekbones, a flawless complexion, and eyes that shimmered like sapphires. Her enchanting presence resonated with the timeless elegance of her Mediterranean roots, evoking a sense of allure and grace that left all who beheld her spellbound.

Francois interrupted Alastriona's brooding when he said, "We'll be ready, sir."

The captain was satisfied. "Very well. Dismissed."

Alastriona remained in her seat as the others got up. A wave of loneliness washed over her heart. In some ways, the Requiem had always remained within her. What made the forsaken creatures that lived there so terrifying was the pain of desolation that surrounded them. She closed her eyes, wondering if the memories about the Requiem were real, or if they were just terrifying nightmares. *I have always been there and always will be.*

An icy wind brought her back to the present. She opened her eyes and stood up, trembling against a sudden gust of cold air. *The air conditioner is set too high in here.* Most of the other officers had already gone out. However, before she could head for the door, the captain said, "Miss DeTroyes, could you remain here for a moment?"

Maximo said, "I'd like to stay too, if you don't mind."

Hugging herself, Alastriona noticed that Von Meyer didn't leave either. He didn't even bother to ask, but as the highest ranking officer on board the *Tycho Brahe*, he was in charge of the mission. Letting her arms drop down to her sides, she nodded at the captain and remained where she was, trying not to shiver.

After everyone else had gone, the captain said, "Miss DeTroyes, did you attempt to transfer a data file with Imperial technology to the Kishtatu?"

Alastriona was completely caught off guard. "How did you—"

Captain Winters interrupted her. "I think you need to answer my question, Lieutenant."

Maximo tried to intervene. "Captain, I'm certain that she did nothing wrong."

Von Meyer interjected. "Come, now, chief inspector. Don't pretend that you're not biased regarding Miss DeTroyes. You came here to get to know her, didn't you? Aren't you two getting married?"

Alastriona gave Von Meyer a dark look, while the chief inspector ignored the remark.

Maximo said, "There is a secondary reason I am here on the Tycho Brahe. I'm investigating the covert transfer of Imperial technology to aliens. Someone on board is a traitor."

While the captain didn't react at all to Maximo's statement, Von Meyer raised his eyebrows in surprise. He took a step back and sat down in a chair by the conference table. A robot approached him with a cup of coffee but he waved it away.

Maximo and the captain glared at each other. The tension in the room had shifted, like a passing storm, from Alastriona to the captain.

In a quiet voice, Maximo stated, "You don't seem surprised, captain."

"I'm not. I know everything that happens on my starship."

"Do you?"

Captain Winters continued to stare at Maximo. "As Von Meyer said, you're biased. Should you be investigating this case at all?"

Caught off guard, Maximo remained silent.

The captain grinned and nodded. "So you're here to look for a traitor." He pointed at Alastriona. "There she is."

Alastriona found her voice. "I'm no traitor, sir."

The captain turned away from Maximo and looked squarely into her eyes. "I need you to complete our mission, but when we return to the Imperium there will be a full, impartial investigation. Now get out, all of you."

*　*　*

As they left the captain's cabin and walked down the short hallway to the quarterdeck, Alastriona stopped Maximo with a touch. "What's going to happen now?"

Maximo placed his cane squarely onto the deck "This is like a game of chess. Our traitor is bound to make a mistake, and when it happens, I will be there. Don't worry."

He went out onto the quarterdeck and down into the lower decks. She stood there at the entrance to the quarterdeck, next to the helmsman, listening to Maximo's cane click against each step on the staircase. Telling her not to worry didn't do any good. *He's so distant. Are we all lab animals in a cage?*

The space outside the hallway from the captain's cabin was an area enclosed on three sides that contained the wheel of the *Tycho Brahe*, which looked out onto the quarterdeck. Two cabins stood on either side of the wheel. One held the captain's secretary and the other housed Sailing Master Jabulini Dlamini. As the *Tycho Brahe's* navigator, he was in charge of sailing the starship. Boatswain William Davies, the Deck Boss, was directly under his command.

The helmsman stood at the wheel, idle, since there wasn't anything for him to do while they sailed through hyperspace. To his credit, he ignored everyone's conversation.

The binnacle in front of the wheel displayed a holographic image of their destination, the two of stars of IK Pegasi. The image had been updated with the latest observations they had taken from 34 Pegasi. Alastriona noticed a cloud of objects encircling the red giant. Wondering what they were, she stared at them for an instant before walking out onto the quarterdeck.

The energy dome covering the outside of the starship was invisible. Beyond, there was nothing at all except the darkness of hyperspace. A dim glow, left over from the Big Bang, cast illumination into the darkness within the wormhole. Her mind drifted into the void. *And the light shineth in darkness; and the darkness comprehended it not.*

Von Meyer was waiting for her to come outside onto the quarterdeck.

Badly unnerved, Alastriona felt like running away and hiding in a dark hole, where it was safe. She could be facing a court-martial and imprisonment. She hoped Von Meyer wouldn't notice that she was shaking. She stepped out onto the quarterdeck. "What is it, Legatus?"

Von Meyer spoke in a low voice. "I told you not to do it."

"I didn't do anything."

He shook his head. "I saw your message. It contained blueprints for advanced hypersails and the technology to open wormholes."

"I never sent a message to the Kishtatu."

Two bells sounded from the belfry on the fo'c'sle.

Von Meyer looked out onto the star deck and watched several star riggers climb down the ratlines from above. "After I left you in the communication center, I saw that starsinger, the one you have a crush on, just outside. He was waiting there. I bet he was the one that informed the captain about what you did."

"Francois would never—you did it."

Von Meyer shook his head. "I'm afraid not."

Her world was spinning out of control. "Why would he tell the captain?"

Von Meyer shrugged.

Was Francois scheming to orchestrate her expulsion from the military, to pave the way for her to be with him? It took effort for Alastriona to keep her voice down. "Now, Captain Winters thinks I'm a traitor."

With a smirk on his face, Von Meyer put a hand on her shoulder. "Don't worry," he said. "I will take care of everything."

Alastriona shoved him back. "Get away from me!"

Von Meyer chuckled.

She ran off down a flight of stairs to the decks below.

*　*　*

That evening, she went down to science lab housing the neutrino detector. Alastriona couldn't take her mind off of Francois, sitting next to Angelica. She could see an intimate connection through their mutual smiles. She wondered if her future life with Maximo would ever offer her something beyond nothing. *I'm like the neutrinos, untouched by reality. Somewhere, anywhere, all at once. Nowhere. Alone.*

While staring at the giant pearl hovering in the chamber, Alastriona bit her lip. She wondered if this neutrino detector would give them enough time to escape if the white dwarf suddenly turned into a supernova. She shook her head. *Nonsense. What's the probability of it exploding while we are here?* Activating it was merely a safety precaution.

Francois came to the doorway and knocked.

Her heart skipped a beat.

But she didn't want to talk to him. She focused on her work, checking to see if the neutrino detector would function properly. She did, however, allow a distracted murmur to escape her lips. "Yes?"

He walked in and stopped a few paces away from her. "You've been avoiding me."

Without turning away from the holographic console, she shook her head. "Not really."

"Then what?"

"What do you mean?"

Francois took a few steps, closing the distance between them. "Do you blame me for what happened to you in the cathedral?"

All of the data on the console lost its luster. The hologram displayed a cloud of numbers, dead, cold, uninteresting. She couldn't look at it anymore. Alastriona shut the console off and turned to look up at him. Electricity passed between their eyes, and it struck her heart. For an instant, they stared at each other, lost in the promise of a shared connection. "What?"

"I told you, I was called away by Tinibu."

She always had trouble concentrating around him. "Oh."

"After you recovered—" He didn't finish.

Closing her eyes, she shook her head. "Francois, what are you doing here?"

"I wanted to see you."

The words would hurt her more than they would hurt him. "You should stay away."

"You have been avoiding me," he said. "Why?"

Alastriona crossed her arms. "Someone told the captain that I was considering sending technology to the Kishtatu. Was it you?"

Francois shook his head. "No. But I saw what you were doing. So I went in after you had gone and I disabled the communications array."

"You stopped all messages from going out."

"Yes."

Anger simmered inside, threatening to boil over. *He took away my choice.* Another thought competed with her fury, and it touched her heart. *He wanted to protect me from myself.* "Well, for your information, I never sent any signal."

He didn't respond.

There was more, though. Was she angry at him for trying to stop her, or for something else? Another troubling thought touched her heart. *How far would he go to protect me?* She decided to make it bigger than herself. "You would condemn an entire race to extinction."

"They're in no serious danger of that. You said so yourself."

No answer came out of her lips.

He continued, "You never even tried to send the message. So it doesn't matter what I did, does it?"

She didn't want to think about it anymore. With a sigh, Alastriona turned the console back on. "I'm very busy, Francois."

He wouldn't let it drop. "You're afraid of life, afraid to live." He took another step closer. "You're afraid of love."

She closed her eyes, wishing she could find somewhere on board where the light would never reach her. Some place safe.

As if he sensed what she was thinking, he said, "You can't hide in the darkness forever," he said. "Flowers need light to grow."

A touch of light found her heart. *He's comparing me to a flower.* Opening her eyes, she resisted giving him a smile, but she didn't say anything.

Recognition dawned in his eyes and mingled with surprise. He whispered, "You're afraid of me."

Alastriona sighed. "I have work to do, Francois."

"Is it really that important?"

She whispered, "Yes."

He shook his head. "What's more important than love?"

Francois walked out.

She watched him go and felt a terrible sinking sensation. Putting her emotional armor back on, she thought of the life that a mere provincial would lead and how it would affect her family. They needed her to marry a Pure Strain Human. Too many people, like her sister, had engaged in unrealistic romantic love affairs. Such a notion was preposterous. After he had gone, she glared after him and whispered, "You're just not good enough, Francois."

From that moment on, Alastriona knew that she would always be alone.

* * *

**3221 A.D. — YEAR OF THE GOLD OX (NINE YEARS AGO)**

**THE REQUIEM**

A profound silence had settled over the dark forest. Swirling shrouds of mist veiled the black trees and pale, lifeless leaves were scattered all over the forest floor. The cold, white sun had drained all of the color out of the landscape. It cast colorless beams of light down through the twisted branches onto the forest floor like spotlights.

The exiles splashed through a shallow pond, heading into the fog, trying to hide from the light. Alastriona walked amongst them, one hand holding her rag doll, the other holding the hand of Elise. The woman had found her a year ago in the Requiem and had always protected her from the Nameless Ones.

They came to the edge of the forest and looked out over a pale garden. Night jasmine scented the air among evening primrose, white orchids and moonflowers. A black pyramid loomed on the other side of the garden. The blinding light of the white star gleamed off the ancient black stones.

Nicolas stood at the edge of the forest with one hand on the dark trunk of a tree, staring at the pyramid. "There's too much light here," he murmured. "We'll never make it to the gateway. It was reckless to suggest that we come here, Elise."

Elise let go of Alastriona's hand and went over to the edge of the trees.

Closer to the shadows inside the forest, Alastriona sat down with her back to a tree trunk. She cradled her rag doll in her arms and whispered words of encouragement. "Don't worry, Nanette. I will protect you."

Her only friend, Timmy, came over and sat down next to her. Although he was two years younger than she was, it was hard to tell. All sense of time had faded away inside the Requiem. Immersed in a world of everlasting shadows, they never seemed to get hungry or thirsty. Timmy had learned to be quiet. Those who had made too much noise had always been taken away by the dark things. Timmy whispered, "I'm afraid, Alastriona."

Fear. For a year she had been smothered in it. The best way she had learned to deal with fear was to let it live inside. She had always been able to wrap herself into a blanket of shadows, to hide from the Nameless Ones when they came. She whispered back, "I am too."

A terrible scream pierced the silence of the forest. All of the people around them froze. Several people slipped away into the shadows, hoping to escape. A few of them drew their batons and transformed them into pale swords, hoping to defend themselves.

Leaping away from the tree, Alastriona ran into the field, threw herself into a bed of pale flowers and lay still.

Timmy had looked away at the screaming woman. Her shriek had been cut off suddenly. A withering sound, like air slipping out of a balloon, came from the tree where the woman had been standing. Timmy remained there, staring at the dark thing which had drifted close. A horrid sucking sound came from the thing and the woman fell down into the flowers.

The air had turned cold, as it always had done so when the dark things were around. So cold that it seeped into the bones. The frigid air came after the dark things had sucked out all of the little warmth there was in the Requiem. With every icy breath, a frosty cloud puffed out of her lips. Sometimes, the dark things caught people because they could see the little white puffs coming from their hiding places.

Alastriona held her breath.

The dark things had always lurked in the shadows of the Requiem. Their ethereal presence devoid of solid form, they haunted the forests of solitude with silent anguish. They always moved with a fluid grace, weaving through the emptiness that left a chill in their wake. Sometimes, in quiet moments, she could hear their whispers echoing through the empty spaces of the Requiem. Their forsaken cries seemed to draw strength from their own isolation. Their delicate whispers became a song of tormented lamentations. The exiles had many names for them. Some called them the Nameless Ones, while others called them the Waiting Ones That Abide. But Alastriona had always called them the Dark Things.

A wind caught an overhead branch and slivers of light fell down on top of Timmy, bathing him in brightness like a spotlight. Alastriona lay there among the white flowers, hoping Timmy would run, hide, get away from the dark thing. But Timmy was too terrified to move, even as one of the creatures drifted over to him.

Timmy did not cry out. He choked as the dark thing engulfed him in its cold embrace. Timmy began to shake uncontrollably.

There was a horrible slurping sound and his skin turned black. Like a brittle leaf crushed in one's hand, Timmy's body simply shriveled up and withered away.

For a moment, Alastriona was unable to look away. At last, after Timmy had faded into black dust, she shut her eyes. Her spine tingled as a wintry gale seemed to blow across the flowers and away into the light.

*　*　*

## 3230 A.D. — YEAR OF THE METAL DOG (PRESENT)
## BLACK TORTOISE OF THE NORTH
## IK PEGASI

There was a frosty chill. Alastriona opened her eyes to the frozen darkness. Shivering, she pulled up her blanket but it brought her no warmth. For a moment, she lay there, terrified, hoping no one would find her. Alastriona's heart was racing. Disoriented, she peered into the darkness. There was a window with stars shining outside. She closed her eyes. *I am in space, aboard the Tycho Brahe.*

With a sense of relief, she sat up. An icy band encircled her right forefinger. She raised her hand to look at her silver ring, which always turned cold when she had one of her nightmares. She inhaled slowly and then let it out again. Unwilling to turn on the lights in her cabin, she got out of bed, pulling the blanket around her shoulders. She walked over to the window and looked outside at the stars, finding some comfort there. She had suffered and survived the night.

A moment of clarity washed away the terrors.

They had arrived.

A light appeared in the darkness of her cabin.

Alastriona blinked, as her eyes adjusted to the sudden radiance. The little ball of light had returned. She let out a satisfied smile. *We're out of hyperspace. This will all be over soon, and then I can go back home to Scylanthia.*

* * *

Wearing her white uniform, Alastriona walked down a hallway on the science deck, followed by the little light. She arrived at the observatory and went in. A huge hologram of the IK Pegasi star system floated in the center of the room. Most of the fifty scientists from the *Tycho Brahe* were already there, including Thando Mthembu and Nils Ostergaard. Saila was there, too. Since she was merely a contact scientist, Saila sat in the corner, trying not to get in anyone's way.

Alastriona took a seat at her desk, and smiled at Lieutenant Heikkinen. "I'm really glad you're back to normal, Saila."

Saila returned the smile but didn't say anything.

Since light from IK Pegasi took nearly 57 years to reach 34 Pegasi, the data collected there was out-of-date. With a wave of her hand, Alastriona activated a console and began to study the new data they were now collecting, while the little light hovered over her shoulder.

The white dwarf danced around the primary star, the red giant. The little star was surrounded by a gaseous accretion disk as it drew hydrogen off the red giant. Their orbits had shrunk and they were getting closer together. They were dancing faster now. The white dwarf was particularly intense. Its core was close to reaching the ignition temperature for carbon fusion. The little star would soon flare into a supernova that would outshine the entire galaxy.

With the wave of her hand, she activated the neutrino detector. A holographic viewer showed the chamber housing the massive instrument. The white pearl emerged from the ring on the floor and it pulsed with silent purpose: To detect sudden bursts of neutrinos that came from an exploding star. The neutrinos were able to penetrate the layers of the star before anything else because they had only weak interactions with matter.

Beyond the two stars, there were ten planets. Two molten rocks were inside the gaseous envelope of the red giant. Next, came a green mini-Neptune, a Super-Earth, an asteroid belt, a blue mini-Neptune, another glacial Super-Earth and finally, three more rocky planets, covered in oceans of nitrogen ice. Scans showed there had once been a thriving civilization on the first Super-Earth, but it was now frozen and uninhabitable. They had even detected a pyramid there. The ancients had built pyramids all over the galaxy.

Turning her attention back to the two stars, she saw an massive ring of objects around the red giant. It was a cloud of millions of parachute-shaped satellites. They rose up and away from the star, retracted their parachute-like structures, and then dropped down towards the star again. The satellites were arranged in several rings that encircled the star. They performed an intricate dance, up and down. Over the poles of the star, there were millions of objects arranged in an immense ring, one above the star, the other ring below it.

Alastriona stared at the star in wonder.

*It's a megastructure.*

*   *   *

"What's a megastructure?" asked the captain.

Alastriona stood on the poop deck next to the captain. He was looking through his spyglass at the Super-Earth that they were sailing towards. Though it had once held an alien civilization, it was now a frozen world, incapable of supporting life after the habitable zone around the star had shifted. A few thousand years ago, observatories on Earth had recorded a hot, Type A blue star here, along with the white dwarf companion. Somehow, it had expended most of its fuel and it had swelled up into a red giant, turning the two closest planets into molten rocks in the process.

She had an impulse to grab the spyglass out of his hand. *Why is he so obsessed with that dead world?* Rather than indulging in her whims, she answered his question "A megastructure is a massive object, such as a Ring World or a Dyson Swarm. They're theoretical ideas, mostly. The Imperium has constructed some, like the orbital rings around our capital world, Novus Constantinople, or the chandelier cites over the gas giant, Galileo. But some types have never been encountered before. Presumably, they were made by the ancient races, the Archons, the Eloieion, or the Celestials."

Captain Winters lowered the spyglass and turned to look at her. "What is it's purpose?"

Alastriona brought up a holographic image of their latest observations. It floated in the space between them like a djinni just out of the bottle which had imprisoned it. She zoomed in on the objects surrounding the red giant.

This megastructure was composed of a series of orbital stations, set up in rings, with particle accelerators powered by the light of the star. The stations shot streams of charged ions between each other to create a ring of current. The current allowed the orbital stations to magnetically float over the star. Periodically, the orbital stations would turn off the current and begin to fall. Once they picked up speed, the ring current was turned on again and the orbital station flew back up and away from the star.

This generated a squeezing action on the star that pumped the atmosphere up through the poles. The rings of orbital stations were arranged to create a well-coordinated pumping action. Another ring of giant magnetic rocket nozzles were placed over the poles. These created magnetic fields that directed the plasma into giant collectors.

Alastriona said, "This one is used for starlifting. Stripping matter off of a star."

"So the ancients are the ones that killed this star." The captain smiled. "There's your answer, Lieutenant."

A puzzled expression covered her face. She didn't answer.

He raised his eyebrows. "What is it?"

Alastriona shook her head. "Stars are mostly made up of hydrogen, the most abundant type of normal matter in the universe. They convert that into helium to produce energy for nuclear fusion. When helium builds up in a star such as this, it leads to a process that will lead to the destruction of the star. In simplistic terms, helium is like a poison that kills a star."

He crossed his arms. "So?"

By removing some of the helium and dumping the hydrogen back down into the atmosphere, you could extend the life of a star. Alastriona explained, "Theoretical models of starlifting show that it can be used to extend the life of a star, not shorten it."

She zoomed in on one of the orbital stations. Scans revealed that they were also helium fusing stations. After converting hydrogen into helium, the helium was dumped back down into the atmosphere. "Whoever built this megastructure wanted to shorten the life of the star. Why would someone do that?"

He turned his back on her, picked up his spyglass and peered at the Super-Earth they were approaching. "That's for you to figure out."

It took a few hundred billion joules of energy per kilogram to lift matter off a star. However, fusing hydrogen into helium generated more than enough energy for this. Starlifting could remove about an Earth's worth of mass every century, so it should have taken ten or fifteen million years to take apart this star. The numbers didn't add up. A question plagued Alastriona's mind. *Where is all that matter going and what is it being used for?*

Captain Winters activated the intercom. "Primus Muller, I'd like you to assemble a surface deployment force for a landing on the uninhabited planet."

Helmand responded over the intercom. "Aye, aye, sir. How many others are going?"

"Bring a security detail, Lieutenant Ostergaard and the archeologist, Warrant Officer Taichi," said the captain. "I want to have a look at that pyramid."

"Aye, sir."

Alastriona crossed her arms, wondering why the captain hadn't asked her to accompany the surface deployment force.

As if he could hear her thoughts, he turned to face her. "I'm sure you have plenty of work here, Miss DeTroyes. Carry on."

"Aye, sir."

Alastriona went down to the science deck, full of unanswered questions.

*   *   *

**BLACK TORTOISE OF THE NORTH**

**IK PEGASI / ICE PLANET**

The holographic images of the star system continued to update in real time as they approached the planet. Alastriona continued to examine the megastructure while listening to Sailing Master Dlamini and Davies, the Deck Boss, exchange remarks over the intercom. They were tacking, sailing upwind in a zig-zag pattern towards the Super-Earth close to the red giant.

Dlamini shouted, "Run out the stuns'l booms and set studding sails."

Davies replied, "Aye, aye, sir. But if the wind picks up, the stuns'ls and royals will have to be brought in quickly."

"Don't you worry yourself, Davies," said Dlamini. "This pitiful, pasty star isn't providing enough wind to propel a cutter. While we're sailing close-hauled, the captain has ordered the sails trimmed in tight until he says to change it."

"Very good, sir."

A porthole in her office looked out into space. In the distance, she saw their approach to the Super-Earth. The *Tycho Brahe* settled into orbit while one of the longboats was brought out. Feeling like a forgotten puzzle piece, Alastriona watched the longboat descend to the ice planet with a sense that she was missing something important.

*　*　*

Several hours later, she was calculating the rate of removal of mass from the red giant when she noticed a sudden shift in the gravitational patterns around the star. She switched on the multispectral imaging system. A massive vortex came into view above the poles of the star. She switched on the tachyon detection array and it went wild.

Thando Mthembu walked in and noticed what she was staring at. He said, "That's a  gateway, transferring stellar matter into another realm."

She leaned back in her chair. With deft fingers, she gathered her wild hair into a bunch. With a twist and a gentle tug, she tied it into a ponytail. "How do you know that, sir?"

Thando pointed to an indicator. A stream of matter swept up

from the poles into the collector rings and then vanished. "There is a consistent, unidirectional flow with no return activity."

Surprised, Alastriona stared at the assistant chief science officer. *I suppose even the dimmest bulbs can flicker occasionally.* She nodded. "This is a one-way gateway into another dimension."

Mthembu wondered aloud, "Why siphon off hydrogen from a star and pump it into another dimension?"

Alastriona shrugged. "Perhaps to provide a power source for something."

Over the intercom, they heard an announcement from Lieutenant Ro. "Attention, all stations, incoming longboat from the fourth planet has entered the launch bay. Standby for arrival procedures. Prepare for immediate processing and debriefing upon landing."

Mthembu said, "Why don't you take a break, Lieutenant. Go see if the captain has brought anything interesting back from the planet."

*       *       *

Alastriona was walking towards the entrance to the launch bay when Nils emerged from the hatch just outside, wearing a space suit. He had his helmet retracted. She looked into his weary eyes. "How'd it go, sir?"

Nils shook his head. "That planet was one of the coldest places

I've ever been to. Taichi found an entrance to the pyramid. He and the captain went inside and brought this out."

Nils has holding a box in his hands. He handed it over. "Here, take this up to the captain's cabin."

"Yes, sir."

Emerging onto the star deck, she walked past the helmsman and went up to the sentry standing outside the hall leading to the captain's cabin. It was the centurion, Ethan Taylor. He shook his head as she came up to the door.

Alastriona raised the box a little and adopted an innocent expression. "I'm just taking this to the captain's cabin."

He shook his head. "Sorry, Lieutenant. No one is permitted past this point."

"Oh, so you want me to take it back to the captain in the launch bay?" Alastriona glanced over her shoulder dramatically. "I'm sure he'll thank you for your diligence."

She turned around and started to walk away when she heard him sigh out loud. She turned around again just as he said, "All right. But be quick about it."

*　*　*

Setting the ancient box down onto the sturdy wooden desk in the captain's cabin, Alastriona paused to admire the artifact. Crafted from an unknown material, it was covered with intricate adornments of sacred geometry. Each symbol revealed a mesmerizing pattern, a symphony of lines and shapes woven together in perfect harmony. She ran her hands along either side of the box. Smooth and cool, it had the touch of something solid and luxurious. It was a fortress of elegance, a treasure trove of secrets.

It was irresistible.

Dare she?

With a quick glance over her shoulder, Alastriona lifted the lid.

A material like golden silk had been carefully folded up, concealing an object underneath it. She took the cloth up between her thumb and forefinger. It possessed a golden luminescence that shimmered like the reflections from a swimming pool. It appeared to have delicate, yet resilient fibers that encased its precious cargo in a timeless embrace. It remained pristine and unyielding, luminous and beautiful. It was as if gold had been transformed into silk.

Lifting the fold of the cloth, she uncovered the object underneath. It was a crystalline  artifact that pulsated with an otherworldly glow. Its surface was adorned with intricate symbols, reminiscent of ancient hieroglyphs, yet it bore a sophistication far beyond anything known to humanity. Every facet of the crystal seemed to hold the secrets of the universe within it's crystalline depths. But it looked incomplete, as if was only a piece of a larger object.

Alastriona glanced around the cabin and spotted the reliquary from 34 Pegasi sitting on the captain's desk. The Vesica Piscis symbol on the reliquary lingered in her thoughts. *Two realms, brought together with a portal.* She tapped her translator earring. "Computer, what did Shar-Kali-Sharri say when he gave this reliquary to the captain?"

The computer whispered the answer into her ear. "May this gift prepare you for your journey into the realms of night."

A shiver danced its way down her back, leaving a trail of tingling sensations in its wake.

There was a package sitting next to the reliquary. It was wrapped in the same golden silk that was inside the box taken from the pyramid of the Archons down on the deserted planet. It was identical to the package that Von Meyer had taken out of the museum on Sigma Pegasi. Alastriona looked down at the crystal resting inside the box. She had the sense that it was something very dangerous.

*What is the captain collecting?*

Like the onslaught of a winter storm, the temperature in the cabin dropped suddenly. Alastriona shivered. A plaintive whisper made her jump. It was like the cry of a wounded animal, pitifully sad, deserted and forsaken. She turned to see where it had come from and saw the little crystal sphere in the cabinet. Like a moth to a flame, she was drawn inexorably towards it.

Letting the lid of the box down, Alastriona walked over to the cabinet and peered inside at the crystal sphere. Resting in the center of the jewel, was the essence of innocence itself, shimmering with a gentle radiance that belied the darkness it harbored within. The faceted surface was a window to a realm veiled in shadow and mystery, where echoes of forgotten whispers and haunting specters lingered in obsidian depths.

A tiny whisper, no louder than a sigh came from the sphere. "Help me!"

Alastriona's heart pounded inside her chest. Her breath came in gasps, as if she had just run a marathon. No longer a nightmare, no longer a veiled memory, the Requiem was real. It was wrapped up inside a crystalline cage. Alastriona opened the cabinet door and touched the crystal, intending to pick it up.

All at once, the shadows came rushing in.

*　*　*

# ONE

## Aleya

**3221 A.D. — YEAR OF THE GOLD OX  (NINE YEARS AGO)**

**THE REQUIEM**

The pyramid was made out of black stones that absorbed all of the light around it. Standing out in the middle of a field of pale wildflowers in front of the pyramid, Alastriona inhaled a aromas of sweet jasmine, exotic gardenia and the lemony scent of magnolia.

Holding her doll, Nanette, close to her chest, she waited there, all alone. She whispered to the doll. "Don't be afraid, Nanette. I'm here."

Her friend, Elise had told her to come here and wait for them. They wanted to try to get to the gateway, to escape. Elise said that all of them had to make their way alone, so as not to draw attention to their approach.

A wind came on, and it brought with it the whisperings of the dark things.

Alastriona peered into the darkness and saw Elise and Nicolas standing near the entrance to the pyramid. They were staring at her. Alastriona started to walk towards them and noticed their gaze shifting. Nicolas pointed beyond the spot where Alastriona had been standing.

A troupe of the dark things was all around her. Both Elise and Nicolas smiled. With the entrance to the pyramid unguarded, they went inside.

The shock of what they had done struck Alastriona like a thunderbolt. She had been used as bait to draw away the dark things. Worse still, she had been abandoned. Alone in the quiet emptiness, each breath felt like a whisper of time slipping away. A sense of helpless isolation engulfed her. The bitter taste of betrayal mingled with a longing for the warmth of her only companions. In the cold embrace of solitude, she realized that she must face her journey alone. Each passing moment was a reminder of the emptiness that was about to consume her.

Without realizing it, Alastriona dropped Nanette onto the ground. Abandoned, the doll fell into the dirt and rolled over onto its back. A single jasmine flower touched Nanette's face, as if the doll were breathing in one last aroma before it was no more.

Alastriona ran through the field of flowers towards the pyramid, pursued by a throng of shadows, intent on devouring her soul. Like a pack of bloodhounds, they went after her. No louder than a storm of whispers, their cries of hunger were carried forward by the wind. She came to a small hill that was covered in wildflowers. She dropped down and lay still.

Alastriona closed her eyes and listened to her heart racing. Breathing in and out slowly, she let her heart quiet down, wondering if the dark things could hear it beating. Laying still, she let all of her emotions drain out until her heart was empty. To survive the Requiem, she had learned to lose all sense of connection with others. Alastriona wrapped solitude around her like a blanket. The dark things never took the lonely ones. Desolation had become a survival tool.

A cold wind blew through the flowers and flew away towards the pyramid. It carried away the dark things that called out into the night, forever hungry and alone.

Alastriona breathed a sigh of relief. Togetherness had always been a lie. She had finally become the embodiment of quiet indi-vidualism. Solitude  unexcelled. *I am safer alone.*

*    *    *

## 3230 A.D. – YEAR OF THE METAL DOG (PRESENT)
## BLACK TORTOISE OF THE NORTH – IK PEGASI

A tiny light called out into an ocean of darkness. Though it was terrifying to approach the light, it was the only way out of the abyss. Alastriona swam up towards the illumination and broke through the surface and into the daylight.

Opening her eyes, Alastriona took a deep breath. Although her right hand was entirely numb, her index finger throbbed with life that emanated from the icy band around it. Bright illumination made her squint. She raised a hand up to shield her vision and noticed that the brightness came from her little companion. A smile touched her lips when she saw it.

There was another warm touch which she became aware of. Someone was holding her hand. Alastriona turned her head to the left and saw Francois standing there with a hopeful grin on his face. Unable to filter out her emotions, to quiet them down to a more measured response, she simply smiled back at him. "I'm glad you're here."

Francois squeezed her hand. She noticed that the feeling was returning to her other hand while the cold which wrapped around her index finger melted away. She flexed her right hand, shook it a little bit and looked at it. The numbness was going away and was replaced by an intense tingling sensation, like an arm or leg that had fallen asleep. *Do fingers ever fall asleep?*

Alastriona sat up and noticed that she was in medical. The top of the biobed she was laying on rose with her and she leaned back against it as it came up.

A robot nurse glided silently into view and went over to a row of biobeds, occupied by some of the officers who had not yet transformed back into humans, and a few other crewmen with minor injuries. The robot's sleek, metallic frame reflected the turquoise glow of the overhead lights. Equipped with precision sensors and multifunctional appendages, the robot attended to the diverse needs of the patients with calculated efficiency. It stopped in front of one of the monkey-like creatures and extended a mechanical arm to analyze the patient.

All at once, the monkey creature moaned and writhed about. Like a flickering mirage, the creature suddenly transformed back into a human. It was Dmitry Petrov, the maintenance chief. He sighed and sat up, feeling his arms and legs, as if he wanted to know they were still attached. A smile crept into his face and he had a look of relief. Healer Silva walked over to check on him.

Finished with his examination of Petrov, Silva walked over to Alastriona's biobed. "Feeling better?"

"Yes, I think so," she said. "What happened?"

"As far as I can tell, it was a psychic or a spiritual attack of some kind." He took a reading from the instruments on the biobed and glanced at the little ball of light. "This fellow brought you out of it, I believe."

Alastriona smiled. "That's my friend, it's an entity that followed me onto the Tycho Brahe from my homeworld, Scylanthia."

Silva raised his eyebrows. "I don't think second lieutenants are allowed to keep pets."

"It isn't a pet. It's intelligent," she said. "I wish I could figure out how to talk to it, though."

Francois reached up to touch the little flame. It danced away from his finger. He moved his hand around, trying to touch it, but the sphere wouldn't let him. Francois laughed out loud. It was a game.

Alastriona smiled at the two of them. Francois gave up. The tiny sphere drifted closer and hovered just over the healer's shoulder.

"What do you remember?" asked Silva.

Alastriona frowned. "There was a lost child in the captain's cabin. I heard him call out to me. I think the voice came from the inside of a crystal. I walked over and tried to pick it up—"

Her words stopped there. To talk about the Requiem was to make it real, and she didn't want to go there anymore. In response to her silence, the little ball of fire blinked out.

"The captain is the one that carried you in here," said Francois.

"He found you in his cabin, unconscious."

The doors to the medical center opened and Maximo walked in. He glanced around and, noticing her, came over. He did not click his cane this time, opting to simply carry it. He nodded towards Francois. "Hello, Mr. Chevalier."

Francois let go of her hand and took a step back. "Hello, sir."

Maximo continued to study Francois, as if he was mentally painting his portrait.  "Tell me, is Von Meyer the one that broke your arm?"

Francois didn't reply.

"Why not report him?"

"He's a legatus, sir. I'm just a starsinger."

"Did he threaten you?"

"He asked me to stay away from Alastriona." Francois smiled and turned to look into her eyes. "I didn't listen, of course."

"So he broke your arm."

Francois shrugged. "Not exactly."

"Let me guess," said Maximo. "He threatened you, and you assaulted him."

If it were true, Legatus Von Meyer could have had Francois court-martialed. The starsinger didn't give an answer, so Maximo continued. "I have not seen Von Meyer's android bodyguard around him lately."

Alastriona didn't bother to try to guess how he knew about the android. She admired Maximo's insightfulness.

Francois held back a grin. "Perhaps it's out of commision."

A smile lit up Alastriona's face. "Did you break his android?"

"It was self-defense," said Francois.

"So the robot broke your arm." Maximo turned to look into Alastriona's eyes. His tone carried a hint of scorn. "You shouldn't encourage Von Meyer."

Alastriona flexed her fingers, which were no longer numb. The tingling sensations had faded, too. "Von Meyer doesn't need any encouragement to harass me."

"I will speak to him," said Maximo.

"He's the traitor," said Alastriona. "Von Meyer must have contacted the aliens so that he could send them high technology. He knew they would use it to destroy their neighbors. Then he could build his colonies on their planets and make a huge profit."

Maximo laughed. "Leave the investigating to me."

"Who else could it be?" she asked.

He didn't answer. Turning to the healer, he asked, "In your report, you mentioned a spiritual attack."

Silva nodded. "Yes. Both a psychic assault and a spiritual attack. Miss DeTroyes just stated that it occurred after she had touched a crystal in the captain's cabin."

Maximo raised his eyebrows and gave her a questioning look.

Alastriona sighed. "I heard a child call out to me. The voice came from a crystal sphere in his cabinet."

"A child?"

"Yes."

Maximo had found another puzzle piece, but he was trying to figure out where to put it. "You should stay away from the captain's cabin for now," He turned back to the healer. "Who is the chief lookout on the Tycho Brahe?"

Silva shrugged. "I forgot her name."

Francois gave the answer. "The chief lookout is Warrant Officer Ngozi Adichie, but Isabela Vasguez is the chief protector on board. She's in charge of all the ESPers."

"Thank you, Mr. Chevalier." Maximo smiled at Alastriona. "Once you're back on your feet, how about dinner?"

Alastriona let go of Francois' hand and nodded. "Yes, I'd like that, Maximo."

"That's the wonderful thing about you," he said. "There's a serene elegance in your manner, a genuine authenticity that sets you apart. I still find myself spellbound in your presence."

Francois smiled. "Yes, she is pretty, isn't she?"

Alastriona gave Francois a "quit-it" stare. *Don't encourage him.*

Maximo nodded. "This one is a radiant, glorious queen. Don't ever treat her like any other woman."

Francois didn't take his eyes away from hers. "I won't."

"Until tonight." Maximo nodded politely and went out.

Francois and she exchanged moody glances. "The chief inspector doesn't seem to care about our relationship," he said.

Alastriona sighed. "He thinks you will go away with time. Provincials aren't really worthy of his attention."

Francois laughed. "I don't plan on going away, ever."

Raising her hand to look at the silver ring on her forefinger, Alastriona said, "May I ask you something, healer?"

"Go ahead."

"I've been having nightmares, ever since I came aboard," she said. "You think they might be related to whatever attacked me?"

Leonardo Silva closed his eyes. Delving deep into the recesses of Alastriona's soul, he sought to unravel a faint whisper of darkness amidst the usual currents of emotion and memory. He shuddered, and all of the color went out of his face. His brow furrowed and for a moment he seemed to have trouble breathing. He raised a hand in a protective gesture, and then began a sweeping motion with the hand, repeating it several times. After a few moments, he calmed down again. Peace settled into his expression  and he opened his eyes.

Alastriona felt lighter, as if a heavy burden had been lifted from her spirit.

"A dark entity has been stalking you," he said. "It's an elusive shadow, hovering at the edge of this dimension. I sense it watching and waiting with predatory patience. But it is unable to reach you. I put up a white shield around you, just in case."

Instinctively, Alastriona reached out to take Francois' hand into hers again.

*　*　*

The hologram of IK Pegasi occupied the entire room of the stellar observatory. Millions of the orbital stations swirled around the red giant like a swarm of bees. An immense stream of hydrogen was swept into the two rings above and below the poles. All of the gas vanished as soon as it touched the threshold of the rings. *Were these portals to another dimension?*

Alastriona sat there, studying the pair of stars like a bird dog watching pheasants about to take flight. Through a porthole window, she could see one of the orbital stations grow in size as the *Tycho Brahe* sailed towards it. Nils had chosen the satellite, presumably, because it was one of the more prominent stations. He had called it a command center, but the idea was spurious. She shook her head. Military minds always thought in terms of a leader. This was a network, not a hierarchical system.

*It's fascinating how these educated fools manage to find new ways to disappoint.*

As soon as the thought had come, she chastised herself. *What am I thinking? Now I'm being petty. Nils is a fine officer and a friend.*

But the touch of remorse faded as soon as it had come. *His scientific incompetence is a dark cloud overshadowing my brilliance.* Sometimes, intelligence was a curse. It put her in a cage. She longed to have a conversation with someone as smart as she was. She was so tired of dealing with mediocre minds. Most of the time, she found herself in a sort of numb-like state, pretending to be interested in the mundane things that occupied the shallow waters of everyone's mind: Sports, drinking, food, sex, entertainment, partying, fashion.

A smile slipped into her face. *No, I give fashion a pass. That's all about being beautiful.*

There was a simple solution to her intellectual solitude. Alastriona muttered, "I wonder if Maximo is interested in astrophysics?"

Lieutenant Heikkinen sat there too. "Pardon?"

"Nothing."

There was a tiny flash of light.

Saila stared at the little ball of fire, which had reappeared over Alastriona's shoulder.

Turning her attention away from Maximo and the red giant, Alastriona gave her friend a pensive look. She had an urge to tease her about being a monkey but thought better of it. "Saila, how do you know, if you're in love?"

Saila shrugged. "I think you just know."

"Thanks," grumbled Alastriona. "That really helps, Saila."

Lighthearted laughter escaped Saila's lips. "When you're in love, you're always thinking about them. You want to be with that person all the time. When you're together, it feels like a field of flowers in the sunshine."

Alastriona bit her lip. *Why am I wasting my time, thinking about Francois?*

Sensing her friend's reticence, Saila made a suggestion. "We could explore a method rooted in resonance and vibrational frequencies."

Alastriona raised her eyebrows, curious.

Saila continued, "Given that your little friend likely interacts with the environment through energy waves and oscillations, we might develop an apparatus capable of emitting resonant frequencies that align with it's natural vibrations."

Modulating the frequencies to encode information would be like a musical language. Alastriona nodded. "Yes, we could potentially establish a form of harmonic communication."

Saila crossed her arms. "It would require an in-depth knowledge of mathematics, stellar physics, and the precise frequencies at which your little friend resonates."

"Naturally," said Alastriona.

"Here." With a wave of her hand, Saila transferred a stream of data to Alastriona's computer. It was the linguistic database for every society in the Imperium.

"Merci." Picking up an omniscope, Alastriona took a reading from the ball of light. She activated a console and went to work.

Saila got up and came over to look. "What—"

"Shh!"

Saila went back over to her seat and stared at the cloud of orbital stations as they did their dance to squeeze hydrogen off the star. Several minutes passed. A pair of robots came in, summoned by Alastriona. They went to work constructing a device. Saila was obviously enthralled. The communicator was being made right in front of them.

When it was complete, Alastriona waved away the robots and went over to it.

Saila stopped her. "Can I activate it?"

"Since I am the one that built it," said Alastriona, "I should be the one to turn it on first."

"But it was my idea."

"What do you know about stellar physics?"

"I provided the language parameters," said Saila.

"I have access to the Imperial database, too."

Saila crossed her arms. "All right then. Go ahead, turn it on."

Alastriona sat down with a sigh. "No, you're right. It was your idea. You do it."

"You just want to blame me again if it doesn't work."

"It'll work."

"That's what you said the last time."

"All right," said Alastriona. "I will turn it on."

Saila got up. "No. I'll do it."

Saila walked over to the device and pressed the button.

Nothing happened.

"No luck." Saila sat down, dejected. "You didn't build it right."

"I built it perfectly well."

"Then why doesn't it work?"

Alastriona was silent.

The little ball of light went over to the device, hovering above the box. It emitted a series of fiery flashes and immediately, a voice came out of the communicator. "I greet you in the love and the light of our Infinite Creator."

Alastriona and Saila exchanged excited glances.

Saila whispered, "Ask it something."

For once, Alastriona's mind was blank. "I don't know where to begin."

The little ball of light flashed again. "I have been observing you since our first encounter. I was not certain you were intelligent entities. I have noticed the frequent repetition among your kind, of a vibratory complex of sound which you call name."

Alastriona nodded. "That's right. I am called, Alastriona. My friend here is Saila."

"You may call me, Aleya."

Alastriona smiled. "Hello, Aleya. Can you tell me where you come from?"

"Before our meeting, I lived inside the star near your world."

Alastriona's mind went awhirl with theories of life that could exist inside a star. Could the basic building blocks for life be made out of a metal, like tungsten?  Such metals could remain solid at the surface temperature of a star, though many other metals would become a liquid.  Perhaps such liquids would serve a purpose similar to water. She imagined immense beings made out of hollow metal spheres. Stars were huge and there was plenty of room for such life forms.

Alastriona said, "Since the temperature of my star is so hot, are other life forms such as yourself composed of metals?"

Aleya responded. "We are composed of love and light."

Alastriona sat down. "Love and light?"

"Love is the manifestation when light has been impressed with love. Love is the enabler," said Aleya. "Love uses light and has the power to direct light."

Saila asked, "What do you do inside your star?"

Aleya said, "We spend our existence sending love and light as pure streamings to those to call. Entities such as ourselves exist within every star."

Saila whispered, "Pure, undifferentiated love."

Alastriona said, "The temperature of HD 84117, the star illuminating my world, is 6,100 degrees Kelvin, how is it that you can exist inside the star?"

Saila frowned. "What are you talking about?"

Aleya flashed. "Love creates the vibration in space and time in order to form what you call the photon."

"The basic particle of light," said Alastriona. "Why did you follow me?"

"The darkness inside you drew me to you," said Aleya.

Saila asked, "Why did you follow us to this star system?"

"One of the stars here is about to change," said Aleya. "You are to witness the transformation."

Alastriona asked, "Why is a supernova important to you?"

Aleya said, "I am here to bring light and love to the universe."

A whistle from the intercom interrupted their conversation.

Aleya blinked out.

It was the captain. "Winters here. I'm sending an expedition to one of the control nodes surrounding this star. Chief Engineer Li, Lieutenants Taichi, Ostergaard, DeTroyes, and Mthembo, report to the launch bay. Lieutenant Chevalier, I'd like you to accompany us, too. Primus Muller will lead the military escort."

*   *   *

**BLACK TORTOISE OF THE NORTH**

**IK PEGASI / MEGASTRUCTURE**

Lieutenant Iveta Balina, their pilot, had to concentrate. Maneuvering the longboat to match the movements of the orbital station was tricky because the ancient satellite bobbed up and down. The station was equipped with solar power collectors, arranged like an umbrella. While they were fully extended, the photons from the star pushed it up. Once it had reached a peak altitude, the collectors retracted, and the station dropped down again towards the star. In addition, the stations had particle accelerators which fired streams of charged ions between them, creating a ring of current. This allowed the stations to magnetically float over the star while they were switched on.

Alastriona sat in her seat among the rest of the deployment force, staring at a computer readout that analyzed the ancient station in detail. She sat next to Francois and had to resist an urge to hold his hand. In the seat across the isle, Chief Engineer Jun Li smiled at the two of them.

Finally, she gave into the impulse and took the starsinger's hand into hers. She could barely contain her excitement. They were further out than anyone had ever gone before, 154.2 light years from Sol. They had discovered a prehistoric space station, presumably built by the Archons, the ancient race which had conquered the entire galaxy tens of thousands of years before humanity every came to the stars.

What wondrous secrets did it hold?

Francois squeezed her hand and they looked into each other's eyes.

The orbital station looked like a spinning top that hovered over the giant star. The longboat had landed on the top of the structure, next to what looked like an airlock. The longboat touched the doorway and an atmospheric seal formed at the point of connection.

Everyone on the deployment force remained in their seats as Mthembo checked out the readings from inside the station. The captain was sitting next to the pilot at the front of the cabin. Alastriona noticed that he was holding a hyperspatial bag in his hand. Folded into a small cloth, the container could have held anything. Presumably, he had brought it so that he could bring back artifacts of interest.

The captain looked over his shoulder at Von Meyer, who sat just behind him. "You should've remained on board the Tycho

Brahe, sir."

Von Meyer grinned like a child who had found a new toy to play with. "I want to see it. This ancient fortress built by the gods. I want to see everything."

"The atmosphere has a few contaminants, but it's breathable," said Mthembo. "Be on the alert, though."

Taichi asked, "Should we keep the helmets of our spacesuits activated, sir?"

"Yes, for now."

They stood up and went through the door. Balini remained behind. The captain rose from his seat by the pilot and followed the rest out.

*　*　*

They stepped into a circular chamber, ringed by high windows that looked out into the darkness away from the star. They were on top of the station. Light came from the star, below. The light flickered on the ceiling and walls of the chamber. A central ring in the middle of the room housed a large crystal that pulsed with blue light.

Taichi, the archeologist, said, "This station has been altered." He pointed at the large crystal. "That is not Archonian technology."

Alastriona frowned. "I thought this station was built by the Archons?"

"It was," said Taichi. "However, there are modifications to the structure. The technology came from the Nameless Ones, the Eloieion."

"Who?" asked Nils.

"The enemies of the Archons," said Taichi. "The Eloieion were shadowy beings that lived in the darkness. They nearly defeated the Archons."

A sinking feeling came over Alastriona. She shut her eyes and looked away from the crystal. *No. I don't want to hear this.*

Nils asked, "What happened to them?"

Taichi said, "They disappeared from the galaxy."

Lieutenant Li examined the crystal. "I wonder what these modifications do?"

Taichi shrugged. "You're the engineer."

Suddenly, lightning swept through the entire room. It vanished as quickly as it had appeared. Though no one was harmed, it was a bit startling.

"What happened?" asked the captain.

Alastriona examined her omniscope. "An electrical current has just passed through the entire station," she said. "The electricity has split the oxygen molecules in the air and they've recombined into ozone. I think the station was cleaning the air for us."

Nils nodded. "Yes, there's plenty of breathable atmosphere in here, and the gravity matches Earth's 1G. The station must have analyzed our biosignatures as we came aboard." Pressing a button on his space suit, Nils deactivated his helmet and it slipped into a pocket dimension. He took a few careful breaths. "It's safe."

Everyone else turned off their helmets.

Alastriona noticed that the air had a sharp, clean scent, like just after a rainstorm.

An arched doorway led down, deeper inside the station. Captain Winters motioned towards the archway and gave an order, "All right, everyone, disperse and conduct thorough searches. Form teams of two and report findings accordingly. Taichi, you're with me."

* * *

Alastriona and Francois entered a wide corridor that was lined with windows along one side. They could see some of the solar collector panels outside, and they were fully extended. Suddenly, the panels began to retract. Mthembo's voice came over the intercom. "The station has reached it's peak orbit. We're going down again."

Although there was no sensation of falling, Alastriona knew that the ancient station was falling into the inferno of the red giant below. Eventually, the station would reach speeds of over a hundred kilometers per second before the solar panels would extend. At that point the light from the star would literally push the station up again.

As they entered another corridor, they could hear the others over the intercom. The engineer, Lieutenant Li, said in an excited voice, "I've found the power distribution center."

A hologram appeared in her helmet's Heads Up Display and Alastriona transferred it to her omniscope. With the wave of her hand, the hologram appeared in the air in front of her. She paused in the middle of the corridor to examine it.

Towering crystalline structures, pulsating with ethereal light, absorbed solar energy through translucent canopies in a giant ring. Li said, "Light is being funneled into quantum resonators embedded in the station, where exotic minerals resonate with the hum of subatomic particles."

*Wow.* Alastriona whispered, "I have to see this."

As they made their way towards the power center, they entered a dome-shaped room with crystal panels lining the circumference. The room was surrounded with archways that were blocked up with solid stone walls. A central dais in the middle of the room contained a large spherical crystal. Francois walked up and waved his hand over it.

Light came up from the sphere and a hologram appeared in the chamber. They both stared at it in wonder. Little islands of spinning lights hovered in the air.

"This is a map of the Local Group," she said.

"Yes, it looks like a star map," said Francois.

"More than that, even." She pointed. "Look, this is the River of Heaven, which our ancestors called the 'Milky Way,' and here are the satellite galaxies that surround it." She pointed at another spinning disk, encircled by a cloud of little balls full of stars. "This is the Andromeda Galaxy's satellite system. Smaller galaxies, globular clusters, everything. A hundred of the nearest galaxies are here."

Francois smiled. "Superb."

"Let's try something," she muttered. Alastriona stepped close to the hologram and waved her hands in a separating motion. The star map zoomed in. With a little effort, she could examine any part of the River of Heaven and she could even focus on a single star system. Picking one at random on the other side of the galaxy, she found a yellow star encircled by eight worlds. A soft glow surrounded one planet. She touched it.

One of the stone walls inside the archways vanished. The view was replaced by a simple doorway that led out to a world covered by green forests. She could barely contain her excitement. "This room is a transportation hub."

Francois started to walk through the archway.

She shouted, "No, wait."

Francois halted just in front of the archway. Wind brushed

against his hair, knocking a lock of hair into his eye. He smiled. "There's a breeze coming through. I can smell the ocean."

Alastriona swiped the hologram and the image zoomed back out. The passage through the archway turned to stone. "Let's get back to the others."

* * *

Metal arches ran down the length of the passage. The walls were transparent windows that looked out into space. Illumination from the red giant star made the corridor look like they were walking through a tunnel of fire. As Alastriona and Francois moved down the passage, she couldn't resist looking outside, at the beautiful star down beneath the station. They floated over a massive pit of fire, which drew the station inexorably down towards a stellar inferno.

Alastriona activated her communicator so that she could talk directly to Lieutenant Ostergaard. "Nils?"

After a short pause, she heard his reply. "So nice of you to call, Alastriona. What is it?"

"How did you choose this station?"

"I didn't."

"What do you mean?"

"The captain chose it," said Nils. "He was rather insistent, too."

Francois had paused in the hallway. He closed his eyes and tuned into the red giant. A contemplative expression settled on

323

his face. As he touched the spirit inside the star, his lips moved soundlessly at first, and he formed a soft hum that emerged from deep within his chest. The hum became a melody.

She could have listened to him sing all day, but something told her to keep going. Alastriona took a reading from her omniscope and spoke into the intercom for everyone to hear. "The passages on this level are like the spokes of a wheel. We're heading for the center."

"We're already there," said Nils.

Alastriona's ring on her forefinger turned cold.

*   *   *

There were a dozen corridors that led into the room. The central chamber inside the orbital station was surrounded by windows looking out into space. White illumination flooded into the room from a ringed light-fixture on the ceiling. There were also several large crystal spheres attached to the top of the chamber. Purple lights flickered from within, and it threw dancing shadows across the room.

On one side of the room, stood a massive circular gateway. Turquoise lights went around the ring. The opening was sealed with a massive blue-white crystal plug. There were three spherical indentations in the center of the seal, arranged in a triangular configuration.

Taichi, the archeologist, stood to the side of the gateway, examining it. "This ring is covered with inscriptions," he said. Withdrawing a hand computer, he began searching through data. "The writing is Archonian."

When she saw it, Alastriona stopped.

Whispering voices slipped out of the gateway.

Francois turned to face her. "What is it?"

She didn't answer.

Sensing an ocean of solitude on the other side, Alastriona felt her heart begin to race. The ring on her finger had grown so cold, it spread ice throughout her body and she trembled. Each heartbeat pounded in her ears, a drumbeat of impending doom. She had trouble breathing. A haze of panic clouded her mind and she had an overwhelming urge to run away.

A tiny, terrified whimper escaped her lips.

Francois took her into his arms and embraced her in a warm hug. She held onto him like a liferaft. Warmth came back into her body, pushing out the frozen terrors. But it took several moments for her to calm down enough to think clearly and catch her breath.

"I can feel your heart beating," he said. "Even through your spacesuit."

The rest of the deployment force came into the room from different corridors. Von Meyer grinned, walked up to the gateway and put his hands on his hips. "Wow."

Alastriona let go of Francois and took a step back. "Merci, I'm all right now."

Captain Winters took out the hyperspatial bag and withdrew three objects, wrapped in gold, shimmering cloth. He stepped up to the crystal seal and placed a sphere into one of the indentations.

All that Alastriona could do was whisper, "No."

Captain Winters withdrew a second crystal and inserted it into another cavity.

Alastriona shouted, "No, captain!"

Undeterred, Captain Winters took out a third sphere and placed it into the third spherical cavity.

All of the lights in the chamber went out. The only illumination was the glow coming from the pit of fire beneath the station. All of the windows vanished. A whirlwind rushed out into space.

Alastriona's helmet automatically activated. Magnetic boots in her spacesuit kept her firmly on the floor as the air in the space station rushed out into space. However, several of the deployment force were swept out into space. Francois held her against the archway of the corridor until the air had gone out of the room.

To her horror, the crystalline seal in the gateway was gone.

The captain stood in front of the open gateway, waiting.

Looking around the room to make a quick head count, Nils

spoke into the intercom. "Mthembo, Taylor, turn on your gravity belts and make your way back to the longboat."

Mthembo's trembling voice replied, "Yeah, I'm coming. Wow, what happened?"

Nils said, "The satellite shut off life support and opened the station up to space."

"Obviously," grumbled Mthembo.

Nils turned to the captain. "What were you thinking, sir?"

Alastriona felt their presence before anyone else. She stared at the open gateway, wanting to run away but too terrified to move.

A shadow incarnate slithered out of the gateway. Born of pure hatred, the twisted entity was steeped in centuries of isolation. A tentacle like thing stretched out and grabbed Taichi. Over the intercom, Alastriona could hear him choke and it was followed by a horrible sucking sound. He let out a moan like a balloon that was losing all of its air. Through his space helmet, she could see his face wither and turn black.

The horror had shocked everyone into a state of paralysis.

Alastriona's reaction was purely instinctual. Years of stifled fear erupted from her in a primal scream. It was like a storm which had finally broken free. Her voice, raw with emotion, shattered the silence which had masked years of pent-up anguish and dread.

As if they had awakened from a nightmare, everyone reacted at once. The Marines drew their weapons and fired blaster rifles and lasers at the Dark Thing, but their weapons were useless. Captain Winters drew his Vajra Thunderbolt, transformed it into a sword, and struck the entity, which let out a horrible scream as it faded away.

More of the Dark Things emerged from the gateway. One of the entities grabbed a Marine and he withered away like a piece of fruit which had turned black in the heat of the sun.

The ancient station would soon be full of the monsters.

The captain shouted an order. "Everyone, back to the longboat."

Alastriona stumbled backwards and fell down.

Francois pulled her to her feet. He shouted, "This way!"

Alastriona found her feet again as they ran down the corridor. The surface deployment force followed. She could see the lights from lasers and blasters reflected off her space helmet. When they came to the transportation hub, she stopped. "Wait, we can't let them in here."

Captain Winters had a bewildered expression on his face. "Why not? What is this place?"

"It's a transportation hub," she said. "They can invade the galaxy from this chamber."

Without warning, there was a brilliant flash. Ethereal columns of light materialized in the chamber. Their luminous forms pulsated with an otherworldly glow. Standing tall and slender, the light columns emitted an aura of formidable presence.

Primus Muller and two of the Marines raised their rifles and pointed them at the columns of light.

Von Meyer asked, "What are they?"

"Possibly some kind of probe," said Nils. He raised an omniscope and took a reading. "They're composed of high energy plasma." He smiled. "Light Ghosts."

A tendril of light from one of the columns flashed out and struck Nils, who screamed and fell down. A hole in his spacesuit smoked.

Captain Winters gave an order. "Everybody, out! Back to the longboat."

The Dark Things entered the chamber and the Light Ghosts attacked them. Soon, the entire chamber was engulfed in a desperate battle between the Dark Things and the Light Ghosts. It was like being in the middle of a macabre dance.

One of the Light Ghosts moved towards Alastriona. Francois stepped in front of her, just as a tendril of energy flashed out. It struck him and he fell down.

Alastriona shouted, "Francois!" She took him into her arms.

The Marines opened fire. Pulses of laser light passed harmlessly through the Light Ghosts, striking the walls of the chamber or passing out into space. Bolts of energized atomic particles from Primus Muller's blaster rifle struck one of the Light Ghosts. A silent burst ripped through the chamber as the particle exploded.

Alastriona and Francois were thrown out into space.

She felt an eerie calm wash over her, despite the chaos of debris hurtling through the darkness. The violent explosion had thrown them clear of the orbital station. She watched in awe and horror as bits of equipment drifted away like scattered leaves in the wind. Spinning around in a disorienting ballet, she watched the red giant and the stars alternately appearing and disappearing in her view. One moment, she had to squint against the glare of the red giant, the next, all she could see was a whirl of stars resting against the backdrop of infinite black.

Her heart raced with adrenaline. Alastriona held onto Francois tightly and looked into his helmet. He gave her a warm, reassuring smile, which calmed her down. "Don't worry," he said. "I've got you."

But the moment was lost. His face twisted into a grimace of pain and he drifted away into unconsciousness. She could feel his grip loosen and let go.

"No!"

Alastriona held him tightly and activated her emergency suit thrusters to stabilize their trajectory. The spinning stopped. Closing her eyes, she took a moment to steady herself. She activated her gravity belt and maneuvered to the top of the station where the longboat rested. She entered through a side airlock and dragged him over to a seat.

Mthembo and Taylor were there already. Ethan came over with a combat medical pack. "Move aside," he said.

Alastriona moved away to another seat, unable to concentrate on anything other than Francois. The centurion seemed to know what he was doing. She glanced around and noticed that everyone had come back, except for Taichi and four of the Marines. Primus Muller carried Nils in and placed him in a seat. Captain Winters was the last to come inside the longboat. He turned to Iveta Balini. "Take us back to the Tycho Brahe."

"What about Taichi and the others?" asked, Von Meyer.

Muller shook his head. "They're dead."

Closing her eyes, Alastriona could only think of Francois.

*　*　*

Alastriona sat in her office, staring out into space. Healer Silva had asked her to get out of the way.  So she had returned to her desk, with nothing to do except for studying the data collected on the two stars. The white dwarf was close to exploding, though it would probably still take a few thousand years to ignite. Calculating the exact time remaining in the star's lifetime was complex, but it should have been easy for her. Alastriona wasn't able to concentrate. The only cold fact she cared about now was whether Francois would recover or not.

Francois had saved her life when he had stepped in front of her. *Why did he do that?*

Alastriona threw her omniscope across the room and it struck the far wall, just as Saila came in. Saila looked at the scratched device and took a seat. The redness around her eyes revealed that she had been crying. "Nils is dead."

"I know."

Alastriona swam in an ocean of sadness. She held back her tears, though. The promise of holding Francois in her arms again was the only thing holding her together.

Saila looked hopeful. "How is Francois?"

Alastriona shook her head. "I don't know. Silva threw me out."

"I heard that the healer is done." Saila looked down at the floor. "Angelica is there now."

Resisting an urge to run down to medical, Alastriona turned her attention back to the stream of data on the holographic display.

Saila said, "You should go."

"Why?"

"You know why."

The little ball of light appeared near the porthole that looked into space. A ghostly trail of plasma swirled after it like a comet's tail as it flew over to Alastriona. It turned pink. She felt warmth from Aleya, and it was soothing. The sphere of light flashed and pulsed out a signal.

Forgotten, the communicator came to life suddenly as it translated the pulses of light from Aleya into words. "I greet you in the love and the light of our Infinite Creator."

Alastriona smiled at Aleya. Shaking her head, she wondered aloud, "How can you exist?"

Aleya said, "Light was used to create a sufficient purity of environment for this entity so that my consciousness could be placed in this carefully created light vehicle. Thus, I may move and interact with beings that exist outside stars, such as yourselves."

Pushing the worry about Francois out of her mind for the moment, Alastriona asked, "Why have you come here?"

Aleya was silent for a time before relaying a response. "I have studied your language and I have discovered a word which more accurately defines my function. It is what I am."

"Yes?" Alastriona raised her eyebrows. "What is that word?"

"Detonator."

*　*　*

# ZERO
## Light


**BLACK TORTOISE OF THE NORTH**

**IK PEGASI**

Through the porthole in the stellar observatory, Alastriona could see that the *Tycho Brahe* was sailing away from the red giant. The orbital station was rising up from the star again. All of the windows in the station had rematerialized. Light Ghosts could be seen patrolling around the main ring that went around the station. When encountering a Dark Thing which had passed through the gateway, there would be writhing dark shapes and flashes of light as they fought one another. The Archons were still at war with the the Eloieion. She wondered if the ancient guardians could keep the

Dark Things away from the galactic transportation hub for long. Alastriona watched as the station shrank smaller and smaller until it became lost among the hundreds of thousands of other orbital stations around the red giant.

*Where is the captain heading?*

Aleya pulsed with fire.

Saila stared at the flaming plasma entity and then turned a bewildered expression towards her friend. "What did it say?"

Alastriona looked at the tiny ball of burning plasma. "Could you repeat that, Aleya?"

Aleya flashed and it's words were transmitted through the communicator. "Your language has a paucity of sound vibration complexes for the specific context. In simple terms, I am a detonator."

Alastriona crossed her arms. "Am I correct in assuming that you came here in order to make contact with the white dwarf star?"

"You are correct."

"What will happen when you touch that star?"

"I shall touch infinity."

Alastriona raised her eyebrows. "Infinity?"

Aleya said, "The first known thing in the creation is infinity. The infinity is creation. Intelligent infinity chanced upon a new concept. This concept is finity. Infinity considers finity. It is a primal paradox."

They exchanged expressions loaded with caution and curiosity. Alastriona asked, "Intelligent infinity seeks to explore limitation?"

"Yes," said Aleya. "This exploration continues infinitely as an eternal present."

Alastriona thought the idea sounded rather like a child hiding in a closet. "So, will anything else happen when you touch the star?"

"Love shall come into light."

Saila and Alastriona were silent for a moment.

Saila spoke first. "The star will detonate?"

"Yes."

"Nonsense," said Alastriona. "IK Pegasi B will not reach the ignition temperature for carbon fusion for at least two thousand solar years. I'm just now running the calculations."

Soft flashes emanated from Aleya. "I shall accelerate the process. It will occur immediately when I touch the star."

Saila asked, "Why would you do this?"

"The origin of all energy is the action of free will upon love," said Aleya. "The nature of all energy is light. Love shall come into light."

Alastriona shook her head. "So you're a Will-o'-the-wisp after all. You have come here to destroy everything."

"Destruction is not my purpose," said Aleya.

Alastriona walked over to another console and activated it. She began to enter data.

Saila said, "We are not the same kind of life forms as you. We will not gain love. We will be destroyed."

Aleya considered Saila's words a moment. "You are indeed primitive. However, when I touch the star, there is a possibility that you will ascend."

Alastriona shook her head. "We will not ascend, Aleya. We will die."

"Life is an eternal dance."

*How many civilizations will die out when the star explodes?* Alastriona shouted, "But I brought you here!"

"You have my thanks."

Silence filled the room for a moment. Sadness touched Alastriona's heart. "You have always been kind to me, Aleya. I thought we were friends."

"We are friends."

"Then how can you leave me?"

"You, and one other among you, have lived among dark entities," said Aleya. "Light will drive them away."

Alastriona thought of the gateway to the Requiem, standing wide open, inside a megastructure built by the ancient Archons. "Aleya, can you sense an opening to another dimension close by?"

"Yes."

"Do you know what is beyond?"

"It is a realm of negative entities."

Alastriona thought of the ancient transportation hub. She imagined the Dark Things coming into this dimension and using the station to travel all over the galaxy.

Aleya interrupted her musings. "This vessel approaches a portal, which exists inside a ring over the celestial polar region of the star. This vessel moves away from my destination. I shall leave you now."

Alastriona activated the program she had been working on. "Computer, erect a quantum resonance enclosure around Aleya."

A force-field appeared in the chamber, placing Aleya inside a globe of energy.

Aleya touched the inside of the force-field and there was a flash. Aleya retreated to the center of the sphere that surrounded it. "Why have you detained me?"

"Aleya, I need you to wait."

"You are afraid of light and love," purred Aleya. "Be at ease. All of the problems in the universe come from light being withheld. Let there be light and love."

"How am I withholding light?

"You carry lingering grievances."

Alastriona shook her head. "You think I need to forgive someone?"

"Most likely, your progenitors, your immediate ancestors."

They had abandoned her. Alastriona remembered standing in the Requiem as a child, clutching her doll in one hand.  Amidst the stillness, she stood alone, grappling with the harsh reality of being left behind, surrounded by the tainted memories of her childhood. She whispered, "My parents?"

"When you forgive, you create light," said Aleya.

Alastriona sighed. "Aleya, wait."

"No," said Aleya. "Release me."

The light inside the force-field dimmed for a moment, but it came back, brighter than before. Aleya had tried to blink out, but was unable to. The tiny ball flared up and struck the barrier of the force-field. A bright flash filled the room, accompanied by a loud, "Crack!"

Bouncing back to the center, Aleya rammed into the barrier again, holding there while a sizzling sound pierced the air. The light became unbearable.

Alastriona and Saila ran out of the stellar observatory and paused just outside the door, shaking. There was another, "Crack!"

Alastriona's hands trembled uncontrollably. She pressed herself against the cold, unforgiving wall, her breaths were shallow and rapid. Like a drumbeat of impending doom, her heartbeat thundered in her ears. Her nerves were electrified and jolts of panic swept through her body. Her legs were unsteady and she slipped down to the floor.

The weight of guilt bore down upon her. Alastriona thought of the tiny sphere of light, always friendly, always warm and loving. Ever since they had met, her little friend had always been there for her. In her mind, she went over and over the memory of what she had just done. Tears welled up in her eyes. She whispered, "I'm sorry, Aleya."

Obviously terrified, Saila was no better off. She sat down right next to Alastriona.

A long buzzing and hissing noise came from inside, accompanied by flashes of light.

A silence, and then another, "Crack!"

They both jumped.

Saila calmed down enough to ask a question. "What is it? What did you do?"

Alastriona tried to sound calm but she couldn't keep the quiver out of her voice. "It's just a little something I put together. It's a force-field. It uses a quantum harmonic field generator that resonates with the energetic frequencies of Aleya."

Saila was incredulous. "You designed a force-field while we were talking?"

"Naturally." Alastriona explained, "It has a multi-phasic energy shell. It's designed to withstand intense energy fluctuations for a time. I hope I got the adaptive resonance calibration right. That's what keeps it stable."

"How long will it last?"

"Not long."

* * *

The red giant star, IK Pegasi A, was underneath the *Tycho Brahe*. It was like sailing over an ocean of fire. She could see the star's surface as it rotated beneath them. Jets of fire erupted into space like water spouts. The largest of these, filament eruptions from coronal mass ejections, rose high up into space like fiery tentacles from a massive sea monster. Occasionally, a tentacle of fire would reach out to grab one of the orbital stations. As the flames reached an ancient satellite, a shield would appear in a bright flash, and would surround it in a protective bubble. The star monster would try to grasp the prize, and failing to catch it, the fiery tentacle would drop down into the ocean of fire once again.

The white dwarf lurked in the distance on the horizon, leering at the red giant like a hungry wolf. A river of hydrogen from the red giant surged forward with relentless energy, racing away and swirling into flaming whirlpools as it hastened towards the tiny star to be gobbled up. The white dwarf had gorged itself on the stellar fuel for centuries and it gleamed with a deadly pale light.

Alastriona stepped out onto the star deck and she saw that the crew was up in the rigging, adjusting the solar sails. Dlamini stood on the quarterdeck next to Davies. They were both looking up into the main mast. Though Dlamini spoke into the intercom, he still shouted out his commands. "Look alive, Jonesy! Drop the main sail peak."

Davies shouted, "You, Simmons, clew up the foresail." The Deck Boss shook his head. "I'm going up there." Davies climbed up into the rigging.

For a moment, Alastriona stood there, admiring the crew as they manipulated the solar sails as if they were a troupe of dancers performing an ensemble. Over the intercom, she listened to the star riggers as they sang melodies to fine tune the solar sails. The sail picked up as it caught the solar wind and their music turned into a chorus. She had an urge to climb up into the rigging herself and join them in song.

They were sailing perpendicular, at nearly a right angle to the rotation of the star, heading for the celestial north pole, where millions of giant magnetic rocket nozzles were arranged in a massive ring that captured the star's fuel. An immense river of hydrogen and other gases from the red giant were drawn into the ring. Once the hydrogen reached the membrane, all of the gases disappeared into another dimension.

Her smile faded away. *Why are we sailing towards the boundary surface leading into another dimension?*

Dlamini noticed her presence. "What are you doing here, DeTroyes?"

"I need to give a report to the captain." She frowned and changed the subject. "Where are we sailing to, sir?"

Dlamini nodded towards the massive ring over the star's celestial pole. The *Tycho Brahe* was tilted on it's side, with the star underneath it. At that angle, it looked like they were sailing towards a massive circular archway over a sea of fire. The rest of the ring was hidden below the burning horizon.

"That way," he muttered. "'Tis death, sure and certain."

Alastriona whispered a reply, "That's a true word, sir."

Would they all soon join Nils in death?

A heavy fog settled over her heart, suffocating, obscuring clarity and weighing down every one of her thoughts. She missed Nils more than ever and felt sorry for the way she had treated him during their voyage.

Dlamini came out of his reverie. "If you have a report to make, the captain is in his cabin with Von Meyer and a few of the officers."

"Thank you, sir."

* * *

Alastriona walked by the helmsman, who was standing by the ship's wheel, on her way aft. A hologram of the star system hovered just over the binnacle in the wheelhouse. She glanced at the two stars in the center of the display, wondering if the *Tycho Brahe* would have enough time to escape if the white dwarf exploded. The force-field around Aleya wouldn't last long.

Centurion Ethan Taylor stood outside the hallway leading to the captain's cabin. He blocked her entry.

"Please stand aside, Centurion."

Ethan simply shook his head.

Alastriona had an urge to go back down to the science deck, to hide away in an ocean of numbers. "I have a report to give to the captain in person." She raised her eyebrows and softened her tone. "It's important."

Ethan hesitated a moment. Coming to a decision, he let her pass.

Alastriona walked down the passage and paused outside the captain's cabin. She heard several voices inside. She had the feeling that she was walking into a lion's den. What will they do to me? She took a deep breath and knocked.

"Come in."

Alastriona entered, came to attention and saluted.

Captain Winters sat at his desk. Von Meyer and First Officer Tinibu were sitting in chairs facing him. Maximo sat over on the leather couch, watching their conversation.

A hologram over their heads displayed the red giant, the megastructure of orbital stations, and the rings above and below the celestial poles of the star. A current of hydrogen gushed away from the red giant towards the tiny white dwarf, no larger than a planet. A tiny hologram of the *Tycho Brahe* sailed towards the giant ring, tacking back and forth along the circumference of the red giant. They were sailing into oblivion. *What madness is this?*

The captain looked up at her impatiently and returned her salute. "At ease."

Alastriona adopted a parade rest posture with her feet slightly apart and hands clasped behind her back. The crystal which she had touched sat on top of the desk, right next to a picture of the captain's wife, Eleanor. A tingling sensation slipped down her spine at the sight of the globe. She thought she could hear a faint whisper coming from it, too.

"What is it, DeTroyes?"

"Sir, I have a report to make."

"Go ahead."

She told him all about Aleya.

Captain leaned back in his chair and steepled his hands. "You admit to bringing a dangerous life form aboard the Tycho Brahe?"

When Aleya had first appeared, she thought the tiny ball of fire was cute. What's more, it had warmed her heart. *I was lonely.*

"I didn't know it was dangerous, sir," she said. "In any case, I didn't know how to tell it to go away."

"How long will your force-field hold?"

"Not long, sir. Perhaps an hour or so."

The rest of the officers present were alarmed by the news. Maximo simply sat there, deep in thought. Von Meyers was angry. "So, you have endangered the *Tycho Brahe*, the mission and our lives."

Lieutenant Tinibu said in a calm voice, "She may have endangered the Imperium itself. If we remain here, that life form will eventually escape and will destroy the star. If we return home, it will destroy one of our stars and everything within thirty light years."

In the hologram, she watched as the *Tycho Brahe* sailed past the white dwarf, which was about to go supernova, towards the massive ring over the red giant.

"Sir, Aleya is not the cause of what's happening to these stars."

Legatus Von Meyer looked nervous. "What is the cause?"

Alastriona said, "These stars were rapidly aged by the Archonian megastructure. It was altered by the Dark Things on the other side of the boundary surface, a portal to their dimension,  which we're approaching now."

A shadow of apprehension surrounded the captain. He whispered, "Dark things?"

Alastriona nodded. "Aleya said that two on board have touched the Requiem. I am one."

"What is the Requiem?" asked Tinibu.

"A realm of darkness, where the Nameless Ones dwell," she said. "I was sent there as a child, to escape the devastation from a comet which struck my homeworld, Pleione."

None of them said anything.

Alastriona looked into the captain's eyes. "Your wife, Eleanor, found a portal to the Requiem when she was exploring the ancient ruins on Pleione. How long ago was it?"

Captain Winters lowered his hands to the table. No longer steepling them, he rubbed them together, anxiously. "Too long."

Alastriona explained, "The Archons built this megastructure to capture hydrogen fuel to power their transit portals, which connect to all of the stars in the galaxy and even beyond that, to other galaxies. The enemies of the Archons modified the technology of the megastructure, siphoning the fuel off and directing it into the other dimension, the Requiem. But the ring portal is uni-directional."

"It's a one-way door," said Von Meyer. "They can't enter our universe."

She shook her head. "No, they can't."

"Is that why you're helping them?" asked Maximo.

Captain Winters looked at Maximo is surprise. "What?"

Maximo stood up and leaned on his cane. "You have been

using courier drones to contact aliens. You made contact remotely and learned their languages. But you had to make deals with them. Imperial technology in exchange for what you wanted."

Alastriona remembered the objects the captain had acquired from the planets they had visited on their way here. "You were collecting components for an ancient device, a set of keys to open a new two-way gateway. The keys were found by the aliens in the prehistoric settlements of the Archons."

"It didn't go as you planned, though," said Maximo. "The Kishtatu were too warlike. Shar-Kali-Sharri destroyed the civilization on Sigma Pegasi with the Imperial technology you gave them."

Alastriona remembered the shock on the captain's face when he had learned of the dead world. "You thought no one would notice that it was destroyed with Imperial technology because Sigma Pegasi is so close to the region of Ash Worlds."

"Just another dead planet," said Maximo.

Alastriona said, "With an open gateway into our dimension, the Dark Things can invade our galaxy. They can use the transportation hubs here to travel to every star in the galaxy."

Von Meyer leaned back in his seat. "So what?"

Alastriona shivered at the thought of horrors that went beyond the boundaries of mortal comprehension. The memory of her friend Timmy, shriveling away under the touch of the Dark Things tormented her soul. She remembered Timmy's haunted shell as he turned black and withered away. She closed her eyes. "The Dark Things devour souls. It's a fate worse than death. If they come here, they will wipe out all life in the galaxy."

No one spoke.

Alastriona gazed into the captain's eyes. "You are their servant, though I know not why."

"That's a preposterous suggestion," said the captain. "How dare you. As a captain in the Imperial Star Force, I'm sworn to protect the Imperium. Why would I do such a thing?"

They were silent.

The captain continued, "DeTroyes here is the one that transferred data to the Kishtatu." He turned to Maximo. "You two are engaged to be married, so you're covering for her."

Alastriona and Maximo exchanged glances.

"Healer Silva said that you've been having nightmares," said Winters. "You even passed out, right here. Furthermore, you have brought an alien life form with you to destroy this star system."

A cold murmur made Alastriona's spine tingle. It came from the crystal on the captain's desk. She shook her head. "But I saw you place the keys into the gateway on the Archonian station."

Captain Winters laughed. "No, that was you. That's why you demanded to go on this expedition, isn't it? You wanted to collect keys to open the gateway. You want to go back there."

Alastriona shuddered and shook her head. "No. I never want to return to the Requiem." She turned to the others. "You were all there on the station. You all saw it. He opened the gateway."

Von Meyer shrugged. "I'm sorry, but I don't remember any keys."

The captain said, "Warrant Officer Yize Taichi, the archeologist, was an expert on ancient civilizations. He warned me about you."

"Too bad he didn't survive," said Maximo.

Captain Winters glared at Alastriona. "Accusing a senior officer is a serious offense."

The murmur from the crystal turned into a whisper, barely audible. "Help me!"

It suddenly dawned on Alastriona, why the captain would aid the Dark Things. It was an act of desperation. It was an act of mercy. It was an act of love. "They have your son!"

All of the leaves fell out of the captain's tree.

Alastriona's voice turned gentle. "Captain, you can't help them."

Captain Winters stood up. "We'll see about that."

He activated his communicator. "Dlamini?"

The Sailing Master's hologram appeared before them. "Yes, sir?"

"How long?"

"We're nearly there, sir. Just a few minutes."

"So it is very well," said the captain. "Take us in."

"Aye, aye, sir."

Captain Winters shut off the hologram and turned his attention back to Alastriona. "For now, you may return to your station, Lieutenant. I will consider whether or not to charge you after this mission."

Alastriona gazed at the others in the room. "Wait, you can't do this."

"You are dismissed, Lieutenant."

"You're taking the Tycho Brahe into the Requiem!"

"I can order this starship to sail wherever I choose."

"You wife and your son are dead. They're gone."

"No, they are not. I'm going to find them and bring them home."

She shook her head. "You can't. No one survives the Requiem for long. Their souls have been devoured."

"No, they haven't. My son is here," said the captain. "Now get out!"

Alastriona pointed at the crystal and shouted to Maximo, "Destroy it!"

Maximo raised his cane and struck the crystal.

Captain Winters stood up. "No!"

It shattered on impact and there came a whooshing sound,

followed by a quiet whimpering. The fragments looked like broken glass at first, but they soon faded away, like melting ice. Wisps of vapor drifted into the air.

Captain Winters sat down into his chair with a lost expression on his face. "What have you done?"

Alastriona sighed. "That crystal only held a soul fragment of your son. It was just an echo," she said. "It's all that was left after they consumed his soul."

Captain Winters leaned onto his desk with hands clasped together. He closed his eyes.

Maximo nodded. "Yes, the Dark Things used the crystal to send orders to him."

A shiver went up her spine. "You mean they've been talking to him, all this time?"

"Yes," said Maximo. "When he realized you were on to him, he sabotaged the cathedral while he called Mr. Chevalier away. He tried to get rid of you. He tried to kill you."

Alastriona couldn't believe it, but it made sense.

Maximo said, "Captain Winters, I am arresting you for treason."

Von Meyer and Tinibu looked at each other. Von Meyer shook his head and activated his communicator. Centurion Taylor's holo-gram appeared. "Yes, sir?"

Von Meyer said, "Centurion, come inside. We are placing the captain under arrest."

"Aye, aye, sir."

The hologram showed the Tycho Brahe moving closer and closer to the dimensional portal. Alastriona turned to the first officer. "Sir, I believe you are now in command."

Tinibu nodded. "Yes."

"Might I suggest, sir," said Alastriona, "that you alter our course?"

Tinibu smiled. "Of course, Lieutenant." He activated the intercom. "All hands, stand by to come about. Lively now."

Von Meyer looked at the cloud of ancient Archonian stations. "What do we do about the gateway that Captain Winters just opened?"

Tinibu said, "I'll deal with that after the Tycho Brahe gets some distance away from that portal ring."

Maximo and Alastriona looked into each other's eyes, feeling a connection there unlike any they had experienced before. It was as if they had finally found one another after being lost in the wilderness.

*   *   *

The stellar observatory was quiet. The hologram of the IK Pegasi star system floated in the center of the chamber. To one side, the little ball of light hovered inside the force-field. Aleya was acquiescent and simply waited there.

Saila sat at a desk, observing the tiny sphere.

Alastriona walked in and halted in front of Aleya. "Any news?"

Saila shook her head. "No. Aleya stopped trying to break free."

The tiny ball of fire had become her closest companion. Alastriona had grown fond of it. She closed her eyes, not wanting to let Aleya go. She whispered, "What will I do without you?"

Aleya flashed in a pattern. The communicator said, "I, too, am sad to leave you, but I must go. It is my purpose."

Saila asked, "Will you cease to exist when you touch the star?"

"No. I will transform. I will give love and light to the galaxy."

Alastriona sighed. "Computer, deactivate the force-field."

There was a whooshing sound as the light in the room darkened slightly when the globe surrounding Aleya vanished. Aleya blinked a few times but did not move. Alastriona raised her arms and cupped them in front of her. Aleya drifted over and hovered just over her hands. Alastriona could feel the warmth in her palms and her fingers. Tears came as she whispered, "Don't go, Aleya."

The little ball of light didn't answer.

Alastriona cupped her hands around the ball, brought it up to her heart and closed her eyes. Warmth, light and love touched her there. The dark universe was a lonely place. She imagined how wonderful it would be to give this love to everyone else. She opened her hands and lowered her arms. "Go, spread light and love to the universe."

Aleya said, "All is well. I leave you, my friends, in the love and in the light of the One Infinite Creator. Rejoice in power and in peace."

The little ball of light drifted out of Alastriona's hands, whirled around Saila in a friendly dance and then whisked towards the wall and passed right through it. In the porthole, they watched as Aleya drifted away into the night.

Silence filled the stellar observatory.

The door opened, Angelica walked in and sat down. She said, "I thought you'd like to know that Francois will be fine."

"Thank you, Angelica." Alastriona wiped tears from her eyes. "That's good news."

Angelica looked at them and raised her eyebrows. "What?"

Saila shook her head and got up. "Nothing." She activated a console that tracked Aleya's progress towards the white dwarf. "I'm glad that he'll recover."

"It was kind of you to come," said Alastriona, "but shouldn't you be tuning the hypersails?"

"No," said Angelica. Tinibu wants us to stay here for a time to allow you and the other scientists to study these stars. Isn't that why we're here?"

"Computer, activate the neutrino detector," said Alastriona.

A holo-display appeared of the chamber housing the neutrino detector. The huge white ball raised up out of it's housing. The large-scale, high light yield scintillator detector would discover neutrinos when they were emitted by the supernova. As the neutrino flavor composition was distorted by perturbations induced by quantum gravity, the detector would probe the structure of spacetime. It would give them the first sign of the supernova detonation.

Angelica frowned. "What are you doing?"

Ignoring her, Alastriona activated her communicator.

Lieutenant Tinibu's voice came back. "What is it, Lieutenant?"

"Sir, the white dwarf should detonate soon."

"Soon? How soon?"

Alastriona looked over at the hologram. Aleya was rapidly approaching the white dwarf. Traveling at the speed of light, it wouldn't take very long. She made a sarcastic mental note to herself: *Next time, release the detonator of a supernova further away from the star.* As she was watching, Aleya struck IK Pegasi B.

The neutrino detector went wild.

"It's happening now, sir."

"What?"

"IK Pegasi, the white dwarf star, has started burning carbon," she said. "The star has detonated. It's a supernova now."

His command was broadcast over the intercom. "Action stations. Action stations. Set condition one. This is not a drill. All hands, man your battle stations. The white dwarf is turning into a supernova."

Angelica's eyes widened.

Alastriona said, "Shouldn't you be somewhere?"

Angelica ran out, headed for the cathedral. She would have to tune the hypersails and then open a hyperspace vortex. If they couldn't make it outside the termination shock, the region at the edge of the star system, before the shockwave, they would be destroyed.

For some reason, Alastriona was quite calm. She remained in her seat, looking at the wealth of data as it came in. Saila went out, heading for the star deck. Tinibu's voice came over the intercom. "All hands, make sail. Draw on every strand of aetherium the yards will hold."

Sailing Master Dlamini's voice came over the intercom. "Run out the stuns'l booms and set studding sails." Moments later, the *Tycho Brahe* was sailing large, at full sails, with every solar sail deployed.

Alastriona observed the hologram of the star system. Even though they had reached incredible speed, they were still sailing away from the white dwarf at too slow a pace. Red stars simply had weak astrospheres, which meant that the solar winds were insufficient to give them much speed. What's more, the crystals lining the solar sails were not even calibrated for these type M stars.

A moment later, Dlamini gave another order, "Deploy the electrostatic tether system."

The series of charged lines extended out from the solar sails, electrifying the lines and giving them more propulsion. A glance at the hologram showed that the *Tycho Brahe* still wasn't sailing fast enough.

Over the intercom, Tinibu asked, "How much time do we have before the shock wave strikes us?"

Alastriona raised her eyebrows and gave a clinical response. "In a type Ia white dwarf detonation, most of the energy is directed into heavy element synthesis and into the kinetic energy of the ejecta. The time it takes for the shock wave to reach the surface of the star and then propagate through the surrounding material can vary significantly, depending on the density and structure of the stellar envelope."

Tinibu repeated his question, "How long, Lieutenant?"

She made a mental calculation. The shock wave was traveling quite slow, at roughly six percent of the speed of light, nearly 18,000 km per second. Alastriona shrugged. "Two or three hours, perhaps, but we're in more danger from the gamma rays and x-rays, which travel at the speed of light."

She heard the voice of Davies, the Deck Boss, "What's going on with the lookouts?"

Dlamini said, "What do you mean?"

Davies said, "They're acting strange. It's as if they're happy or something."

Alastriona saw a burst of light come in through the porthole. They were out of time.

Min Ji Ro's voice came over the intercom. "We're going to burn a sunstone to get to lightspeed quickly. Hold on."

Since the *Tycho Brahe* had inertial dampeners and gravity control systems, Alastriona couldn't sense their sudden burst of speed at all. Tinibu's calm voice sounded over the intercom. "All hands, prepare for an incoming burst of gamma rays from the supernova. We're diverting our remaining energy to the shields."

Alastriona closed her eyes and smiled.

Light. Alastriona stood enveloped in a shimmering cascade of illumination and passion. Rays of luminance rippled through the starship, dappling her in golden hues, while what seemed like a gentle breeze caressed her skin. It was the most wonderful feeling she had ever felt. It was like standing in a field of wildflowers, where each blossom gave off a delicate fragrance that enveloped one in a sweet, soothing embrace.

Love came into light.

*   *   *

## HYPERSPACE

When Alastriona had opened her eyes, a new world greeted her. Everything seemed lighter and brighter. The rest of the crew felt it, too. Everyone was happy and calm as they went about their business operating the starship on their way home.

Angelica had managed to open a wormhole, propelling the *Tycho Brahe* through hyperspace. They traveled to the nearest star systems and deployed a series of robotic  science probes which would keep an eye on the expanding supernova. The light from it would take years to reach the various star systems, of course. Courier drones housed inside the science probes would periodically travel through hyperspace to the Imperium with the latest data. New courier drones would return to the probes, replenishing the stockpiles.

Alastriona sat in her office, studying the data on the supernova. It was unlike any other supernova in the universe. The gamma rays had not killed the crew at all. Rather, they had all been bathed in the sensations of love and light. She picked up a pencil and twirled it around her fingers. The ancient stylus wasn't necessary, but she had always liked to write with them. Newly printed from her personal files, a picture of her parents sat on her desk now. Leaning back in her chair, she looked at them and smiled.

They hadn't abandoned her at all. They had sacrificed their lives to save her. She didn't even realize that she had resented them until the light and love from the supernova had engulfed her. It had reminded her of the feelings she had felt for them when she was a little girl. She would never forget that feeling. Their love was inside her heart now. It would never fade away.

Alastriona closed her eyes. *Thank you, Aleya, for this gift.*

A knock came at the door. It was Saila, wearing her dress uniform. "Ready?"

Nodding her head, Alastriona shut her computer off with a wave of her hand and got up. She retrieved her white uniform jacket and put it on. Without thinking, she switched to French and said, "Oui. On y va."

* * *

Robotic bees and butterflies flew through the air of the arboretum. Birds sang happily from the tree branches. The sound of running water from a stream grew louder as Alastriona and Saila walked along the trail on their way to the ceremony.

All of the officers and crew had assembled in the garden of the *Tycho Brahe*. They got into formation at the head of their respective commands and stood at attention. Acting Captain Salisu Tinibu stood at the head of the assembly. The entire crew was present. Captain Winters was there, too, next to a Marine guard. He was a broken man. Alastriona realized why he had done what he had, and didn't blame him for it. His story was the saddest of all.

Her gaze fell down to the line of coffins. Nils was there.

Second Lieutenant Étienne Leclerc, the *Tycho Brahe's* priest, gave a eulogy for their fallen comrades. It was a beautiful ceremony.

As for herself, there was really nothing to say. One day Nils had been there, the next day, he was gone. Alastriona would miss teasing him about his lack of understanding in astrophysics.

After the ceremony, they all gathered in a clearing in the garden. Robot slaves served drinks. Part of being in the military meant that there was a risk that one might not come back. Even on a science vessel, the dangers were real.

Legatus Legionis Kevin Von Meyer walked up to Alastriona, accompanied by his secretary. The android was shadowing him again. "What will you do, when you get home?"

Alastriona raised her eyebrows and sighed. "I'm still assigned to the Imperial Science Institute on Scylanthia. I have a lot of new data on supernovas to go over. You wouldn't believe what I've learned so far. I sometimes wonder if its too much for me."

"Now, now. Humility is not one of your virtues." Von Meyer gave her a warm smile. "I'm sure you'll be up to the task."

He held out his hand and she took it.

"I'm sorry if I was too much for you," he said.

She didn't know how to respond.

He leaned in close and whispered into her ear. "If you ever get tired of your home on Scylanthia, come find me. We're building a new colony on a perfect world we found in orbit around the star 59 Virginis."

She gave him an awkward smile and noticed that he continued to maintain his grip on her hand. She looked down and gave a shake. "You never let go, do you?"

"Never."

Her mind was filled with a single thought: *Love is gentle.*

As if in response to her thoughts, Von Meyer finally released her hand.

He returned to the crowd, shadowed by his ever-present android secretary.

Saila was standing next to Nil's coffin, silently saying goodbye to her friend. Alastriona went over to a chair by some rose bushes and sat down. Their aroma permeated the air and it made her smile. She heard the approach of someone walking with a cane. Not bothering to turn her head to look, she said, "Hello, Maximo."

He sat down next to her, placed his cane on the ground and inhaled the clear air of the garden. "I should have spent more of my time in here."

"What's going to happen to Captain Winters?"

"He'll go back to stand trial," said Maximo. "That civilization on Sigma Pegasi was destroyed with the technology he gave to Shar-Kali-Sharri. The Kishtatu may prove a danger to us in the future. Treason is a serious crime."

In a gentle sigh, a breeze caught the leaves in the trees. The garden on the *Tycho Brahe* made one forget that you were sailing through space. Her voice dropped to a whisper. "But they forced him, didn't they? I wonder what I would have done if the Dark Things had captured my family."

Maximo shrugged. "The law is the law. Without it, humanity would descend into chaos. That's a darkness I'd rather avoid. Still, they might grant him some leniency. It's out of my hands, now."

The wind had blown a lock of hair into her eyes. Her fingers deftly swept aside the errant strand from her eyes and she looked at him. "What is your full name again?"

Maximo sat up a little. His eyes went up into the trees. "I am Don Inocencio Maximo Navarro Ayala De Coronado," he said. "You'll get used to it, after awhile. When we are wed, your name will become, 'La Radiante Alastriona DeTroyes Navarro Ayala.'" He leaned closer to her. "I hope you don't mind me calling you, 'La Radiante.'"

Alastriona dropped her gaze down to a pink rose blossom. "I can't marry you, Maximo."

He remained silent. He didn't ask the typical questions. His silence was enough.

"You're just not good enough for me."

"Ridiculous."

He was really perfect for her. He had everything: Intelligence, wealth, reputation, a fine career, and they were so much alike, too. Yet, their differences were also finely tuned. Life with Maximo would be like an exquisite dance.

But what he offered would never be enough.

"I'm sorry."

"No." He stood up. "I want you to be happy, after all." He touched his cane to his forehead. "Give my regards to your family."

Alastriona couldn't look at him. She nodded. "I will, when I get home."

*　*　*

Imperial Courier Drone: 7C29F6D8

Origin: Copernicus / Maria Celeste / HD 84117 / Scylanthia

Destination: Helvetios / Pegasus

June 5, 3235

*Dear Alastriona,*

*I just received all of your letters and I am sad that you have chosen the path set out for you by our parents. You have no idea what true love is like. I would caution you to wait for some time before jumping into a marriage you may regret. I should let you know, however, that shortly after you departed for your journey to IK Pegasi, I broke up with Decimus. He was a little crazy. He wanted to experiment on my DNA! It's all right, though. Romance is still better than computer love! I have been praying for you every day. One morning, after coming out of the cathedral, a tiny ball of light appeared. It brought warmth to my heart. I am reassured that you will be all right now. I can't wait for you to get home.*

*Hugs and kisses!*

*Julie*

Secure Data Transmission Encrypted

Imperial Regulations Compliant

*   *   *


## BLACK TORTOISE OF THE NORTH

## HELVETIOS / PEGASUS

Five bells rang out over the intercom. Two sets of dings, followed by a single note. After spending twenty-eight days in hyperspace, the *Tycho Brahe* emerged from a mandala of light outside the astrosphere of the star system, 51 Pegasi. The starship began to retract the immense hypersails.

Through the transparent dome inside the cathedral, Alastriona stared at the stars, which were steady points of light. Without a planetary atmosphere to cause distortions, they would never twinkle in space. Rather, they shined with a constant brightness. They gave off continuous, unchanging, steadfast illumination. Light and love.

Francois walked over to the central console in the cathedral. Sheets of the solar sails hung down from the overhead dome. The crystals covering the sails looked like glittering stars. He held out his hand.

Alastriona walked over to him and took his hand into hers. He looked down at the infinity bracelet around her wrist. "What's this?"

Alastriona looked down at the golden bracelet studded with diamonds. "It was a birthday gift from my sister, Julie."

They smiled at one another and he said, "I can't wait to meet her."

She whispered a question. "Is it difficult, tuning into a star?"

He shook his head. "Close your eyes."

When she did so, she heard his voice. "Concentrate on the star."

"I don't know how this works."

"Then pretend you know."

She took a deep breath and imagined the star, 51 Pegasi, whose formal name was Helvetios. It was a yellow ball of fire in the darkness. Hotter and older than the Sun, 51 Pegasi was the star where the first extrasolar planet was discovered.. Dimidium was what they had called it. The massive planet was too close to the star to host life. At over 5,100 degrees Kelvin, the star –

She heard his voice, "Stop thinking."

She opened her eyes. "I don't know how to do that."

Francois was mirthful. "Yes, you do. Now close your eyes and just imagine the star. Nothing else."

Alastriona nodded and let out a sigh, concentrating on the golden disk.

Silence.

Francois began. A faint murmur emerged from the stillness. Barely perceptible at first, it was like a gentle breath of wind brushing against the silence. Gradually, the murmur rose into a soft hum which permeated the air. The hum turned into a melody.

Alastriona listened, at first, not knowing when to join in.

A moment later, she felt resonance, light, music.

At first, she hummed along. Then she broke into her own melody, singing in harmonic counterpart. Their voices intertwined like an intricate dance among the stars, creating a tapestry of sound that enveloped the cathedral in a moment of shared togetherness.

As their music faded to silence, they were looking into each other's eyes.

Francois smiled. "You see? Perfect harmony."

His hand moved tentatively to brush a lock of hair from her

face and the touch sent shivers across her skin. In that moment, nothing else mattered except the warmth of his hand on her waist and his beautiful eyes. Her heart raced with anticipation.

He leaned in.

Alastriona closed her eyes.

THE END

# MARK O'BANNON
*Biography*

Mark O'Bannon is an American novelist, screenwriter, and game designer best known as the author of the science fiction series *Imperium* and for three fantasy series: *Whiskers, Aia the Barbarian,* and *Shadows and Dreams.*

O'Bannon is the CEO of Shadowstar Games, which publishes the Interactive Storytelling Game (a Pen & Paper Role Playing Game), "Fantasy Imperium."

O'Bannon is an advocate of Self-Publishing and teaches workshops to aspiring authors on how to publish, market and promote their work.

Born in San Diego, California, O'Bannon is the grandson of the famous aviation pioneer, Reuben H. Fleet (who acquired the Wright Brother's airplane company Dayton-Wright along with Gallaudet Aircraft and formed Consolidated Aircraft, the makers of the famous B-24 Liberator bombers and the PB-Y Catalina flying boats from WWII).

O'Bannon is a registered Libertarian and runs a non-profit, Mapping Freedom, which teaches Free World Theory (FWT), an exploration of the freedoms protected by the U.S. Constitution, and new scientific discoveries of freedom, coercion, property, slavery and intellectual property.